DIVER

Books by Lewis Buzbee

The Yellow-Lighted Bookshop
Blackboard
Steinbeck's Ghost
The Haunting of Charles Dickens
Bridge of Time
After the Gold Rush
Fliegelman's Desire
First to Leave Before the Sun (with Dave Tilton)

DIVER

a novel by

LEWIS BUZBEE

PALMETTO
PUBLISHING
Charleston, SC
www.PalmettoPublishing.com

Paperback ISBN: 979-8-8229-4684-2

Diver is a work of fiction

Cousins

Judi, Chuck, Ricks, Joanna, Lory, Meri, Diana, Cara

All this, the Troy of my childhood, no longer exists except inside my head. I will rebuild it there while I still have time, I will not forget a single stone, a single incidence of light, a single laugh, a single cry.

Christa Wolf

DIVER

Monday, May 4, 1970

It was the day they shot the students. By the six o'clock news, Pacific time, we were already watching the clips, which Cronkite explained for us, four college students killed, nine wounded, by the Ohio National Guard at Kent State. The night before my father and I had seen a report about the protests that weekend and knew that martial law had been declared. That morning the students showed up anyway. They were protesting the war.

We ate dinner at the kitchen table, the four of us huddled to one side for a clear view of the television, Sparky at our feet, patient for scraps. This was who we were, a TV family, watching the news during dinner and talking about everything we saw, riots and assassinations and dead soldiers and dead babies. We rarely turned away and sometimes ate from TV trays, inching closer.

All through that dinner we talked about the shootings, then on into the evening, gathered close to the TV, waiting for the eleven o'clock news to watch the clips again.

To that day's daily death toll, how many soldiers had been killed in Vietnam, four others were added, civilians. Children, my father said. Puffs of smoke from rifles, a body on the ground, a girl begging for help.

It was a late bedtime for me, but the day was deemed too important.

My father, my mother, my brother Ricks, me. Gathered in the blue light.

Except for my sister Judi, of course, long married with kids of her own.

Ricks had just left the Marine Corps after four years of volunteering to go to Vietnam, but the Hawk missiles he worked on were under Army command there, and he was never sent and felt cheated, still Gung Ho about the war. My father, retired career Navy, had softened in the last few years, I knew because he told me, and now saw the war as a colossal error, too many boys killed, and now this. So there was tension that night, and I kept expecting it to foam into rage, as it had before, but nothing. We had killed our own, that was too much for each of us, even for Ricks. My father and brother seemed exhausted. My mother could only be shocked and saddened. I was twelve and had begun to look around at the world, and was outraged.

But we were together again, and there was pleasure in that.

Then we went to bed, and in the dark, played a family game we hadn't played in a long while. One of us, most often Ricks, who loved making my mother giggle, a form of torture, would call out a number into the shadows of the hallway. Number 64, now that's a funny joke, he would say. There was no joke, of course, to correspond with number 64, that was the game. Then a pause. Then another number, Number 39, what a hoot! I might yell. A classic, my father might add. Soon my mother would start to chuckle, and within minutes would surrender and collapse into a high-pitched giggle, which made us all laugh, which made her laugh more, and we kept calling numbers from bedroom to bedroom to bedroom in the dark house, until, exhausted, we slept. That night my mother tried to call out numbers of her own but did not get through a single one without breaking up.

Out of sleep, a commotion. The lights on in my parents' bedroom, and my father coughing, desperate, drowning. Ricks was with them, and I knew they were all squeezed into the tiny master bathroom. I raced, and there he was, my father, in the white bathroom in his white terry robe and white t-shirt and underwear, but all of it, that stunning white, spattered with brilliant flecks of blood.

My mother hushed me back to bed, while my brother shouldered my father, still in his robe, to the garage. They would take him to the fire station, it was closer than the hospital, and I should stay in my room and wait, it would all be okay. My father had had a heart attack five years before and lived.

I lay in bed, lights on, staring at the cottage cheese ceiling.

Later, my sister-in-law Jan arrived, she and my brother had remarried recently but were separated again. Jan sat on the bed and made me look at her. Her eyes were shining and empty, her face pulled apart. Your father is dead, she said.

I turned to the wall because there was nothing to see in the world.

Before dawn, we drove the few miles to my aunt's house, where the family would gather.

My aunt Mimi hugged me silently, led me upstairs to the guestroom, and urged me to sleep.

I spent an unknown amount of time there, then made my way downstairs. The gray-blue haze of dawn saturated the rooms and hallways, as if the house were dipped in dye. I heard cracked soft voices from the family room but was alone in the kitchen at the blue Formica table. On the table was a plate stacked with cinnamon-raisin toast, warm and drenched with butter.

The memories began then, assaulting me, in shards, and the questions I needed to ask my father, and all the stories he'd told me, these flew at me, surrounded me.

Hunger overcame me, and I ate bite after bite, slice after slice.

Stories

You told me every single one of your stories.
Whenever and wherever I asked to hear them.
Though mostly when it was the two of us alone together.
In your favorite bar or late at night in the family room
when Mom was already asleep.

Somehow it was easier for you to tell them when we
were alone. The stories then were more detailed, and
more fantastic, nearly incredible.

Stories about your life before I was born, or before
I could remember. It was your stories about scuba and
deep-sea diving that most compelled me. I devoured them.

Even when the stories changed, from telling to telling,
and often got mixed together or were told completely out
of order, I didn't object, because I heard the truth in your
voice and knew that, if I listened closely, your life could
be found there.

And the stories you told wrapped themselves around
where and when we were when you told them, on a boat

at sea or standing on a lakeshore or simply driving in the car, the places and times we shared, each day and all the hours.

Whichever story I asked to hear, you told me, and I tried my best to remember everything.

Fair

When we got to the fairgrounds that Saturday, early, I was burning, impatient and clear-eyed. I could smell the shape of the day, everything that waited. I had been to the Santa Clara County Fair the year before, when I was almost six, and all the year since, I remembered everything. Today, walking with my mother and father across the gravel parking lot, I actually did smell it, the day ahead, a cloud of grilling meat and dense sweet sugar blowing around us.

We passed under the blue steel arch and got in line for tickets. The fair's mascot, a wooden cutout of a hillbilly in overalls, white beard, straw hat and yellow jacket, corncob pipe, toting a carpetbag, waved at us. This year I could read the painted words he was saying. I tugged my father's hand and pointed to the cut-out. Hi, Neighbor, Come to the Fair. That's right, my father said.

Once we were admitted, melting into the crowds, I seemed to see everything from a distance. I was already

9

looking forward to the evening, when, as part of a Navy recruiting demonstration, I was going to put on a Jack Browne mask and dive with my father and brother, in a tank of water thirty-feet deep. My first real dive.

My brother and his girlfriend Jan would meet us later, so my parents and I set out to see the fair. I had no choice.

The open barns of pigs and cows and sheep, and the 4-H kids who raised them and showed them, the sweet tang of manure. The endless auditorium of fresh vegetables, preserves, quilts, handmade baskets, and acres of lattice-crust pies. Blue and red and yellow and green and pink ribbons hung from each stall and pen, as though every entry had won.

Then the midway, the unruly square of carnival rides. With my parents I rode the Ferris Wheel, Tilt-a-Whirl, Octopus, and went by myself on the Clown Coaster and some motorboats that went round and round in murky water. I did not ride Rock-O-Plane or Space Race or Round-Up. Those rides were too fast and too loud, but that didn't stop me from standing before them and wishing I were older.

The grid of carnival games. Fish Bowl Toss, Balloon Races, Ring-a-Bottle, Sharpshooter, Batter Up. I won nothing, but my father won a Kewpie Doll at Sharpshooter, which he gave to my mother, who giggled.

The long lane of food stalls. Hot dog, Polish dog, hamburger, taco, pizza, enchilada, tamale, grilled corn. Cotton candy, soft-serve ice cream, saltwater taffy, strawberry shortcake, churros.

And the crowd growing and swirling around us. Troupes of teenage girls, phalanxes of teenage boys, teenage couples carrying giant stuffed bears or crocodiles. Families with kids pinballing in and out of range. Soldiers and sailors in uniform on leave.

The noise kicked up like the dust we kicked up, and rose in clouds and funnels of sound, the clang and groan of the ride machinery, Top 40 blaring from every concession, riders screaming for their lives.

Even though it was daylight, scorched and dry, the lights on the rides were lit up.

I couldn't think about anything but the dive.

It didn't make much sense to me, though I didn't care, that the Navy had decided to put on a diving demonstration thirty miles from the ocean. The Chief in charge, CPO Ghilotti, had dived with my father in Key West, and had called a few weeks before to invite my father to join the crew. At dinner one night my father asked my brother, if he wanted to dive too, and of course he said yes.

My brother started diving with my father when we were transferred to Key West, the year I was born, when my brother was twelve. We lived in Navy apartments then, two-story beige clusters built on a naked expanse of crushed white coral. Our backyard was a rugged beach that eased into a shallow reef, and that's where my brother learned to dive, with scuba tanks my father borrowed from the Navy, On a semi-permanent basis, he said when he told that story. We even had our own compressor, for refilling the tanks.

My brother and father dove and collected dinner off our backyard. Bright orange Longoosters we grilled. Conch, which we hung for hours from a clothesline, a hook dug into its flesh at one end of a rope, the other end of the rope attached to a cinder block, until finally the animal released itself from its shell. Both my father and brother had been bitten, Nipped, my father said, by barracuda in our backyard.

At least these were the stories they told.

I often swam with my father, and must have in Key West though I couldn't remember, but in San Jose we swam in pools, sometimes from the beach in Santa Cruz. I was a good swimmer, at ease in the water, Since the day you were born, my father said, but that was swimming, not diving, and I had come to realize that my father, retired now, would not be diving with me, that that time had passed. Though maybe not.

At dinner the same night, my father turned to me.

Well? he said.

Me?

Only if you want to.

Yes, sir.

My father looked over at my mother, waited for her approval. This was an old trick of my father's, offering me the treat then asking my mother's permission, making it impossible for her to refuse.

Only, she said, staring coldly at my father, If you're very very careful, then I suppose.

My mother, oddly enough, had never learned to swim.

After we'd worn out the fair, the sun about to dip behind Mount Umunhum, the day's heat releasing a deep breath, we made our way to a field in the far corner of the fairgrounds that was shielded by a grove of blue-gray eucalyptus.

The diving tank was battleship gray, and as tall as the eucalyptus, and near the base of each broad side was an enormous viewing window, a square fishbowl. A steel sea-stair ladder rose to a small platform at the top, where a group of divers congregated. In the tank two scuba divers turned somersaults and tied underwater knots. From the platform, a diver used a microphone to describe what the divers were doing and how scuba worked.

Ricks and Jan were already there, and we were all introduced to Chief Ghilotti.

These your divers? he asked my father, then shook my hand and my brother's hand. Good to see you boys again, sprouting like weeds, I see. Ready to do a few tricks, Mac?

While the two divers ascended and climbed out of the tank, my father and brother went behind a Navy truck and changed into their trunks. They didn't need weight belts, as they would in the ocean, because this was fresh water and they would sink.

They climbed the ladder and strapped on Jack Browne masks. Chief Ghilotti spoke to the thick crowd.

Ladies and gentlemen, for our next demonstration, we'd like to present the Jack Browne mask. The Jack Browne is a triangular mask that covers the diver's entire face and is attached to an air hose that's fed oxygen from our compressor. This mask offers the diver more freedom to work underwater, no cumbersome tanks or heavy suits. And I'm pleased to announce that our first Jack Browne diver is Chief Petty Officer Mac Macoby, Master Diver. Mac once held the record for the deepest dive by a scuba diver, until I broke that record of course. Mac's retired now but you can't keep an old Shellback out of the water. Chief Macoby, everyone.

There was a beach wave of applause. I slithered my way through knees and elbows to a viewing window and looked up.

The ladder curled over the edge of the tank and continued into it for six feet or so, and my father was climbing down it, releasing himself into the blue water. He floated to the bottom, flapping his arms like a baby bird, and the crowed laughed. He landed on his tip toes, no flippers.

He swam from window to window, pretending to shake hands through the glass. When he came to me, he bopped me on the nose. He then swam around the tank, twisting like an otter. A basket appeared next to him, dangling from a rope, and from it he pulled a bottle of Coke, a church key, and a banana. He bowed like a magician.

He adjusted the exhaust valve on the Jack Browne, the stream of bubbles tapered off. He held the Coke upside down, snapped off the cap with the church key, pulled the mask from his face, and drank the Coke in three gulps. I watched his Adam's apple and counted. This was his favorite trick, he once told me, drinking Coke underwater.

More applause.

He replaced the mask, re-adjusted the exhaust to full flow, and peeled the banana. Then he stoppered the exhaust again and removed the mask, and as casually as if waiting for a friend on a street corner, ate the banana.

Chief Ghilotti continued to narrate, but I did not hear him.

The crowd applauded. I wanted to tell them that that man right there was my father.

Ricks splashed into the tank.

And here we have, Chief Ghilotti said to the crowd, Mac's oldest boy Ricks, a real son of a diver.

Ricks floated to the bottom, bringing with him a basketball, but one partly filled with water so it would not float away. He and my father played a scrappy game of one-on-one, dribbling and shooting at an invisible hoop.

My father came to the window, pointed to the top of the tank, gave me a thumbs-up. It was my turn.

I moved to the foot of the ladder and slipped out of my clothes. All day I'd worn my swimsuit under my jeans. My mother held my clothes, Jan kissed me on the head, Good luck.

A sailor trailed me up the ladder, and by the time I reached the platform, my father had surfaced to meet me.

You ready, ya bum?

I was able to nod.

The people looked tiny, the top of the tank much higher from up here than it had seemed from below.

You scared, Robert? my father said, looking me in the eye.

A little.

Good, he said, you should always be a little afraid of water. Capiche?

Capiche. You can drown in an inch of water, I said.

That's my boy. Now, whaddya say?

I nodded.

The breeze up here made me shiver a bit.

Okay, my father said.

He strapped the Jack Browne over my face. This one was made for a child but was still huge and heavy. He pulled the straps taut, checked the seal, adjusted the exhaust valve, and cool clean air filled the mask. I knew I was supposed to breathe normally, so I did.

He rapped his knuckles on the face plate three times, the diver's signal, all ready.

Chief Ghilotti was saying something to the crowd, and they applauded, but I could not hear over the pressure and exhaust of the mask. I liked wearing the mask, it made the people on the ground seem not so far away.

My father lowered himself down the ladder a few rungs, then waited for me. I stepped as close to the edge as I could without stepping over it. Looked down into the dark gray-blue water, my brother waving to me from far away.

I did not move.

My father rose up before me again.

Here, he said, let me help, it's okay.

He held my forearms and tugged me forward, until I finally set one foot on the top rung, then down to another, until I was in the water up to my waist.

Good, he said. I'm going to go down and I'll be there, you'll see me, and you know I'll catch you, nothing to worry about. Just push off, like at the pool, it's just like the deep end of the pool.

He released and fell back.

My brother and father were there, in the depths, waving at me, beckoning. They wanted me to join them. I could see the bottom of the tank but I did not believe in it.

The bottom of the tank, the blue water in the blue evening, was every ocean my father had once dived, that dark blue endless column of water, where one floated alone, San Diego Harbor, Espiritu Santo, the Hudson estuary, up and down the Atlantic coast, all over the Mediterranean, Key West, Saudi Arabia, all the oceans and all the depths, right there in that tank. My brother and my father still waved for me to join them.

I did not push off.

After far too long, my father ascended and helped me up the ladder and back onto the platform. He removed my Jack Browne, then his own.

Chief Ghilotti spoke into the microphone, and the crowd offered polite applause.

My father began to say something to me on the platform, kneeling in front of me, the crowd looking up at me. But he stopped, I was crying, shaking, I could feel the hot tears on my cold cheeks.

He wrapped me in a towel and helped me climb back to the ground. My mother and Jan were moving toward us, but my father held up a hand, gestured for my clothes, and led me behind the Navy truck, where we got dressed. For a few moments, we were both naked and shivering in the gray and blue dusk.

Why are you crying? he asked me, pulling me close.

I got scared, I couldn't do it, I said. Then I was really crying. He held me for a while, while I tried to get my breath.

It's okay, it's okay, he said, it's my fault, don't you worry. Next year, he said, you'll be ready for sure, and we'll practice a lot.

I nodded.

Tell me, he said.

I'm okay, I said, my chin up.

C'mon, ya bum. Next year.

We went to find my mother and Ricks and Jan. My tears had dried, though I could feel where they had evaporated.

All that night, as we moved about the fair, and on the drive home, and getting ready for bed, I pretended that what had happened was no big deal. And so did my father.

Strawberry

I could not find him. It was late, dark, cold outside and a little cold inside the big cabin. The other Scouts and their fathers were already getting into their bunks. I looked everywhere, in the bedrooms upstairs, down in the kitchen, and the big rooms below it, everywhere, but I did not find him.

It was snowing last night when we arrived, a lot, but not today, and the road from the highway down to the cabin, steep and twisted, was now iced over, so after burgers and beans and Cokes, we sledded and saucered by ourselves in the fresh dark until we were sweaty. I learned poker after that, and that's when I could not find him.

I went out to the road and headed up to the highway. It had started to snow again, and it was beautiful and quiet, but empty and scary too. The road was gray-white, the sky darker gray, and all around, the forest was black. Except when I passed another cabin and the yellow lights whispered.

At the edge of the highway finally, a big rig passed, two cars right behind it, then nothing. In the bright white parking lot of the Strawberry Lodge, the snowflakes seemed to be falling faster. He was probably here.

Up the four big stone steps to the only part of the lodge still lit, then the door opened, and the orange and blue neon breathed into the night, and there he was, of course, at the bar, with his drink and a new friend, and the TV black and white and snowy, and the red jukebox playing a song we always listened to together.

Labor Day 1969

My brother would be there. Labor Day was always a big to-do in our family, but this year Ricks was coming, on leave from Yuma. I'd seen him earlier that summer, when we visited Yuma, and there was that bloody platoon fight and he got a tattoo, and all weekend he insisted, repeatedly, on listening to The Beatles' Get Back and I was still trying to figure out what was that look in his eye when he heard the song. He was driving up with his buddy Brophy in his red and white Fairlane station wagon and would join us late in the day.

It was at Uncle Frank's too. Always fun at Uncle Frank's. My mother's sister's husband, he worked for the City of Santa Clara, in the sewers, but he also had a cocktail lounge he'd made up in a spare bedroom, complete with a wet bar and a candy-apple red drum kit. He played weekends in a wedding band, a red velvet tux with black lapels. Like my father, he'd been in the Navy, two ships shot out from under him, one at Pearl Harbor, the other in the Philippine Sea. He was the only person I allowed to call me Bobby.

My mother and father and I were the first to arrive, we always arrived first, and went straight to the kitchen, where Aunt Carol, in apron and mitts, stood over the stove. She squealed and pulled each of us in for a hug, then sat my mother down at the kitchen table. I dropped off the trays of food we'd brought, and my father and I went out to the backyard.

Just beyond the covered patio, Uncle Frank stood at the BBQ, moving coals around with tongs. The sharp scent of Kingsford charcoal lighter. Frank wore plaid Bermuda shorts, a white t-shirt, black socks, black dress shoes.

Mac, you Okie son of a bitch, grab a beer!

Frank, you old Portagee malingerer you.

Bobby, my uncle said, grab a couple of beers, will you, get yourself a soda. Diana's in the garage, go say hi.

I retreated under the green fiberglass patio awning, pulled three ice-sweating cans from the aluminum cooler. Yanked off the pop tops, then carefully placed the razor-sharp rings into the bottom of the trash can. I'd nearly cut off my little toe earlier that summer, when I stepped on a pop top in a friend's driveway, and at Moffett Field had it stitched up by a Corpsman-in-training because the doctor on duty had left early to play golf.

My cousin Diana, just a year older, sat on a folding chair in the shadowed mouth of the detached garage, listening to 45s on the record player she'd brought out from her room. There was a chair for me too. In the garage, out of the lazy sun, her hair and skin looked much darker than usual, but her teeth were sharper and brighter.

Cousin, she said.

We leafed through her singles. The Temptations, Aretha, Sly and the Family Stone, Creedence, The Zombies. We were too old, we imagined, to run around and play any longer, that was for little kids. Diana's sister Joanna and her Air Force husband had recently been stationed in Italy.

My sister's family poured out the back door, my brother-in-law Dave, former Navy too, served aboard an ice-cutter in the Arctic Circle, and my nieces Deby and Cathi, five and three. Dave joined my father and Uncle Frank at the BBQ with a fresh round of beers. All three men were smoking. My sister, fourteen years older than me, was still in the kitchen with Steve, just a year old.

Deby and Cathi sat on the garage floor next to the record player, trying to be interested in Diana's 45s, but gave up half-way through Honky Tonk Women and ran to the side yard.

The food began to emerge from the kitchen, and Diana and I were recruited to help. Macaroni salad, potato salad, dishes of black olives, peanuts, strawberries. Green beans with almonds, refried beans. Lime jello with floating grapes, orange jello with mandarins. Tortilla chips and guacamole, potato chips, pretzels. Deviled eggs sprinkled with paprika. Hamburger and hot dog buns, chopped onions, sliced tomatoes, catsup, mustard, relish, butter pickles.

Chocolate cake and devil's food. There was ice cream in the freezer, Rocky Road and Tropical Swirl sherbet.

Stacks of paper plates, bundles of napkins, trays of real silverware.

Plates of hamburger patties, chicken breasts, hot dogs, and ears of corn were set on a TV tray next to the grill.

Diana and I dropped folding chairs around the lawn. One easy chair was brought out from the house and set in the shade for Grandma Cleaves.

Uncle Frank turned up his radio, the Giants vs. The Expos. White-blue smoke swirled into the white-blue summer sky.

Aunt Mimi and Uncle Don, her third husband, arrived with two-year-old Cara, who chased after Deby and Cathi's shrieks. More trays of food. Watermelon slices and Caesar Salad and garlic bread. Aunt Mimi retreated to the kitchen, but not until she hugged me to death.

Then my cousin Chuck came out of the kitchen, with Grandma Cleaves on his arm. She was nearly bent in two and depended on a wooden cane.

Diana and I took her from Chuck and got her to her easy chair under the olive tree in the back of the backyard. We fetched ice tea and potato chips for her, bowls of olives and peanuts. Then we sat around her, not merely dutifully, but mostly. Her iris beds, she told us at some length, were suffering in this nasty heat.

I watched the men at the BBQ. Beer, cigarettes, loud.

Chuck, Mimi's son from her first marriage, had been an Embassy guard in Burma, chosen for the position because of his height and good looks. He'd left the Marines several months earlier, but his stance remained formal. He looked like he might salute at any moment.

Uncle Don stood apart from the others, though leaning in and listening and smiling. He'd been a Navy pilot in Korea, and once landed his jet upside down, no injuries, but the jet was ruined, and he was discharged. My father thought Don was crazy, and pretentious, though he tolerated him for Mimi's sake. Don liked to talk about other things, painting and music and books, and was, my father once confided, from a wealthy family in New Jersey. It made me sad to see him there, not shunned but clearly distanced.

Rooster-tail clouds froze in the sky. The afternoon sagged.

Diana and I decided we needed squirt guns. For the little kids. It was too hot not to. We begged coins from our fathers, and Diana gave me a pump on her bike to the Spee-Dee Mart. We bought a package of eight guns in neon colors, blue and orange and red and green. Diana and I bought ice cream sandwiches for ourselves and sat at the edge of the store's parking lot and tried to eat them before they melted.

By the time we got back, everyone else had arrived. Except for my brother.

My cousins Lory and Meri, Mimi's daughters with Uncle Nimion, my father's brother who I'd never met. Meri had just graduated from high school and was engaged to Larry, another sailor, but he had shipped out to the Mediterranean.

Lory and her husband Mike and their baby David. Mike was Beach Boy hair and tan, white jeans, huaraches. It wasn't until I saw him standing with the other men that I realized he was the only one who had never been in the military. Because of his young son? Or was it something else?

Diana and I filled the squirt guns from the side yard hose, the water warm at first. We gave guns to Deby and Cathi, kept one each for ourselves, then gave them to the adults who wanted them. Lory and Meri, who were suddenly not old anymore. Grandma Cleaves and Uncle Frank.

We hid, chased, ambushed, annoyed. A swirl of colors racing around the yard, fine strings of rainbow-tinged water soaking dresses and shirts and pants. When anyone came within striking distance of Grandma, she let them have it. Always went for the ear and had great aim.

Aunt Carol put an end to the fun. It was time to eat. The day was thickening now, golden and rich.

We piled our plates, grabbed sodas and beers, found spots at the picnic tables under the green fiberglass. The glow there made us look like fishes in a tropical aquarium, languid in this last splinter of summer.

My mother and Cathi and Deby sat on blankets near Grandma Cleaves, and from where I sat, they looked like exotic birds who'd alighted on the lawn.

I saw him first, coming in through the other side yard. My brother. He was with Brophy, Sergeant Brophy, my brother's best buddy.

My brother was wearing a long-sleeve Pendleton shirt and stiff, straight Levi's. Yuma was a desert, and he was always cold when he came home anymore. The sleeves were rolled up, though, showing off his Semper Fi bulldog, left forearm. His hair was regulation.

Brophy was different from the last time I saw him, down in Yuma, he looked different. A yellow USMC sweatshirt, with red emblem and lettering, but the sleeves were cut off at the shoulders. His hair was a mop, black and curly, a huge moustache. Dark sunglasses, hippie sunglasses, and a golden chain with a golden razor blade.

I stood and waited.

Little brother! my brother called.

So I ran to him, and we collided, and would have wrestled right there except for all the other people who leaped up and surrounded him. My mother elbowed a path to him. My father waited to shake his hand.

Brophy was introduced all around, and plates were made up for him and Ricks, and we all stood by, waiting for stories.

Brophy had just returned from a nine-month stint in Vietnam. He was okay, he told us, but it was a fuckin' shitshow over there. My father and Uncle Frank nodded along. I whispered the words fuckin' shitshow under my breath, to help me remember them.

I stood next to Ricks where he sat, draped over his shoulder, eagerly asked about his platoon, he was a Sergeant now, and the Hawk missiles and Yuma. I asked where his wife and daughter were, Jan and Kim. He only grunted.

Jan and Kim were living in San Jose again, I knew and had seen them, and Ricks and Jan were getting a divorce, and the divorce had something to do with Brophy, I knew that too. But here was Brophy now, so I figured Jan and Kim should come to the party too.

My brother wasn't right, not the brother I'd been expecting. And it all had to do with Brophy, that was clear from the way Ricks kept looking at his best buddy. But whether it was about the divorce or about Brophy's stint in Nam, that confused me. Brophy had been to Nam, and Ricks hadn't. Since he'd graduated from Boot Camp, five years before, Ricks repeatedly volunteered to go to

Vietnam, but the missiles he was trained on, Hawks, surface to air, were under command of the Army in country. I had a G.I. Joe version of the Hawk missile in my bedroom.

Why was Brophy even here?

The stories Brophy and Ricks told simmered down.

Then it was time for ice cream and cake.

Diana and I carried her record player from the garage to one of the picnic tables, at Uncle Frank's request, he had a surprise. He held a 45 close to him, hiding it, and with his other hand asked for quiet.

You all like Johnny Cash? he said.

We did.

Here's his new song. I think you'll appreciate it.

With a perfectly sober expression, he lowered the needle into the groove.

It only took three verses of A Boy Named Sue to break us into stitches. Johnny's deep voice, his complaint about being named Sue. By the end of the song we were weeping.

Everyone applauded Uncle Frank. He took a bow, then he bellowed, Give me another Schulz! And he almost toppled over.

The laughter brewed up again.

A Schlitz, he wanted a Schlitz beer. We thought this was even funnier than A Boy Named Sue.

We settled and drifted into smaller floes, bright murmurs of chatter. The men gathered around the picnic tables, the women floated out to the lawn.

I didn't see how it started.

I was sitting at one end of a picnic bench, watching the little kids run and crawl and climb, watching my mother and my aunts, my cousins and my sister and all their talking.

I felt it in the air, crackling on my skin.

The first blows, bodies pushing and shoving, all behind me, and I ducked before I turned, and when I turned all I saw were the men, scrapping and punching, a heap, and it was like a cartoon fight, there should have been a cloud of stars and exclamation points and asterisks. I only saw colors, no faces, only motion, swift and frightening. A chair was thrown. A picnic table and all the food on it got knocked over, and bodies fell on that. Diana swooped in to save her record player.

The women yelled at the men to stop.

My mother pulled me away, pulled me off the patio and onto the lawn. Shade covered the lawn now.

It ended as precipitously as it began. The bodies separated and stood, moved away from one another. No one spoke, no one shook hands.

Brophy, my brother, and my cousin Chuck left by the other side yard. Brophy stomped far ahead of Ricks, Chuck grudgingly brought up the rear.

I had seen fights like this. I didn't want to ask what had happened.

Then everyone else left. We all said goodbye, with quiet smiles, until I started saying Schulz instead of goodbye, and that earlier laughter circled back.

My mother and father and I stayed, though, my mother helping Aunt Carol in the kitchen. I helped for a while too, picked up plates and napkins and cans from the lawn. Uncle Frank scoured the BBQ with a steel brush, drinking another Schulz.

I hadn't seen Diana for a while, so went looking, and found her in the other-other side yard on the far side of the garage. She was leaning against the garage, one foot braced against the wall, and smoking. The orange cherry glowed. She flicked a Zippo open and closed.

Want one? she said, and held out a crumpled L & M, one of Uncle Frank's.

Nah, I said, I'm cool. I'm gonna go help some more.

Right on, Cousin, she said, and flashed me a peace sign.

My father sat in Grandma's easy chair under the olive tree. He was drinking a beer and smoking, tapping the ashes into an abalone shell.

I sat on the arm of the chair. We looked back at the house, all the windows lighted.

You have a good time, ya bum? my father said to me.

Mostly.

Don't worry. Everything's going to be okay.

Where did Ricks go?

He'll be home when we get there.

Uncle Frank went into the house. We were alone in the fresh night.

Make her dance, I said to my father.

My father pulled up his sleeve and there was the Hula Girl, faded black ink, nearly blue, though visible in the dusk.

He flexed his bicep and the Hula Girl danced.

Where did you get it? Tell me again.

In Hawaii, when I was in the Army, on leave in Honolulu. Before I met your mom, before the Navy. I was only fifteen.

Did it hurt?

I don't know, I was drunk. That's how you get a tattoo.

Fifteen?

I lied, he said, so your Uncle Nim and I could enlist together.

In two days, I would turn twelve. That only gave me three more years.

Wildcat

Then the mule died. This was Mac's earliest memory, though he was not yet Mac, still Elwell. He was five.

The family gathered around the bone-stretched carcass and the plow's bleached wood and dull blade, a monument of meager shadow.

Mother and father, older brother Nimion. A dog.

Elwell tried to make sense of the mule, everyone said it was the mule, so it must be, but the gray heap in the middle of the row, Elwell could not make it a mule.

Nimion put a hand on his shoulder, and they all stood around the mule without saying anything.

They didn't bury it, left it to feed other animals, the big black birds already circling the flat, impassive Oklahoma dust. Elwell knew from his father's voice, when his father eventually spoke, that he was simply too tired to bury it, that the death of the mule had killed something else. He knew better than to ask what that might be.

That evening, Elwell bathed in the zinc tub in the front yard, all by himself, under the long and fading shadows of the oil rigs. Then he and Nimion played soldiers in the growing dusk, far beyond bedtime. Their parents were talking in the house, without making any noise.

Their father left the next day, on foot, refusing to say goodbye or answer questions. He disappeared, east, toward Norman, into the morning haze, and in the week he was gone, Elwell began to think his father might have undergone the same transformation as the mule.

But his father did return, and he returned in a jalopy, one that was all black and patched-up gray, one that bounced into and out of the shiny wheel ruts of previous cars and buggies. The car bounced as cheerfully as his father's shouting over the engine. He was home again, Lucky as a penny.

Elwell and Nimion climbed in and through and under the car. Elwell did not know such a thing was possible, not cars but his family's ownership of a car. His father gave them each a nickel, another impossibility.

After dinner that night, Elwell's mother went behind the small barn and visited the graves of Gladys, a sister drowned before Elwell was born, and Baby Macoby, less than a year old and just a baby. He held his mother's hand while she wept.

They left the next morning, left behind the furniture and everything else, took only their good clothes and their other clothes, bedding, a Bible, and preserves and flour and sugar and salt pork, the rest of the coffee, one pan and one pot and a percolator. They left behind the oil fields and the cotton acres and the zinc tub in the muddy yard.

They drove west, the sun chasing them.

Where are we going, Elwell asked.

California.

Dive

Did you know how often I thought about you diving? That you were a deep-sea diver was my great pride in you and my great interest. You told me, when asked, story after story, never failed to. I knew too that diving was your great connection to your life, the spine of your life, how you had found diving and where it had taken you. Even when you no longer dove, several years and one heart attack ago. You missed it, you always told me.

By the time I was old enough to dive myself, scuba or Jack Browne, you had retired, so we did not dive much together. I never officially learned. But water, always water with us. You told me often of my earliest years in Key West and wading in the shallows off that backyard, fresh caught conch and longooster. And I remembered, for myself, in San Jose, the above ground pool on Bel Canto where we lived for a summer before Flood Dr., paddling with you, you paddling me around, teaching me to hold my breath. Shortly after, the community pool near

Almaden Expressway, where one day you simply tossed me in the deep-end, and I swam right off because you had prepared me to swim with all that wading and paddling. We swam together there, and in the pools of whatever motels we stayed in. I often thought we picked our motels for their pools.

Learning to swim from you, I learned badly, no crawl or backstroke or breast, not moving over that surface between sky and water. I much preferred to be under the water, a deep breath, pushing off the wall and gliding and kicking under the surface the entire length of the pool, seal or shark or submarine. Underwater, where you swam and dove. Even when I actually learned to swim, in the Brooks' pool at their house in the middle of the orchards, some teenager teaching a knot of us kids about crawl and back and breast, strokes I picked up easily, still I swam underwater when I could, wall to wall, under the water, that purest element.

Mostly we swam in motel pools, me staying in as long as I could finagle, underwater from shallow end to deep and back, and from the deep end's surface to its deepest bottom. You and I also swam and snorkeled off the beach in Santa Cruz, Mom, who never swam, standing on the beach and vigilant, one hand over her eyes, looking west. Diving into the surf, under it, then up behind the breakers, where we floated and snorkeled and dove into the green-gold, mote-filled bay. Silver fish and transparent jellies, the harmless kind, and sea lions curiously nearby, now and again small sharks. Sharks, you told me, were not to be feared, but barracuda, which did not live on this coast, those were fearsome. We would swim until hunger killed us, body surfing to shore and the promise of fried food and iced soda and beer.

Only occasionally did we swim in lakes, and only briefly because you did not trust lakes, one never knew what was submerged in them, what might grab an ankle and pull you down. The impaired visibility.

Twice you offered me real dives, Navy dives. The first time at the County Fair, when there was a Navy diving exhibition, but when it came my turn, I couldn't go below the ladder's second rung, and I backed out in tears of shame, which you tried to chase away.

Then, last summer, you managed to get two scuba tanks from an old Navy buddy, and we went to Keith Caldwell's house, which was an apartment complex with a pool, all beige stucco bright in the San Jose white-light, that kidney shape of turquoise water all pools seem to be. Brian was my new friend that summer, his parents divorced and his dad living in this complex, and somehow his dad gave us permission. So you and me and Keith spent a day, with no one else from the apartments poolside, in the pool with scuba gear. First you showed us how to breathe, then you showed us signals, then for an hour, Brian and I swam round and round the pool, never once rising for air, the only sound our masks' exhaust. I felt as if I finally knew what it was to dive unmoored. But that was the only time.

In second grade, career day, you came to Miss Cleveland's class and told us all about deep sea diving, the Mark V helmet, forty pounds of brass, the lead belt and shoes, the rubberized canvas suit and gloves, the air and communication lines, comm lines you called them. How slowly a diver had to ascend to the surface to avoid the bends, nitrogen narcosis. The creatures you'd seen up close in the water, everyone shrieking over sharks. No one else's father could compete that day. My pride in that.

All of your stories, how they rapt me, almost as good as diving myself. I cast a net over them all, arranged them into your one story.

Joined the Navy six weeks after Pearl Harbor, you and Mom newly married, you building ships in Vancouver still, Mom with her family in Atascadero. The war. After basic in San Diego, the Navy, because you were a welder and young and strong, assigned you to dive school, there in San Diego, free diving and rebreathers and clunky Jack Browne masks. The war needed men like you, they said, without you ships would flounder. You liked that, repairing the ships rather than riding them. Uncle Frank had already had a ship blown out from under him, Pearl Harbor.

You lost your wedding ring in the silt of San Diego harbor during dive school, and never replaced it, Rings, you said, were not safe for divers or welders. But there, even in the shallow murky harbor and turquoise practice pools, you first felt the freedom of diving, no boundaries, nothing like the lakes and ponds and canals you'd swum as a kid. How it felt to you, as if finally you knew what you were meant to do, after so many years of wandering, and how relieved you were because, you told me, it's hard to get shot at when you're underwater, and you always laughed at that. You liked the rebreathers best, no hoses, no attachment to the surface, Swimming like a seal, you used to say.

Then Espiritu Santo, where you built dry-docks in the water, from underwater, for the ships you would later help to repair, their steel chewed through by enemy steel. Even though it was constant work, you loved it because it was diving, and divers, all the divers, you told me, were a special tribe, dependable to one another. The water of Santo, away from the bustling docks, was as clear-blue as ice but warm too and so clear-blue you could see for miles. Your rare days off you still dove but too often alone.

In May '45, you were transferred to Deep Sea school in Brooklyn, because you were that good of a diver, elevated from Diver Second Class to First. Mom and Judi lived in a tiny Harlem apartment, while you took the subway to the Navy yard each day. Here was an even freer form of freedom. Though tethered to a ship and its air compressor, you could stay down forever, it felt. Burdened with the brass Mark V and the lead boots and belt, that heavy

canvas suit and rubber gloves, you became, you told me,
a citizen of the sea, part of it, not merely passing through.
You passed with flying colors, but the war ended immediately, and you stepped out of the Navy, trying for a year
or two to live back in San Jose, but there was little work
and what work there was bored you and you missed the
diving, so you re-upped and went back to sea.

To Norfolk, Virginia, well, the family at least,
with Ricks now in tow, because you were sent to the
Mediterranean on salvage missions. Clearing harbors of
downed planes and ships, recovering the bodies that lived
there. Detonating mines on beaches and in harbors, the
excitement and dread of it.

Off Sicily one day, a Portuguese Man o' War surprised
you, you failed to spot its purple masts and sails, and
stung you along your right side, from shoulder blade to
thigh, seven puckered welts you showed off your whole
life. How often did I touch those welts?

Tour after tour. Home for two months, then gone
again.

Then the transfer to Bayonne, a mundane posting, but
a diver still, a Master Diver now, a teacher.

Then Key West, where you did submarine rescue,
and fully entered into scuba diving, that aqualung offering time and freedom no other equipment allowed. You
worked with Cousteau on honing scuba technology, and
for a brief time held the world record for the deepest scuba

dive. And making two movies, as a diver, as a technical advisor. All that blue Caribbean to dive in, showing Ricks the ropes.

After you retired, again back to San Jose, but restless, you took a six-month job with an oil company for a year, diving on their rigs in the Red Sea, where you suffered two cases of the bends, too painful to describe, because the foremen on the rigs pressed the divers beyond safety, and then you knew you were done, your body twisted and in pain from all those pressures in all those bays and seas and ocean. You were done.

But the one dive I always imagined, which you never told me about if it ever did happen, was you alone, in the Mark V helmet, descending, hundreds of feet below the ship, so far down the ship only an idea, no idea even of the surface and its swells and storms, and below you nothing but open ocean, and around you no shores or safety, just the ocean, the ocean here as vast as the ocean can be, and nothing but blue, in that high-noon twilight zone, that blue that is only the open ocean. There, on this dive I created, you were simply alone in the watery part of the world, descending, but slowly, happily, hoping only to stay here, submerged.

Aquamarine

There were mornings on the water that I loved, placid surfaces waiting to be smashed. But it was afternoons on and near the water with my father that most occupied me, shards of light and motion bouncing in my head as I made my way through other days, walking home from school in the tree-shrouded autumn, or lying in the back seat of the car with the sky flashing orange through my eyelids, returning to those swells and shores. All those afternoons near the water, one once, one kaleidoscoped day, one long afternoon he and I shared, basking.

Lakes and pools, a few rivers, but mostly the ocean. My family was never far from the ocean.

It was the sun, of course, lowering and lowered, that composed these afternoons, the plush California light dazzling as shadows crept out from under it. It was the sun, of course, that toyed with the surface, of ocean or pool or lake, and carved the water into hollowed scallops that intensified and reflected the light, a single jewel set in each one.

Always in motion, both water and light, the sun easing down the western slope of the day, minute by longer minute, and the ripples and waves, restless under breeze or wind, they cross-hatched and shimmied, sequins on a dancer's blue-green jacket. There was no escaping that light, it came for us, and everything not in shadow was drenched.

The Santa Cruz Beach Boardwalk, our closest ocean, summer and summer and summer. Past the boardwalk's rides and games, a deep beach, yellow-white, the curved bay breaking gently, Monterey just visible through a haze of thirty miles. I always wanted it to be Japan instead. We body-surfed, snorkeled, and floated, and talked about the ocean's many dangers, and my father's adventures on and under it.

Near four or five o'clock, time to head over the hill to San Jose and home, there was always a moment on the beach when we paused and looked back across the bay. The sun laid down a golden sword that chased the horizon, the salt soaked us, and the scintillating reflection of the blue-green sea cured us, preserved the day in our skin. Then we would have to turn our backs on the light and walk away.

Other beaches, from Mexico up to Washington, all that light and always afternoon, and always at least the two of us.

Out on the ocean, fishing, party boats from Princeton Harbor at Half Moon Bay. We started early, at dawn, in pearl fog, rode six miles out, then after a day trying to dredge the deep from the ocean floor, we headed back in, watching as the sun, behind us now, shortened and sharpened what we had left behind that morning, the coastal hills, the thin bead of the small town, the rising breakwater and snug harbor. It all became real again, the world, after rocking over the emptiness.

Those nights, in bed, the boat still rolled under me, swell and release, and I'd return to the harbor's fish cleaning station, where the man in the greasy cap and bloodied apron scaled, cleaned, and filleted our rock cod, ling cod, snapper, sometimes a shark, his knives flashing silver in the air. The silver and orange and golden scales of the catch leapt about, and the afternoon became a mote-storm.

A pier, a wharf, a dock. All good for climbing out of a boat in the late afternoon. The distance from the pier to the boat was not vacant, but a solid brick of light and motion that pulsed. The lead-lines clanged, the outboards gurgled and died, diesel sniffed the air, the surface sheened with gasoline. Nothing was not moving, so we stood still, the better to receive it.

Once, in Monterey, a family outing on the retail wharf, fried clams and crab Louie and artichokes, saltwater taffy, a mystery bag from a souvenir shack. We bought tickets for The Diving Bell, a waterproof elevator that descended a mere twelve feet, tiny portholes. We hoped, I hoped, to see the teeming sea life, the sea life that my father knew so well, but the view was algae-green and empty. Once out of The Diving Bell, though, the afternoon struck us with its honed clarity. Seals barked nearby, and seagulls objected. We stood together on the wharf until the light reclaimed us.

Pinto Lake, Vasona Reservoir, Lake Anderson, Tahoe. Always in the afternoon, fishing done, we stood on docks and waited for the bar to open.

Saddlebag Lake, high in the Sierras, the light a sheet of perfect blue-white ironed onto the lake, until, at dusk, the night seemed to rise up out of the lake and douse all that light.

Loch Lomond, in an aluminum row boat with my father and my brother-in-law and cousin Mike, silver and gold cans of Oly, the tinny pocket transistor hissing a Giants' game, the lake a green gash in the steep green hills, a bald eagle sailing the length of it. The rainbow trout we caught, one each, the long day shining out of their opalescent skin.

Almaden pool, Alum Rock pool, motel after motel, Atomic Motel in Las Vegas or Thunderbird in Redding, the turquoise waters of each an identical hue, each pool a radar dish that gathered the day.

Once. Greg Brooks's pool, in the middle of an apricot orchard on the East Side. Our families were friends, a BBQ and swim day, maybe twenty kids, splash after splash, and vague adults drinking and smoking and laughing. Late again, that shimmering moment, chlorine tang and the dust of August. Shouting. Music from somewhere. I saw my father at the grill, turning the chicken. I was standing at the edge of the pool, the deep end, chilled in the shade, though the pool was under full sun yet. He winked at me, as he always did, raised his beer in salute. I was almost sick I was so tired from swimming. But I curled into myself, one more dive, just one more, hoping that he was watching when I shattered the pool's surface and set free a thousand floating coins.

Oranges

After days of driving through deserts, the family arrived in California and pulled off to the side of the road at the first orange grove they came to. Elwell's parents seemed excited by the orange grove, so Elwell was too, though he wasn't sure why, unsure of what an orange was. The grove was big and bright on top, and shadowy underneath where the trees were weighed down with bright oranges speckled by shade and blazing spots. It was fun to be excited after a thousand miles of heat shimmer rising from cracked asphalt into cotton-colored skies.

His mother shooed them from the car and dressed them in their Sunday go-to-meeting. Right there by the side of the road. Elwell's woolen coat, draped past his knees, was identical to his mother's church coat. Nim and their father wore dark suits buttoned up all the way. They were going to take a photograph, Of this momentous occasion, his father said.

49

Nim flagged down a passing truck and asked the driver if he would be so kind.

Elwell and Nim stood between their parents, the orange trees blotting out the crisp blue sky. They held their breaths and squinted into the sun and tried to smile. Elwell stared at the camera, not into the lens, but at the Brownie itself, puzzled.

There were family photographs, but only those taken by neighbors or relatives, once an itinerant photographer. His mother kept the thin bundle of them in the back of the family Bible. They had never owned a camera. Or a car. Now they had both.

After the truck pulled away, Nim and Elwell ran through the grove, plucking oranges from low branches or scooping them up from the quiet dusty earth, as many as would fit into the old flour sack their mother gave them. After a picnic lunch, bologna sandwiches, right next to the highway, Elwell tasted his first orange. Then several more. An intense light burst inside him. The oranges were worth all that desert.

While the family changed back into their real clothes and re-packed the car, Elwell saw that his father was in a good mood, and he stuck close to him.

Where did you get the camera? he asked his father.

In Norman, when I went to get the car, bought it off a dead Injun.

His father ruffled Elwell's hair.

How did you get the car?

I found it in the street, before anyone knew it was missing.

Elwell slept in the backseat, he and Nim leaned into each other and surrounded by orange peels, the sun flashing orange and yellow in his dreams. When he woke up, at dusk, a close gray chilly dusk, they were in Huntington Beach, though Elwell couldn't see any ocean. He had been to the ocean in Brownsville last year while visiting his cousins, it was pale and warm.

They drove along the coast for some minutes, then stopped at a gate where a guard in a brown uniform passed them through. The oil fields here were too vast for Elwell to comprehend. These fields looked like the one they'd left in Oklahoma, but the derricks and pumps went on for miles, a forest of them.

His father stopped in front of a small office near the camp's main entrance and came out a few minutes later with a map and that big smile of his. In the near-dark they found the wooden house that was their new home, one room, two rickety beds, a cast-iron stove. The shack was cold.

For dinner that night they ate the last of the oranges in the dark.

The next day, though, the ocean was there, dull gray under a silver sky, and far away from the oil fields, past the fence and across the highway and lots of open beach.

Elwell couldn't hear the ocean, but thought he smelled it, salt.

No one was the least bit interested in the ocean. Elwell's father was already out on a rig, after a quick breakfast of fried dough and coffee and a cigarette on the front porch. His mother was busy scrubbing the shack's walls and floors from a tub of soapy water, while neighbor women gathered round and told her where to buy groceries, the company store, and told her there might be extra work doing laundry if she could find a tub. Church was right here, they told her, the same preacher every Sunday and he was good, they said, filled with the spirit, but keep an eye on your purse and your daughters.

Nim raced off directly after breakfast, looking for trouble.

Elwell wandered to the edge of the oil fields and spent the morning staring across the highway at the ocean between the slats of the salt-scorched fencing. Finally the sky cleared, and the ocean showed its true self, dark blue and dark green, the white caps luminescent.

He went to the shack and tugged and tugged on his mother's sleeve, but she brushed him away, she had no time for such foolishness, she would not take him across the highway and he'd better stop thinking that.

After lunch, Elwell tagged after Nim and the gang that had adopted him, six boys, all bigger than Nim, but he refused too, Go away, this isn't for babies, and the gang swirled off whooping. Elwell was stunned, not because Nim refused, but because Nim had always been eager to trespass before. If only Elwell could get across the highway himself.

A few kids Elwell's size came drifting by the shack and shyly tried to catch his eye, not looking at him but around him, so he went back to the fence again and looked through the slats.

Late that night, Nim sweaty and snoring, his parents dead asleep across the cold room, a sudden pocket of silence descended on the oil fields, as if for a moment the voracious machines had been sated, and in the silence, Elwell heard the ocean leapfrogging itself, racing toward the beach, then dragging away again.

What was wrong? Except for one thing, the ocean, California was exactly like Oklahoma, with the derricks and pumps continually at work, the smell of tar on and in everything, the dust and heat once the fog lifted. The food was the same scant food they'd left behind, and there were no more oranges.

He slipped out of bed and onto the porch, and in the clearest of skies, there was the moon, riding west toward the horizon.

Elwell wanted the moon to be an orange, a huge orange, one that would light up the dark, infinite surface of the ocean.

Old Man

I was six, and my brother had just graduated from high school. It was summer again.

My father and brother argued all the time. It had been going on for a few days. Dinners were usually safe, though my brother and father never spoke to each other directly, so my mother and I kept talking and pretending. But at any other time, eruptions, seemingly out of nowhere, sometimes starting in the garage, or at the far end of the house, where they must have thought they had privacy, but the house was too small for that. When the shouting got too heated or too close, Sparky and I retreated to my room and closed the door. I still heard everything.

When the shouting stopped, one of them would leave the house, and the air in the house wouldn't move for a long time after.

It started like this.

My father did not want Ricks to marry Jan, Not just yet, he said over and over. Find a career first, he said, How the hell are you going to support a family?

Ricks was incredulous, could not believe that our father was blind to true love. They would manage, he and Jan, they might be poor for a while, but they would be together. No matter what. That's what Ricks said over and over. And, You should have a little more faith in me.

What the hell did my brother know? He hadn't even begun looking for a job, like he'd promised, he'd been out of school a month already. Did he think someone would come to the door and just give him a job?

My brother was going to go to college in the fall, West Valley J.C. at first, then transfer, maybe Chico State. He'd make a career for himself, not end up in some dead-end job. He wasn't going to get stuck like my father had.

Stuck? Why you little shit. Stuck like everything we've done for you, that car of yours in the driveway, is that what you call stuck?

What could my father possibly know, he was too fucking stuck to know anything.

Watch your language in my house.

Don't mind me.

Jan had stopped coming by, my mother threw herself into her Jumbo crossword puzzle books. Sparky and I hid.

What are you going to study in college? my father said. Underwater basket weaving? My brother didn't need college, what my brother needed was to join the military, it would make a man out of him, the discipline would do him good.

So I can be just like you? No thanks, Dad. I'd like to have a real life.

That morning, a Saturday, started out quietly enough, but by lunch time, my father had started to prowl, into the garage and back into the house, through the kitchen and around through the living room and family room and back to the dining room, rummaging through the closet in his own bedroom. He was pretending to look for something. He scowled at my brother with each pass, a frightening scowl, cold. It was a scowl only ever aimed at my brother. Ricks either didn't notice my father's prowling and scowling, or he did and was trying to rile him.

My brother sat on the family room couch, watching the Giants' game, eating a sandwich my mother had made for him, peanut butter and dill pickle, and reading the paper. I sat in my father's orange chair, half watching the game while vrooming a Matchbox car over my knees.

Reading the want ads? my father said finally. There was a glint of hope in his voice. He was standing in the doorway to the garage.

Comics, my brother said. The taunt was clear in that word, and I wished he hadn't said it.

My father shook his head.

What else you have planned for today? he asked.

Nothin' much. Take a drive with Jan maybe.

God damn it! My father's voice shattered the house. God damn it, Ricks, you told me you were going to look for a job. Now get out there and do something, for Christ sake.

My brother shot up. Fists at his side.

I'll look for a job, all right? But not today. You can't tell me what to do.

I can't? my father said.

No, you can't, old man.

Old man? Who are you calling an old man?

You. Old man.

You think I'm old? You think I can't whup your ass?

I know you can't. Old man.

Let's have at it then. Backyard. Right now.

You got it. Old man.

My mother stormed in from the living room and stood between them and the sliding glass door.

Don't, she said softly, don't, please, not today.

Not now, Olive, my father said, and he and my brother swept past her into the backyard.

My mother stood at the sliding door and watched them go. Without turning, she said, Robert, why don't you go to your room now. You shouldn't see this.

I raced to my room, knelt on the bed, dug my fingers into the windowsill, and pulled myself up just enough to peek.

My father and brother stood in the middle of the back-yard, stripped down to their t-shirts. Ricks took off his glasses and laid them on his shirt.

The gauzy summer sky stretched thin over the deep green grass.

The backyard seemed bigger than I'd ever noticed, two lone figures on a piece of lawn that wasn't very big at all. A birch tree in one corner, a small hand of banana trees in another. We never used the backyard much, except for barbecues. Mostly it was Sparky's place.

Sparky roused herself from under the birch and slunk past the men, tail down. A moment later she came to my room, jumped on the bed, and settled next to me.

My father and brother squared off, like boxers, like the boxers we saw on Friday Night at the Fights. My brother had never boxed, but my father had, in the Navy, in exchange for 72-hour passes. He claimed he never lost.

Fists up, they circled each other.

My father's high-peaked hair, which had always been silver, shined in the stark daylight, a sharp contrast to his deep red tan. He had a beer belly, yes, but his arms were ropy, and he was big, forceful. His hazel eyes were black now, atrocious. Maybe it was the glare and the shade that made his eyes look that way.

My brother was as tall as my father, but he had a boy's frame still, not yet a man, it was clear, slight next to my fa-ther, despite all the sports he played. He had soft eyes and silky brown hair, and Jan thought he looked like Elvis Presley.

My father faked a punch. My brother flinched. Then my father let loose a couple of soft jabs, which Ricks easily ducked.

So, my father taunted, his voice girlish, You think I'm an old man, do you?

I know you are, my brother said. He was sneering and smiling at once.

Well then, what are you waiting for? My father held up his open palms to ask that question.

My brother lunged with his right and walked directly into it. My father's left hook crashed into his jaw, and my brother shuddered, froze, swayed.

Not bad for an old man, my father said. He danced now, shifting from foot to foot.

Ricks lunged again, but with his fists lowered and head down, and he pummeled my father's body, blow after blow. My father could only beat at my brother's back and the top of his head.

Ricks drove through my father, pushing him across the lawn into the fence between us and Mickey Clark's house. One of the boards cracked. Then my father got his fists inside my brother's arms and pushed up and away, and my father's fists would not stop. To the head, the body, my brother helpless, then on the ground, on his back. He was bleeding from his mouth and nose, and my father still assaulted him, and once kicked him in the ribs.

My father was bleeding too, his hands.

My brother struggled to his feet, but my father could not relent, and punched and chased my brother until he was on the ground again. My brother curled up, his arms shielding his head.

My father stood over him.

Be careful who you call an old man, he said.

He left my brother there, collected his own shirt, went back through the house to the garage, started the car and left. I heard all that from my bedroom.

My brother rolled in the grass. My mother came out with dish towels and began to wipe the blood from his face. She drew water from the hose to soak the towels, and I knew that would sting.

During the fight, though I could not see my mother, I felt her, standing at the sliding glass door, watching her husband and son and waiting to clean up their mess.

She knelt next to my brother and dabbed his face. There was one cut, under his eye, that would not stop bleeding.

Then she looked up and saw me in the bedroom window. While she continued to nurse my brother, she shook her head at me, vigorously, curtly, oddly, her mouth a gash.

No, she was saying.

But I did not know if she was saying, no, this never happened, we will never talk about it. Or, no, don't ever forget what you just saw.

Ricks

You didn't hate my brother, I never thought it was that. But there were times you seemed to want to destroy him, and times he wanted to destroy you. It was rage more than hatred, I saw, that drew the two of you into calamity, a rage that lived in you, but which you spent only on Ricks and which he repaid in kind.

Though Ricks did hate you, now and again. I know because he told me, those exact words.

There were so many confusions to parse.

I idolized the both of you. You were my father, big and strong, and had lived, I thought, an heroic life. The war. Your diving. The rootless youth spent drifting across the West, you even worked on a real horse ranch! How much you knew about the big world, a world I didn't think I would ever see, so I depended on you and your stories. You were my best buddy, and you loved me fiercely.

Ricks, twelve years older, was too old to spar with me in the living room or front yard, except playfully, and he never once took advantage of that difference. I was Little Brother, and he watched over me. He was a football player, he had a girlfriend, lots of other friends, listened to and looked like Elvis, had his own car and would smuggle me into the Winchester Drive-in in the trunk, The Incredible Mr. Limpet was one. He taught me to shoot pool, taught me to throw a spiral and how to punt. Let me look through his Playboys when he knew I shouldn't. Then later, he was a Marine, headed off to war. I knew that no one or nothing would harm me if he was near.

I could not fathom why you two were always at each other.

Not always, actually. There were plenty of times when you were father and son without the rage. Normal days. You taught him and cousin Chuck to scuba dive in Key West, and were always on the sidelines of his games. You were proud of him, he looked up to you.

But you almost killed him, too, that time in the backyard. Blood everywhere, mostly his. I saw the whole thing.

It wasn't the booze that released your rage. You were a happy drunk, I never saw otherwise. On the weekends, in your orange recliner, drinking afternoon beers, a big loose grin, petting Sparky and confiding in her, later a long nap. At parties you could be the life, and everyone there was your best friend. In bars, telling outlandish stories of your Navy adventures, stories that always ended with a laugh, mostly at your own expense. My favorite of all your drunks was Christmas Eve, when just before dinner, spaghetti and garlic bread, you'd reach into the cupboard above the stove and retrieve the Snakebite Medicine, celebrating the occasion. Happy and drifting, then after I went to sleep, gleefully setting up, there are pictures Mom took of this, a thousand-piece Army men tableau, complete with tanks and barbed wire. You were at ease.

You didn't come after Ricks when you were drunk, were more inclined to hug him. Not that then.

I used to think there might be some long-standing grudge between you two, an old argument started long ago then continued out of habit, a grudge that began before I was born or old enough to remember. But Ricks was only twelve when I was born, what could he have done to you? I once asked Mom about this, why you two fought so much and so vehemently, but she only said, That was all a long time ago.

I knew you used to beat Ricks when he was younger, when he was my age, with a belt, fists, shoving. Punishment or correction? But what could he possibly have done? I knew you'd beaten him because he told me. He told me to be careful around you, told me to keep an eye peeled. Told me stories.

The most baffling aspect of the rage you carried for him was that you were so tender with me. The proper word. Tender. I knew that always.

Once, though, you chased me through the house, after I called Mom an Old Lady, you snapping your folded-up belt, that harsh thwock, but when you caught me, cornered in my bedroom, you didn't hit me. Instructed me in respect, instead. I was nine then, and it was a terrifying moment, but exceptional. You never once hit me.

And you took me everywhere with you, were interested in what I was interested in, would rub my back at night with all of us in front of the TV. I was your best buddy.

Maybe it was your heart attack that made the difference. That's what Mom used to say, that you'd been a different man since.

I was seven when you were rushed into the ambulance and didn't come home for two weeks. You were going to miss Thanksgiving. But I saw you on Thanksgiving, a black and gold and windy evening, and we ate lukewarm turkey in your hospital room, the whole family, even Judi was there. Ricks had sneaked me up a back stairway, then he and an orderly hid me on the bottom shelf of a food cart. When you finally came home, I spent every day with you, Mom and Ricks both at work, Judi already married and gone. During the months-long home rest, you and I played board games, constructed jigsaw puzzles, tricked up science experiments, and you mastered paint-by-numbers.

But if the heart attack did change you, as Mom said, why did that change fall only on me? You and Ricks continued to fight, no fists any longer, not after that time in the backyard and of course after your heart attack, but louder now and with more explosive words. When he joined the Marines your pride in him swelled, but then the two of you fought about the war for four years. Of course, the war. Everyone was fighting about the war. Ricks saw it as a vital defense against the scourge of Communism. You thought he was too naive to have any opinion about war, where he never did get to go.

How could a heart attack do that, change only one portion of you, while nothing toward my brother softened? It never did soften.

Maybe the heart attack wasn't about people but about the future and the past, the past ending with your heart attack and a new future beginning. My brother the past, me the future.

Were you so tender with me to make up for how you'd treated Ricks?

Still, the rage, I never understood it for as much as I witnessed it.

Maybe he wasn't the son you wanted, or you were trying to mold him into that son, some version of you you had aspired to and failed, and Ricks not wanting to be your compensation.

Or he didn't obey you. Or mocked you. But was that enough?

Or he was Mom's favorite, everyone knew that, especially Judi, and always had been, that jealousy there, did Mom love Ricks more than you? When I was born, perhaps you finally found an ally in the house.

Or our lives were harder back then, when Ricks was small, when all this started, before your retirement and before I was born and we moved back to San Jose. In Bayonne, in Norfolk, in Key West, scant money and living in cramped base housing and no indication yet of that life improving. The big family treat back then, and which we continued to eat after you retired and things got better, open-face bologna sandwiches under the broiler. Did that long frustration, twenty-four years, smelt into rage?

Or maybe it was your father, how he had treated you, though all I knew about him was that he was good at leaving, he left the last time when you were thirteen, and so bad at counterfeiting he spent four years in prison for it. And if it was your father, how did that rage dissolve before it came down on me?

I loved you both so much. I could not bear to see the fear in my brother's eyes, the shame in his shoulders. The atrocity of your gaze.

You should never have hit him.

The Evening News

Ours was a TV family, the TV almost always on, an endless stream, six VHF channels and four UHF. Bonanza, Combat, McHale's Navy, Lost in Space, Star Trek, Laugh-In, Ed Sullivan, Lawrence Welk, Bugs Bunny, Charlie and Humphrey, football and baseball and bowling, every single NASA launch, the moon landing. Always on, and at least one of us watching, or not, but always on, the set warm and humming.

Every night during dinner, we watched the evening news together. Especially after my brother joined the Marines, only the three of us in the house, Judi long married and gone. My father and mother also read newspapers, assiduously, every morning at breakfast, the Chronicle, and the Mercury in the afternoon, and by their example, I joined them, starting with Peanuts and The Sporting Green. After Ricks enlisted, however, my father and mother grew hungrier for news on TV, with film clips showing us undeniable images of what transpired in the world, a world my brother might be sent into any day now.

Our dining room and family room were one long connected room, so when we sat at the round Colonial-style dining table, bronze-maple, we had a good view of the enormous console TV in the far corner. It was my job to race to the TV and change channels when needed.

A lot of my friends were jealous when they found out I was allowed to watch TV while we ate. And it surprised me that so many other families had unbending prohibitions against it: Never ever during dinner, that was sacred family time. My friends spoke of our dining habits as if we were some lawless gang flouting society's norms. What they didn't understand was that TV at dinner was neither diversion nor white noise, no blanket over deep familial silences. The evening news was a keen focus for us, almost like homework. We watched, digested, discussed, so I listened and asked all my questions. Watching the news was deemed essential in our house. You have to know what's happening outside your own little room, my father repeatedly said, one way or another.

I sat facing the family room, my mother nearest the kitchen, my father to my right. At dinner, the TV was turned up louder than normal, as if we might miss the one vital scrap of information that might justify the world. We ate what we always ate, off turquoise and beige Melmac plates. Chicken or liver or chuck, canned corn or peas or lima beans, instant or baked mashed potatoes, a dinner roll and pats of cold butter, iceberg salad with Thousand Island dressing. Ice tea and beer. We watched and ate, and when we were finished, my father smoked, and my mother and I leaned back as if we were smoking too. Sparky slept under the table.

The news rolled in from beyond our seeing. We waited until commercials to speak, Did you see that? What the hell is going on?

We might, especially on hot summer evenings, snap TV trays into place and eat in the family room, my father in his orange Naugahyde recliner, my mother in her Colonial print recliner, me on the matching Colonial print couch. The TV trays were a deep green and golden floral pattern, with a raised lip around the edges. Those nights we didn't eat what we always ate. Sometimes we'd get Crab Louie from Buy th' Bucket, with garlic bread, or on a rare occasion pizza, but most often on these evenings, we ate Swanson TV dinners from their aluminum foil trays. Fried chicken or Salisbury steak, a side of peas, a side of corn, apple pie bubbling in its little foil compartment. I was allowed to drink soda on TV tray nights.

The rhythmic hiss of the evening sprinkler in the front yard, the breeze it created moving through the front door and around the house. No lights on, save the blue fire of the TV.

Riots. There were always riots. Every year, every summer. Race riots, my father called them. I knew what that meant, my father made sure. Rochester, Harlem, Philadelphia, Watts, Cleveland, Omaha, Newark, Detroit, Minneapolis, Chicago, Baltimore.

Nighttime black and white footage. Burning buildings, and racing from and toward the flames, silhouetted by the flames, bodies running and running and throwing things. Police in helmets advanced on the silhouettes, pushed them back, pushed them to the ground, attacked. Night sticks, tear gas, water cannons, live ammunition, vicious German Shepherds. All night these cities burned, or so I had to imagine. Though we only saw one or two minutes of burning cities on the news, I knew the burning didn't stop, nor the police, when the cameras were turned off.

Why, I asked my father, why is there a riot?

Because the rioters are angry, and because they have harder lives than ours, because no one listens to negroes.

But why the fires, why the looting? Looting a brand-new word to me. On the playground at school, many of my classmates condemned the looting, having listened to their parents condemn it.

There's nothing else they can do, my father said, it's the only thing they can do with their anger. Because no one will listen. Because they're too poor.

Can we help them?

I don't know, he said, and I saw that he was defeated by this question.

For many years, we watched riots every night at dinner.

The assassinations. JFK, MLK, RFK. Shock and mourning.

And the war. We watched Cronkite on CBS because my father and mother trusted him, and when he eventually spoke the truth about Vietnam, trusted him even more. Cronkite always looked tired to me, worn out. We watched the film clips, couriered stateside from the night before, then developed and broadcast, so we were always watching the events of yesterday, leaving us to wonder what might be happening today.

Helicopters landed in fields of swaying grass, soldiers with M-16s leapt on or off the helicopters. Stretchers and bodies were loaded into the helicopters. Bandages, bloodstained. Villages burning, villagers haunted and dead. Plumes of napalm imploding the sky. The images never changed, they just kept on arriving. And on Fridays, the weekly death toll.

Why are we fighting this war?

No one really knows, my father said, but it's a war we can't win.

Why not?

We have no reason to be there. These people are defending their homes.

Why don't we stop then?

Because the bastards in Washington are plain stupid and they don't give a rat's ass what happens to other people's sons.

Our sons. My brother. Ricks would never go to Vietnam, despite volunteering over and over, but that did nothing to stop us from worrying. As if he might stow away on a troop transport, get himself to Vietnam and try to win the war single handedly.

What about Ricks? I asked my father.

He'll be okay, he said. He cracked open his Zippo and lit another cigarette.

Once.

June 28, 1968, a Friday. American casualties for the week, 52 KIA, 1 MIA.

Black Velvet

When my father had his first heart attack, in 1964, when I was seven, one week before Thanksgiving, the doctor's orders were clear, six months bed rest. Retired from the Navy only a few years earlier, he was now a welder for General Electric, where he fused mammoth pieces of nuclear reactors one to the other, which hulks would then be shipped to North Carolina or Belgium. My mother, who had never worked outside the house, instantly found a job as a key-punch operator for a credit union. We needed the money.

My job, she told me in the kitchen the night before his two-week hospital stay ended, was to look after my father, make sure he was settled on the couch in the family room each morning before I left for school, and make sure, when I returned in the afternoon, that he was still there and okay. She wanted me to spend time with him, entertain him, and make sure he took his pills, gave himself an injection in his belly fat, and had whatever else he needed.

I was also to make sure that he did not drink or smoke, cross my heart.

Ricks was still living with us, but he was seventeen, a senior, had a girlfriend and a car, and was not around as much as my mother would have wished. Judi was married and living in Seattle with her own family by then.

When Christmas break arrived and I was home all day with my father, I worried, yes, but was thrilled to be with him and proud to be trusted with such an important job. It was a gray and rainy December, and that made it easier for both of us to be happy to stay inside.

Every morning I served him half a grapefruit, usually a Ruby, which I divided into sections with a serrated-edge spoon. I sprinkled liquid saccharine, instead of sugar, onto the grapefruit, then Zwieback toast and a cup of tea, sometimes Sanka. Real coffee was forbidden. He and I ate breakfast together in the family room and watched TV, Morning Movie Time, while he ate delicately and I plunged through a bowl of Lucky Charms.

For lunch there was a scoop of cottage cheese on a bed of lettuce and tomato, and more Zwieback and tea. Some afternoons he convinced me to open a can of sardines, and we'd eat them on Saltines with mustard, washed down with cans of Tab.

Of course I knew when he stepped out to the patio for a cigarette, Parliaments, and would watch him through the curtains, Sparky by my side and equally concerned.

And I knew when he went to the side yard and came back more cheerful, a tang of something clear on his breath. My mother never knew.

All day he told me stories. His life before the Navy, his life in the Navy. I listened to these stories as if I might not hear them again, and he told them as if he might soon forget them. Back in Oklahoma, he'd start, or, Once in Greece, or, Let me tell you about barracuda.

During those weeks we tried to play board games, as if expected to, Park'n'Shop, my mother's favorite, and Mousetrap and Sorry and Candyland. We didn't own Monopoly. These games were pointless, my father and I sensed, though never said aloud, time eaters that always ended the same way, but he would continue his stories while we played, and that was enough to keep me rolling the dice.

We read, too, but the TV always on. My father read to me from his magazines, Argosy and True, tales of treasure and rescue, and I read to him from my Scholastic paperbacks, Murder by Moonlight and Radar Commandos, more to impress than entertain.

My father and I decorated the Christmas tree that year. This had always been my mother's task and joy, but she was exhausted from her new job while still cooking dinners and doing all the laundry, so she thought it might be a nice project for me and him. One Sunday we left my father at home, the first time we'd left him alone since his heart attack, and drove up Mount Umunhum to a lot where you cut down your own tree. In a deep and chill winter fog, my mother and I picked a tree, and sawed at its trunk for half an hour before getting it loose. Up there on that mountain, no one else in sight, and the broad valley shrouded, my father seemed perilously far away.

He sat in his orange recliner and directed, while I hung the ornaments. The glass-blown Santa boot, the glass-blown snowmen and reindeer, the brittle metallic spheres of red and green, the strings of bulbous lights, the blizzard of tinsel, my mother's favorite, which nearly hid the tree, and which we would take down later, strand by strand, to save for next year. When I'd finished, my father placed the lighted star on top.

All during those first weeks, Sparky parked herself next to my father and rarely left his side. It rained every day, the world black-gray and close around us.

There was so much time that year, after Christmas, and we filled it happily and lazily.

Then. Whose idea was it? I suspected my Aunt Mimi, my mother's arty sister, and her husband, Crazy Uncle Don, a weekend painter of paintings none of us understood because they were modern. But one day, a paint-by-number kit appeared in the house, a set of four landscapes, the same image, a stand of vague trees repeated through the seasons. My father completed these quickly but was disappointed they were still so obviously paint-by-number.

He had never before, he told me, painted anything other than the side of a barn or the hull of a ship.

I watched from the couch as he painted the leaves budding, turning brash green, then orange and red, then the bare branches of winter.

Soon after, two new kits arrived. These canvases, however, were not the white cloth-covered boards of the four seasons, but close-cropped black velvet, each one, therefore, a night scene. We often saw black velvet paintings at the San Jose Flea Market, John Kennedy a popular subject, and eagles with snakes in their talons.

The black velvet kits arrived during the longest nights of winter, when the day always seemed one minute past dusk, the Christmas tree lighted blue and yellow and green and red and white, the tinsel trapping snippets of those colors. My father worked under a desk lamp I set up next to his chair. The rest of the room, the house, stayed dark.

There were two black velvet kits, two paintings in each, along with little pots of paint and fine brushes. The first was ducks, three in each panel, the ducks rising against pussy willows and a full moon. On one canvas, three ducks flew to the left, on the other, three flew to the right. The ducks had bright teal bars showing from within their blue-black and dun wings.

The second set was matadors, each silhouetted against yet another full moon, capes swirling, with one matador facing left, one facing right. I could not see where the bulls might be hiding. Everywhere along the matadors' uniforms, vermillion buttons.

My father's blunt fingers held the brushes with a graceful grip, his focus microscopic. I kept as still as I could, said little. The tips of those brushes were as fine as a single hair, his fingernails thick as nickels.

The finished black velvet canvases were immaculate. Not a single stroke visible, not a smudge or overlap, and they didn't at all look paint-by-number. They were real paintings, and the lemon-bright moons in them shone calmly over the ocean-black velvet. My mother hung them in the front hallway.

Those afternoons, close and gloomy and brilliant at once. Those afternoons.

That May, my father was re-hired by General Electric, but only as a gate guard, checking badges at the entrance to the employee parking lot, late shift, four to midnight. He was grateful to be working again.

At least twice a week, my mother and I would drive out to General Electric with a warm homemade dinner for him, liver and onions or meatloaf. From blocks away I could see him in the little guard shack where he stood for hours, warm-lit and yellow, and the dark night all around.

Astronomy

Every year from late July through late August, the Perseid meteor shower is visible across the northern hemisphere. At this point in its orbit around the sun, the earth passes through a cloud of debris left behind by the comet Swift-Tuttle. The comet itself, however, only visits the solar system every 133 years. Out of this long wake, meteors, composed primarily of dust and ice, enter the earth's atmosphere, and the friction of that transit causes the meteors to burn brightly before disintegrating. Shooting stars, falling stars. The meteors may have been waiting centuries in the dark for that single moment of combustion. The Perseid shower's peak frequency occurs on August 12. I read all of this in The Science's Library's Meteors and Asteroids, and spent an afternoon memorizing it on my bedroom floor with Sparky by my side.

So each August, starting when I was nine, my father and I walked the few blocks to Cherry Park for midnight viewings of the Perseids. When we first moved to Flood

Drive, when I was five, Cherry Park had been real cherry orchards, where every spring my friends and I got sick from eating the cherries because we were too impatient for them to ripen. But over the course of one year, the orchards were transformed into an L-shaped lawn big enough for two football fields, and one baseball diamond with backstop and benches. At the far end of the park was a remnant walnut grove, twenty or so trees, and a small playground with monkey bars and swings over beds of tanbark. The park was bordered by identical streets of new houses, the houses that had replaced the cherries.

My father and I took along blankets and lawn chairs, a thermos of coffee and a thermos of hot chocolate. It was rare in San Jose, even in August when the days were suffocating, that midnight wasn't a cooling hour.

We looked up at the stars.

My father graduated seventh grade, this was in Oregon, the farm they'd owned for seven years. Then one morning, his father skipped out on the family, for the last time, so my father and his brother had to work alongside their mother, and school was no longer possible. But whether he was naturally inclined, or encouraged by his Navy training, my father loved the sciences, from the mechanical to the atomic. A diver must be able to perform complex math if he's going to surface alive. A welder must understand the molecular structure of metals.

As a family we of course went to church, every Sunday, United Church of Christ, Dr. Foster presiding, but that was for my mother's sake. My father and I smiled and sang and prayed along in church, and never contradicted by mother's simple and gentle theology, it seemed harmless enough. But my father and I wanted to explore how the world truly worked, concerned most with that which could be proven. My father had seen too much of the world to believe otherwise. I hadn't seen enough.

Though I knew our family didn't have a lot of what my mother called spending money, my father kept finding ways to feed my interest in the sciences.

In second grade, my first chemistry set, a flimsy tin cabinet of vials and test tubes and a plastic microscope with slides. We mixed and combusted chemicals, stared deep into pond water or ocean or blood.

Then the Science Library. Every month a saddle-stitched volume arrived in the mail. Fishes of the Pacific, Cephalopods (two volumes), Cactus, Geodes, Volcanoes, and separate volumes for the sun and the moon and each planet and the asteroid belt. Six volumes fit into a slip-case box with a ribbon pull, and the boxes filled and stacked up in my bedroom. I read each new title cover to cover.

My first telescope, a three-inch refractor on a wobbly stand, perfectly fine for moon viewing, but when my father registered my passion for Astronomy, he managed, somehow, to buy a six-inch reflector, on a weighted, locking stand, complete with various lenses, including a moon filter and a sun filter, and a mount for a camera. Mars, Jupiter, the Rings of Saturn. I used that telescope most summer nights, and once during a 90% solar eclipse in Aunt Mimi's backyard.

A home planetarium too, six plastic sections of dome we screwed together and hung from the ceiling, but with a puny and faint projector. It was cheap but magnificent. In the living room, I gave my parents tours of the constellations.

Then he bought me a better microscope, off a buddy from work. It came in a wooden cabinet, and was steel and black and heavy, and it showed us the tiniest views of life. With this my father included a highly polished demonstration weld he'd made, two inches across and cased in black plastic. Under the microscope it was nearly impossible to find the seam that united the two alloys.

Aquariums. Zoos. Botanical Gardens. Real planetariums. The observatory on Mount Lick and its 36-inch refracting telescope. Riverbanks. Under rocks. Tide pools. The front lawn. On TV, every dawn rocket launch, the first spacewalk, the first moon landing. Everywhere was someplace worth exploring.

The summer I was turning twelve, we went to Cherry Park again, on August 12th, our tradition. No one else was out that night. Everything else was quiet. We set our lawn chairs northwest, ratcheted them back as far as they would go. We located Cassiopeia and drew a line south from her throne to find Perseus, who held the Gorgon's head in one hand, avenging sword in the other.

Soon the first meteor pulled a thread of light out of Perseus and skated toward the horizon. I could almost hear the sound it made, it must have made a sound, burning up like that. Then another meteor, and another. Some were green, some were blue. Some shone for two or three seconds, ice on fire.

That year I had an ambitious plan. I brought along a clipboard and sheets of binder paper I had carefully ruled into columns. Time (GMT), to the nearest second. Duration. Brightness, on a scale of 5. Color. And a space for a name. I would give each meteor a name, unconcerned that what I named would no longer exist by the time I named it.

We sat in our lawn chairs and sipped from our thermoses, called out each sighting. I tried to fill in every row on the binder paper, but soon gave up on naming the meteors, then soon gave up on everything else. There were too many, sometimes three or four a minute, sometimes two or three at once. I was writing the impossible.

I grew frustrated.

Don't worry about that, my father said. Let's enjoy. Make a mark for each one instead.

My father called out each meteor, and I tallied them with hash marks. After more than sixty, I stopped counting.

We settled in to watching, all those bright moments come and gone, all without names.

Mac

Several months after arriving at the Huntington Beach oil fields, living in the cold shack on boiled potatoes and lard-fried dough, and with no visit to the ocean across the highway, Elwell's family suddenly up and left.

On that day, Elwell was throwing rocks at an empty sardine can, trying to knock it off the porch rail, even though his mother, peeling potatoes next to him, kept telling him to stop. Elwell knew she didn't mean it, it was merely something to say, what she said every day about everything.

Then some commotion behind Elwell, as if the air were bending and twisting, made him turn and look. His father held Nim by the scruff, as if he were a puppy, and pushed him along, though he occasionally pulled him back too, if only, it seemed, that he might push him farther and harder.

The knees of Nim's overalls were split open, his shirt torn at one shoulder, hair mussed, face dirty and streaked with tears. Their father's left eye was swollen, blood on his khaki shirt and hands.

The closer they came to the shack, the faster they walked. Elwell started to run to them, but his mother's glare was a lasso.

Nim and his father flew up the three steps, and when they reached the porch, his father shoved Nim hard, to one side, and Nim fell, scraping, to the porch, a heap of sobs.

We're leaving right now, Goddammit, start packing. His father said this as he entered the shack, speaking to no one and everyone in the world. His mother followed, closing the door gently, and they stayed in the shack for a long time without making any noise.

Nim raised himself up against the wall, wiped tears and snot on his sleeve. Elwell sat next to him and awkwardly patted his brother's shoulder.

What happened? Elwell said after a long time.

Nim said nothing.

Then he said, Just don't ever get caught.

The car was nearly packed when a man in a brown uniform with brown patches, and cradling a shotgun, came to the shack, though he stood a ways away, watching them. He stood there until they drove off. Elwell turned and looked back. The man ambled after them until they passed out of the front gate.

Boys, their mother said a few miles down the road, we're going to Los Angeles for a while. It'll be like a vacation for you two. Like when we visit your cousins in Brownsville. You always like that, don't you. Your father and I have to look for new jobs, you understand, don't you. But you boys will stay at a wonderful place, with a lot of other children to play with, and good food too, better than we can afford here, that's for sure.

His mother's words got sucked out the car's open windows and blown over the nearby ocean.

Nim said nothing. Their father said nothing.

For how long? Elwell asked. He was trying hard to imagine what this new place would be like, Los Angeles, but could not. He only heard that he was going where his parents weren't.

Not long, his mother said.

What happened? he asked.

That's none of your damn business, his father said. His words were low and dark and roamed about the car. Mind yourself, his father said. Or else.

It must have been very bad, what happened, Elwell thought.

The highway up the coast veered closer and closer to the ocean, until, at last, it was close enough to hit with a rock. The ocean was sitting there, right there. Elwell knew he shouldn't say anything. But.

Can we please stop at the ocean?

His parents negotiated a treaty with their eyes.

Why the hell not, his father said, and the gloom in the car nearly lifted.

The sand was pure white, the ocean pale blue. From months of staring at the ocean every day, Elwell had noted that the ocean liked to change color.

They ate pork sandwiches, but that was all, no oranges, there had never been another orange. Then Nim stripped to his underwear, so Elwell did too, and they snuck up on the water. Elwell's ankles snapped in the cold, but soon it didn't matter. There was a stiff breeze blowing onshore, the scent of the ocean thick with salt and nearly visible.

Elwell, honey! Stay close! his mother called.

Nim waded into the surf up to his waist, then he dove under and surfaced a few feet beyond the breakers. He waved and whooped and bounced. The sunlight shattered and gathered around him.

Elwell pushed forward.

Elwell! Elwell! No!

He stood in the shallows and watched his brother swimming and diving. For Elwell, having waited so long, months of staring through fence slats, the ocean seemed to double in size and then double again, and again, impossible to gauge, and today he realized for the first time that it was as deep as it was wide.

His father called them back to the car.

Driving through Los Angeles that afternoon, the houses pink and sand-colored, and Easter blue and yellow, Elwell thought, this must be an ocean of houses. The green lawns, what were they?

They parked in front of a big big house, two stories high and five houses wide, a soft beige house with a red roof that curved like waves. Inside the front doors, in a tall empty room, a tiny woman, dressed all in black, sat behind a desk offering up a watery smile. The woman talked to their mother and father while Elwell and Nim sat on a wooden bench and kicked their legs. Elwell heard only silence in their whispers. Finally, the brothers were called forward.

Mr. Macoby, the woman said rather loudly, may we have your children's names and birthdates and birthplace, to register them properly, you see.

Nimion Divine Providence Macoby, June 8, 1916. Elwell Ricks Macoby, April 7, 1921. Brownsville, Texas.

And the reason for bringing them to us today? I must have a reason.

Indigence, his father said.

The woman wrote on her piece of paper.

Elwell understood nothing.

Very well, the woman said, sign here, please, then we'll get the boys settled. It's best for all, has been my experience, to do this as quickly as possible.

At the car, his mother unloaded the black suitcase Elwell and his brother shared.

We'll be back in two shakes of a lamb's tail, she said, so don't go worrying, and remember to have a wonderful time, it's a vacation. She kissed them each on the cheek, then slipped into the car. His mother's face was hot when she kissed Elwell.

You be good boys now, his father said. You hear? He reached out and raised Nim's chin.

Do you hear?

Yes, sir.

Elwell did not like this place. It wasn't at all like a vacation. He didn't like anything about today, didn't even like the ocean anymore. He wanted to run to his mother and fold himself into her.

When the car pulled away, the woman in black put her hands on their shoulders and guided Nim and Elwell back to the building. The sky was the color of the ocean of houses.

You're going to love it here, the woman said, at the Nelly Frank Orphanage. As long as you remember to be good Christian boys. Will you do that for your parents?

The first night, Elwell and Nim slept in the same bed, in their own room, and it was the most comfortable bed Elwell had ever lay on, and it almost made him want to like this new place, but he resisted that thought.

He and Nim did not sleep a wink, however. Nim whispered all night to Elwell, repeating that everything was going to be okay, that he would look after Elwell, that their parents would return soon.

We're not real orphans, Nim said. Remember, it's a vacation. We're only pretending to be orphans.

The next day Elwell was taken to a dormitory, one for the younger boys, rows of three-high bunk beds, flimsy mattresses laid over slack ropes. There was an old orange crate for Elwell to store his clothes. It smelled here, like too many boys, and none of the boys said anything to him.

Elwell almost cried when Nim was taken to the older boys' dormitory, but he knew he shouldn't do that. He didn't breathe until he saw Nim at breakfast in the rotten-egg dining hall a little while later. They ate the eggs and the oatmeal, and the food was not better than his mother's, it was like a crayon drawing of his mother's cooking, paper.

From then on, Elwell and Nim only saw each other at meals, though they had to sit at separate tables, and in the play yard, where a white line divided the big boys from the little boys, and they could only whisper with great caution.

On the fourth morning, out in the play yard, Elwell found himself surrounded by a gang of boys his own size, though they looked much older. The boys wore dull gray and brown clothes, a heap of laundry. Their dirty hands were curled into fists

Elwell the baby! Elwell the baby!

The boys pushed him from side to side. He wanted to lie on the ground and sleep.

Nim tore up, knocking the boys aside.

If you got a problem with him, he said, glowering down on them, you got a problem with me. You, come here. I said come here.

The head boy stepped toward Nim, his face down and flushed with shame. Nim grabbed the boy's shoulders and spun him around, pinned his arms.

Little brother, Nim said. Show him you're no baby.

There was no choice.

Elwell landed a punch in the boy's gut, and he crumpled to the ground. The boy was crying, Elwell saw, but trying hard to hide it from everyone. Elwell almost wanted to comfort him.

Nim made sure everyone in the walled-in and asphalt yard, the knots of gray and brown boys and the white-shirted minders too, everyone, was looking at him before he spoke again. He nudged the boy on the ground with his toe.

His name isn't Elwell, Nim said. It's Mac. Call him Mac. Or else.

His brother had claimed him, saved him, and named him.

Mac.

Nimion

You were always looking for your brother. Weren't you? The last time you saw Uncle Nim we were stationed in Key West, 1960, I was only three. He called from a pay phone just outside base housing, and you met him at the gate and arranged visitor permits for him and his new girlfriend. They would sleep on our couch for a few days, until they settled elsewhere.

Just past Miami, Nim's engine had blown, and they'd taken a bus the rest of the way, but he'd already attracted a handful of speeding tickets by then. Nevertheless, you were thrilled to see him, you always told me when telling this story, opened our home to him, he was family after all. Nim promised he was a changed man, and if you could help him out, just a little, he swore to make it up to you. Mom seemed to know better, you said.

You paid his tickets, co-signed for a brand-new white convertible, passed him a handful of cash to get him back on his feet. A few days later, he left Key West, promising to be back in a few days, he promised, a job prospect he absolutely had to nail down up in Saint Pete. Nim left behind the new girlfriend, and after a week with no word from him, you gave her bus fare to New Mexico and drove her to the station.

You never saw your brother again.

Whenever you told this story, and you told it a lot, to anyone who would listen, you laughed, Crazy old Nim but that's family for you. Whenever I heard you tell this story I knew I was supposed to laugh too, but the look on Mom's face, that made laughing along with you far too complicated.

Before Key West, the last time he'd showed up was in Norfolk in 1949, just passing through, and he begged you to forgive him for all he'd taken from you three years earlier, the truck and the plumbing supplies. You forgave him, naturally, had to, because after you re-upped in the Navy, he'd returned to San Jose, wooed and married Mom's sister, Aunt Mimi, and was living with her and their two daughters, Lory and Meri. You loaned him money, of course, to get him back to San Jose and his family, so he left again. But he didn't go back, and a few days later, Aunt Mimi called to let us know Nim had abandoned her and his daughters when it was discovered he was married to two other women at the same time.

Before that? In 1945, the war fresh over. You and Mom had moved back to San Jose, thinking to settle there, and were building a Sears kit-home on a vacant lot on the East Side, at the foot of Mount Hamilton. You and Mom and Judi, just two years old, and baby Ricks, you all slept at Mom's folks near downtown, then you and Mom hammered and painted all day. When Nim showed up, not even a phone call, he pitched in with the construction, sleeping at the half-finished house for security. He told you all his war stories. He'd parachuted into France immediately following D-Day, and then into Germany, two years later, which was when he'd been shot, in mid-air, in the gut, and had not yet fully recovered. You told him of your war, dive school in San Diego, then Espiritu Santo, then finally Harlem for Deep Sea training. How had so much happened to you both.

You spoke of your father too, dead four years now, not seen since he left the family high and dry in Oregon in '34. You were both in Basic, you the Navy, Nim the Army, when you received notice of his death via Western Union. There was more news, you'd learn through collect calls from Grandma Macoby. Your father had spent four of those missing years at McNeil Island State Prison in Washington, for counterfeiting. This explained the $20 bills he sometimes gave to you and Nim back in Oregon, telling you to buy anything you wanted, just don't forget to bring back the change. Even before he'd left the family, he was counterfeiting. How? That old bastard, Nim said.

But the war was over, the settling could begin. You loved having your brother back, drinking and smoking with him on the unpainted porch of the nearly finished house.

Then one morning your truck was gone, and Nim too, and the water heater, the bathtub and sinks, the copper pipes and copper wiring. Gone, no word.

Six months later, you re-enlisted in the Navy.

And before that, 1939, when you'd both mustered out of a three-year stint in the Army in Hawaii. You and Nim went directly from San Francisco to Grandma Macoby's in Modesto. The two of you made plans, there was work with the CCC, you'd heard, in Yosemite, building roads, honest work. One night Nim went out to meet an old friend and did not return. You went to Yosemite and built roadside walls, stone by stone.

And before that even. You returned to Modesto, August 1936, as you and your brother had planned, after a year spent apart, each of you in search of real work. Nim, you imagined, had been in Southern California the whole time. You'd been working on a horse ranch, and hated to leave it, but you'd sworn to the rendezvous. He did show up, easy as a breeze, with a plan for the two of you to join the Army's last cavalry regiment at Fort Ord. This time the two of you left together, to enlist, even though you were only fifteen.

Before that, the first time he ditched you, you and he and Grandma had just moved to Modesto. This was 1935, late summer, when the three of you had completed the main room of the house Grandma was building of orange crates scavenged from a nearby packing plant. He went out to meet a friend, left a note for you, didn't come back. In his note, he told you to do the same, go out into the world, there was nothing for either of you in Modesto, but made you promise to meet him there exactly one year later.

So you left too, not long after, wandering up and down the valley, looking for work, farther and farther, until you heard about the horse ranch outside Bishop on the other side of the Sierras.

Nim was always deserting, and you always welcomed him without question. You made each desertion into a fairy tale, one of the funny ones.

And still kept looking for him.

So many of the camping and fishing trips you and I took were an excuse for you to keep looking for your brother. I never blamed you for that.

In the summer of '69, you and I drove east and north to Chico, where we did do a little fishing, but mostly you looked for your brother. Nim, you'd heard from someone somewhere, had been spotted this far north in the Great Valley, supposedly working the fields and orchards for pennies a pound. You and he had picked a lot of crops together, he could always fall back on that. But you thought he might be too old now, you were worried about his health, that parachute gut-shot that never healed.

You needed to find him, you told me, did I understand, and I said that I did.

That weekend we stayed at an old wooden motor court, individual bungalows painted white with red trim. There was no pool, but it was right on the river. We fished our first morning there, in an eddied bend, but caught nothing, you and I were always better at lake or ocean fishing. Then you left me alone for the afternoon. I knew where you were going, you were going from bar to bar, where else would you look.

Upstream from the motor court, a hundred yards or so, was a series of broad, stepped waterfalls, three levels of waterfall that fed a deep swimming hole. There were lots of kids there, and their families, I'd be safe, you told me, have fun, you told me, here's a couple of bucks for lunch, a key to the room. You'd be back in time for dinner.

I slid and splashed and basked on the flat smooth boulders, played with the other kids, and made a new friend, Tommy Shaw, whose father invited me to their picnic, sweets and sodas and hot dogs. But by four or so, the world poppy-orange, I couldn't do anything but wait, so I sat at the top of the falls, clearly visible, and watched the other kids and their families, but was only urgently waiting. Hours. Finally, just as dusk had violet-dusted the river, there you were.

We ate at a local diner, you told me Nim stories. You'd found out nothing that day. But you had to go back out tonight, you sensed he was close. Some people thought they'd maybe seen a guy around town who looked like him.

Lock the door behind you, you said, watch TV, I won't be long.

I was asleep when you returned, but the room's lights were all on, and I didn't know what time it was.

You were banging on the door, snuffling like a bear. I took the chain off but didn't unlock the lock. I was certain it was you, but I also thought it couldn't be you.

You tried the lock again, I heard the key glancing off it, but the key wouldn't fit, you shouted my name once, and I finally opened the door. Before I could say anything, you thumped past me, fell onto the bed, and you were gone.

I didn't know why but it seemed important that I get you out of your clothes, so I did. Then I managed to get you under the covers, and I crawled in next to you.

I didn't put the chain back on, or lock the lock, or turn off any of the lamps. In case someone might need shelter in the middle of the night.

Buy th' Bucket

Of all the bars my father took me to, this was our favorite. It wasn't far from the house, just down Curtner, maybe half a mile, close enough we often walked. Once, on the walk home, Sparky met us halfway, and when she saw us coming towards her, stopped, sat and waited, then joined us, a late summer afternoon, gold and purple. But proximity wasn't the bar's only tug. There was the famous Crab Louie our family craved. And my father and I were regulars too, known and welcomed.

Nothing to write home about, my father often said of Buy th' Bucket, but good enough for the Macobys.

It sat at one end of a five-store strip mall, a barber, a drug store, bargain women's clothing, a dry cleaner with 24-hour Martinizing. Plain asphalt parking lot, no trees or light standards. The painted sign on the roof, pin-lighted at night, spelled the bar's name with characters meant to look like pieces of split rail. The two narrow windows, tinted, squinted in the bright San Jose light, a neon Coors

101

sign in one, neon Oly in the other. The facade was otherwise beige stucco and featureless. A bar.

From bright noon through the windowless doors and into immediate darkness, the leaving of that world for this. A moment's pause, then the colors began to seep into the room, the shapes to take substance.

Against the far wall, painted on the far wall, the menu, in fluorescent oranges and greens and pinks, shimmered under the purple glow of black lights, each item painted cartoonishly, title and price beneath. Crab Louie, Shrimp Louie, Garlic Bread, Spaghetti and Meatballs, Hamburger, Cheeseburger, Fries, Fried Calamari, Steamed Clams. I often wished the food was as lurid as the signs.

Above the bar, a television that was always on when a game was on, and on Saturday afternoons, our regular time, there was always a game on, and always one customer begging the bartender to switch to a different game. Boxing or bowling or college football or Wide World of Sports, but never at the expense of the Giants, our team. Next to the TV, a Hamm's Beer sign, with a waterfall that sparkled and rippled, a laughing bear fishing, The Land of Sky Blue Waters.

The bar, the counter, was L-shaped, four seats and eight. Rows of bottles on the back bar, a glowing wall of amber and blue and green and moonlight, as if the light emanated from these liquors. Three taps, Coors and Oly and Hamm's. Rows of glassware, highball and rocks and martini and shot and pints and halfs. Stacks of napkins on the bar, with a variety of risqué cartoons and jokes on them, and I thought I got the jokes but was troubled by the Buxom wenches, as my father called them. Cocktail onions and maraschino cherries and pitted olives and lime wedges, each condiment in a little black trough. Glasses filled with three sizes of straw. The sticky sheen of the wooden bar top.

A jukebox, of course, two songs for two bits, the jukebox trimmed with tubes of bubbling red liquid, like a science experiment. Mostly Country and Western, Eddie Arnold and Buck Owens and Johnny Cash, but also Dean Martin, Ray Charles, Don Ho. Nothing for me, though I played the songs anyway, songs I liked because my father liked them. The drop of the coin, the chunky buttons, A through V and 1 through 9, the flop of the forty-five onto the platter, the click and hiss of the needle, Tiny bubbles in the wine, make-a me happy, make me feel fine.

A pinball machine, Rocket Ship, always the same, and try as I might, I never got past Mars.

Table shuffleboard, a long wooden track, eight steel pucks, four red and four blue, a gutter filled with white slippery crumbs that smelled like almonds and which made the pucks glide. I called it sawdust and that was close enough. No one else played this game on Saturday afternoons, so I played against myself, red vs. blue, never kept score. There was a spotlight that haloed the table, and I could imagine it was any playing field for any sport, and with every match I somehow summoned the skill and endurance to win, at the last second and always heroically.

The rest of the dark bare room was a lazy grid of picnic tables and benches, where sometimes families ate together, or men huddled in conversation, or one man alone needing more space into which he could stare. The floor was cement, painted black.

Someone always at the pay phone in the narrow hall that led to the bathrooms, Gents and Gals.

Chief, the bartender called out when we entered, and he held his arms wide. I loved that moment, the warmth of it, as if the real fun had arrived at last. In return, my father offered a casual salute, along with that smile of his.

And Robert the Bum, the bartender would bark, good to see you, young man. I never remembered his name, but I knew him and liked him, always the same bartender, thin and pale, with an immaculate white apron. I'd seen him welcome a hundred customers with nothing more than a miserly nod. My father was Chief.

Shot and a beer for my father, Roy Rogers for me, two cherries and one olive on the same toothpick, a package of Beer Nuts.

Nothing much exciting happened at Buy th' Bucket, at least not when I was there. Saturday afternoons, slow and simple, all of us indoors against the shrill sun. I played Shuffleboard, Rocket Ship, fed the jukebox. Watched the Giants on TV. Listened to my father tell his stories, Espirtu Santo and Bossy the Cow, the horse ranch on the far side of the Sierras when he was only fourteen, joining the Army at fifteen and getting his first tattoo then in Honolulu, all the stories I never got tired of listening to and always asked for again. On a good day, he'd lift up his shirt and show everyone the trail of scars from his shoulder on down. He'd got these in the Mediterranean from a Portuguese Man-O-War.

My father talked to men he knew from here, and only from here. Victor Davis, hunched and scrawny but a Lockheed engineer, every Saturday, gin and tonic. Alejandro Castro, a welder like my father, almost every Saturday, Coors. Bobby Wilson, of indeterminate vocation, every Saturday, and I suspected, every day and possibly every night as well, something brown with ice and a cherry, Keep 'em comin'. Others my father knew slightly or not at all, it didn't matter. My father told his stories, and he listened to theirs and tucked them away to tell me later or explain to me later.

Rounds of bar dice, the cup slammed down again and again, groans of anguish and taunting victory, a pile of quarters collected, divvied up, shuffled about.

I listened in on the men's stories, but also didn't, bouncing from one station to the other, always ending up on the stool to my father's left, which he saved for me.

Only once was there trouble that I saw. A man at the far end of the bar, no one my father knew, talking loudly about two black men at a nearby table, and spitting, over and over again, the word my father never permitted me to say. Finally my father rose, went to the man, turned him on his stool, and told him to Shut up and shut up now. Never, ever, he stressed, use that language in front of my son. Oh, yeah? the man said, standing, and while he was taller than my father, my father clearly outranked him in fury. Never, ever, my father said, and he pushed the man back onto his stool with one finger. Shut your damn yap, my father said. The bar grew quiet, the man gulped his beer and left. The two men who'd been insulted raised their beers to my father.

A one shot and two or three beer afternoon, that was the usual. Easy.

And the famous Crab Louie, delivered by anonymous hands through the small blue-lighted kitchen's order-up window. Fresh crab from Santa Cruz trucked over the hill, then cooked, cracked, shredded. Drenched in the bar's secret-recipe Thousand Island dressing. To go, packed tight in Chinese food take-out cartons, nothing but crab, why they called this place Buy th' Bucket. We made the salad bed when we got home, and we always brought some home, Hard for your mom to get mad if we bring home the Louie.

Almost always, two cartons of Louie, one large and one small. The large was for home, with iceberg lettuce and hard-boiled eggs and black olives and asparagus. Lemon wedges.

But the small Louie, that we shared seated at the bar, forkful after forkful, guilty because we were hiding our piggishness, but the crab that much tastier because of the guilt. My mother never knew.

One last taste of this luxurious Saturday before stepping out into the sun and what might be waiting for us there.

Sports

My brother played football and baseball, starting at six and all through high school. As a senior, he played the second half of the Homecoming Game against Del Mar with a concussion so severe he did not recall a single snap. We watched him wobble off the field in his purple and gold Camden Cougars uniform, number 64. He was sent back in the next play. He was starting center and they needed his body up front. My mother and my brother's girlfriend Jan were appalled, pale. My father seemed impressed, laughed about it later.

The fingers on Ricks's left hand were permanently spread, two to each side of his palm, like Spock's greeting on Star Trek, shaped by his catcher's mitt and the speed and smack of countless pitches. My father pitched my brother in the backyard, often until it was too dark to see, my father loudly urging him to keep at it, so my brother kept at it.

When he joined the Marines, Ricks was no longer an athlete but a weapon.

My father had not had time for sports in his childhood, nor occasion, having left school in seventh grade to work on the farm in Oregon. But when he joined the Army, at the age of fifteen, 1936, he discovered that he could earn a 72-hour leave if he boxed against another soldier and won. So he donned the company's boxing trunks and gloves and stepped into the ring while a crowd of soldiers bet on the two boxers and cheered heartily for one of them to collapse or at least get cut and bleed. He'd never boxed before, he told me, but had fought plenty, at the orphanage in Los Angeles, on the horse ranch in Bishop, and later, at the CCC camp in Yosemite. Real fights, fisticuffs, he called them, angry and urgent and senseless.

He continued to box when he joined the Navy, one month after Pearl Harbor and married to my mother.

During Navy basic training, a 72-hour leave was enough time to take the train from the base in San Diego up the coast to Atascadero, where my mother was still living with her parents, and later, during dive school, still in San Diego, my mother installed in Navy housing, it meant three days of real R and R.

If a sailor lost a match, the prize was a pitiful 24-hour leave, barely enough time to get to the bars on lower Broadway, get stinking drunk, and find his way back to base. My father claimed he never lost a bout, and there was a picture of him in the album in the living room, gloating over a boxer he'd just knocked out, cheering faces in the background. All in black and white.

Once in Greece, after the war, he'd gotten into it with some Greek sailors, everyone drunk, and fleeing them, leaped over a steel picket fence, caught one of the spikes in his belly and lay bleeding. He was always happy to show off that scar. The Greek sailors caught up with him, beat and kicked him, then left him for the Shore Patrol. Sometimes, he told me, you do lose.

Men were always ready to fight, he told me, but I knew that already, I had seen my brother and my father in the backyard, bare-knuckled and bloody, my brother, that is. But my father never asked me to fight anyone, not even when some older boy beat me up. He seemed to know I wasn't that son.

As a diver, first Deep Sea then scuba, his body was subjected to dangers more brutal than any sport. If a diver rose too quickly to the surface, the Bends twisted him inside out, might even kill him, and my father had on several occasions spent an agonizing 24-hours in the decompression chamber, equalizing the pressure in his blood with the pressure of the world. Also, Barracuda, Man-O-War, sea mines, depth charges, currents swift and unpredictable.

I was never going to be an athlete. I loved playing baseball, but mostly schoolyard with friends, and I was in Pee Wee League for three years, one step less serious than Little League, no real uniforms, only matching hats and t-shirts. There were no try-outs or cuts in Pee Wee League, everyone played at least three innings a game. I was not so much concerned with winning as I was happy to stand with my friends, Rich Davis and Keith Caldwell and Scotty Campbell, on a big patch of grass and dirt under the valley's wide sky, and later go out for ice cream with the team, win or lose. I was a decent hitter but a slow runner, and because there were no home-run fences, I racked up a lot of triples, cut off at third by lazy throws from the centerfield.

In my last year of Pee Wee League, the Fammatre Falcons, my father volunteered as coach, and he treated me as fairly as he could. He gave each boy a shot at pitching during a real game, and I was rightfully pulled after two batters, sent back to first base, where my left-handed glove might be of use. I could anchor a double play, and I did once complete an unassisted double play, snagging a line drive over my head, then casually stepping on the bag at first, a moment of grace.

At the end of the season, when awards were handed out, I received a small trophy, a baseball set in gold prongs above a tiny brass plaque, M.I.P, Most Improved Player. I spent a long afternoon talking with Sparky, the two of us wondering if the trophy were genuine or a gift from my father.

But I stopped baseball after that season, when football suddenly seemed more glamorous.

We had always watched football on TV, my father and brother and I, and sometimes my cousin Chuck. It was what we did on Sunday afternoons in the fall, seasonal and clockwork. My brother and I played a lot of football in our front yard, toss and catch, working on tight spirals. We also ran simple plays, The Long Bomb, often down the middle of Flood Dr., and the Buttonhook, where I snapped the ball to Ricks, ran five yards, stopped fast and turned and gathered the ball into my gut. I learned how to punt too. My brother, twelve years older, was gentle with his blocking and tackling.

And I played tag football with the neighborhood boys, in Cherry Park, but that was tag only, no tackling, casual blocking.

So I thought I wanted to play football. Tackle, with full pads and helmets. And on the first day of try-outs, West Valley Bruins, my father drove me to one of the many lush green public sport fields that quilted the valley floor, and he waited in the car. Us kids, eleven years old, stood shoulder to shoulder while the coach walked past with his clipboard, asking questions, sizing us up like ponies at auction.

There was a break then, before warm-ups began, and my father came to me, cupped my shoulders and gently lifted them until I was at attention, squared.

The sun was summer golden, liquid, a brown haze settled over Mount Umunhum and Mount Hamilton.

I was a chubby kid, husky is what the labels on my clothes said. I knew I was fat.

Keep your shoulders up, my father said. Always be proud of yourself, no matter what.

He jostled my shoulders once, checked my posture, then went back to the car, the maroon Chrysler 300.

I was embarrassed by my father that day, perhaps ashamed, though I knew even then he did not intend that, that his advice to me wasn't about the game or discipline or fortitude.

I quit the team after three practices. We had only run laps and done calisthenics, and I'd yet to see a football. I'd quit before I was asked to hurl myself at another player. I was a soft kid, really.

Things changed for me then, and I never played sports after. Things changed all the time.

Boys

Drew Burgess's big brother, sixteen or seventeen, a foot taller than me, decided to beat me up. We hadn't spoken at all before this day, I just knew he was Drew's brother.

It was spring, seventh grade, and a bunch of us, Drew Burgess and Keith Epstein and Rich Davis, were at the baseball diamond, watching Ida Price play Hogue. We were sitting with Cheri Miller and Candee Hooper and Cindy Roberts, the real reason we were there. It was a school day, so late afternoon, and the sun slanted golden and hazy across the valley, and everything was warm and still, except for all the cars. We were just talking.

Then Drew Burgess's brother was right behind me, I turned and saw him leaning over me, then he started punching me, in the neck and the head and the shoulders, then he threw himself on me, and continued to punch me, kicked me a couple of times in the ribs. I curled up and tried to hide. But that didn't work. I took every blow.

He said nothing the whole time, just beat me. I started to yell, to beg, really, but Drew Burgess's brother was suddenly up and running away, toward Curtner Avenue and down it, followed by three of his laughing friends, all high-schoolers and big.

It hurt, but I wasn't bleeding. All my friends surrounded me, asked if I was all right, even Drew, who apologized for his brother. I had no choice but to pretend I was okay and pretend to vow revenge on Drew Burgess's big brother, even though I knew that would not, could not possibly, ever happen. But I had to pretend, so I did. We watched the rest of the game. I felt the bruises forming, the ache in my ribs, on my face. I was going to have a black eye.

I'd only ever been in one fight before, third grade, when Raymond Aver said something disrespectful of Mrs. Bowman, our teacher, and I told him to take it back, and next thing we were tussling together, trying to hit but not hitting, ending up on the ground and rolling around, until Mrs. Bowman broke it up. Ray Aver was fine, but I was bleeding, from a small cut just below the pinky of my left hand, where my Cub Scout ring had jammed into my flesh. We were sent to the principal's office and made up. The nurse cleaned my cut.

Oh, and once, I called out Rick Siegler, in sixth grade, for some insult, we would fight after school, but never did.

That didn't mean I never got beat up. For several months, in fourth grade, along the blocks between Bagby

Elementary and Flood Drive, a group of boys, always older, and taller and heavier, would suddenly appear when I turned a corner. I wasn't the only one this happened to. I never knew these boys, and my friends didn't know these boys. We only feared them.

I would turn the corner, and there they were, a pack of them, three or four, blocking the sidewalk, and waiting for me to make up my mind. The first time it happened, I immediately knew my options. I could cross the street and hope they wouldn't cross. I could turn and run the opposite way, but that was a fool's game, I knew they would catch me, and somehow that would make everything worse. Or I could walk straight on, try to walk through them, and maybe, just maybe, they'd let me go. I did always walk through them, getting it over with.

The first time I got yelled at, called all sorts of names, Fatso and Pansy and Homo. The boys, there were three that day, also pushed me back and forth, but I kept going and made it through to the other side. It happened a few other times, the same boys, more or less. It got rougher each time. Slaps, tripping, punches to the arm, more names, a new one, Faggot. I tried taking different routes home, but they were always where I was going. Same boys.

My friends and I talked about it, but that never helped. Then it stopped. These boys moved on.

It was just part of it, I knew, these boys, nothing much to do but survive. I never said anything to my parents about them, and my brother was in the Marines by then. I hoped he'd teach me some way of defending myself when he came home next, judo chops or kicks.

Those boys weren't the only ones, there was always some bigger and older boy, who, out of nowhere, from the time I was seven or so, on the playground, in a store, on the street, who would reach out and slap or punch or yell in your face. Just part of it, being a boy.

It wasn't until the game was over, Drew's brother and his laughing friends long gone, that I thought I might cry. I wanted to but didn't. Everyone else peeled off, they were all so nice to me, showed concern, the girls hugged me, Drew apologized again, and Rich Davis walked most of the way home with me. Rich and I stood at the corner of Flood and Leigh and devised the many ways we'd get revenge, we, the two of us, our shouted bravado cloaking our fear. The sky was evening now, purple and red from that day's smog. Rich gave me five and loped off.

As I approached the house, the urge to cry rose up in me again. I was really hurt, physically, and scared, I didn't at all understand what had happened. But I held it in.

My father was home when I got there, just arrived from work, and the minute he saw me, he stopped me, What happened?

Nothing.

You've got a black eye.

Nothing.

Who was it?

Then I cried, and felt foolish, babyish, for crying, sobbing really, but folded myself into my father's embrace. He let me cry it out.

Who was it?

He called the Burgess's, and a few minutes later, Mr. Burgess and Drew's big brother showed up at our front door. Drew's brother looked sheepish, mostly, but he was also grinning, I could see it sneaking out of his face, a grin only I would see. The threat in that grin.

The two fathers spoke briefly, then Mr. Burgess pushed Drew's brother forward. My father opened the screen door, stepped onto the porch, stood nose to nose with him. The smile that Drew's brother had been hiding sprang into the open.

Funny, is it? my father said. Drew's brother's smile evaporated. Here's the thing, young man, my father said, you are going to apologize to my son right now, and you will mean it. Who the hell do you think you are, you little punk, picking on someone smaller than you. Big man, eh? You wanna be a big man, let's go out in the yard, and we'll see who's bigger.

My father and Drew's brother were the same height, but my father towered over him. He was a strong wind pushing Drew's brother off the porch. Drew's brother shrank, and there, I saw the fear I'd wanted to see.

Yes, sir, I'm sorry, sir, Drew's brother said.

My father stepped aside, and I knew I was to step forward now, face to face with Drew's brother.

What do you have to say for yourself? my father said to him. My father was standing behind me.

I'm sorry, Drew's brother said to me, I'm really really sorry. I shouldn't have done that. I'm really really sorry and it won't happen again, I promise.

My father nudged my shoulder, and I knew to put out my hand. Drew's brother shook my hand, sincerely, I felt, if not fearfully. He did not look at me, though, only past me.

Now get on home, my father said, I'm sure your father has a few things to say to you.

Drew's brother slunk off into the evening. Mr. Burgess and my father spoke for a few minutes, low, so I did not hear them. Then Mr. Burgess laughed, turned, waved, and went to catch his son.

The violent sunset had passed already, the sky a uniform blue with one bright white planet, Venus.

My father put his arm around me, and we went back into the house.

The Farm

A year later their parents returned for them.

It was difficult for Mac, he was always Mac now, to believe Nim when he announced their parents would arrive that day and the family would be together again. Even when he saw his parents in Miss Tarn's office, he didn't believe it right away, though these were clearly his parents. The other kids had convinced Mac that his parents must be dead, otherwise why were he and Nim at the orphanage, that's what orphanages were for. Mac told them his parents had been alive when he was dropped off, but the kids said they were probably planning to kill themselves, a lot of parents did that. That year Nim had told Mac a thousand times that their parents would return, and while Mac had wanted to believe his brother, he found it simpler to believe they were dead.

But they were alive and did come back, right there. Mac ran to them, thoughtlessly, hugged them both, and knew he should cry, though he didn't. He could barely look at them, he found. Nim stood by, leaning back on his heels. Their mother wept and pulled Mac to her. Their father shook Nim's hand.

Neither Mac nor Nim asked where they were going when they got in the car, a different car, newer, humped and rat-colored.

Driving north out of Los Angeles, their mother peppered them with questions, which Nim answered, and as vaguely as possible. It was fun, he told them, at the orphanage, they made new friends and played a whole bunch, and school was fun, and Mac was learning to read, but they were also happy to be with their parents again. When Mac tried to say more than that, Nim ground his thumb into Mac's leg. The year at the orphanage had taught them that they only existed together.

Still, Mac wanted to tell them everything. How many times Nim had rescued Mac from beatings by the other kids. How often Nim was beat up by the older boys and Mac couldn't stop them, the long puckered scar on Nim's leg, his broken arm. Hot in the summer, cold and damp in the winter. The thin and scant food, never any oranges. The boredom of the paddlewheel days, that they never once left the orphanage grounds. How hollow the corridors felt in the afternoons. The two weeks in February Mac spent in the infirmary, feverish, hallucinating, riding their old mule, still dead but alive, around the world and under the ocean. Brash bugles kept calling Mac. Nim visited every day.

Mac wanted to tell his parents everything so they would never take them back there.

Elwell, honey, his mother said. She reached back and shook his knee. You're awfully quiet. Tell us about your vacation.

Mac, he said. I'm Mac now, that's what you should call me.

His parents shared a silent chuckle.

Mac it is, his mother said.

The highway was flooded with cars, the sky went on forever, the houses climbed the hills, and over there, a glimpse of the ocean. Mac had forgotten the world could be this way.

Where did you go? Mac said. The only question that seemed possible.

Oh, his mother said, it's so exciting. Zach, you tell the boys.

Well, boys, his father said.

They'd gone to Eureka, up north, where his father got a job in a paper mill. Real money, then a promotion. Weekends he was a short order cook. Their mother found work in town, in a laundry, and on weekends waited tables at the same diner where their father cooked.

It was so cute, his mother said, a diner built right into a hollowed-out redwood trunk. Imagine that. We worked in a tree.

Worked and saved, his father said, worked and saved. And now. Boys, we bought ourselves a farm. In Oregon, right by Medford. It's all ours too, cash on the barrelhead. We're living the good life, I tell you. It's beautiful there. A real home for us, no more moving. And that's a solemn promise.

His father reached back and handed each of the boys a ten-dollar bill.

Nim looked at Mac and shook his head silently. Mac knew the signal, decoded it, there was no farm and never had been, be careful. But after two days of driving and sleeping by the side of the road, they entered a round valley just across the Oregon border. The world was greener here than Mac had ever dreamed.

The farm's house was painted, white with blue trim, fresh painted, and each brother got his own room, unheard of. The barn was enormous, with one entrance leading to a fenced paddock and chicken run, beyond which were several acres of crops, corn mostly, just coming in, and rows of gnarled but verdant apple trees. A truck garden for vegetables. There were two milk cows, a clump of nervous chickens, five pigs.

And a horse, Jody, they had their own horse. She was a red horse, but old and orange and gray-muzzled now, bent but sweet, and that first night before dinner, Mac and Nim rode her up and down the orchard. He had a horse.

All around this brief plain, oaks rose up to ridges of tall pines.

But everything on the farm looked lived in, a working farm, ready for the next day. There was a bed of blooming yellow roses by the front door. Mac wondered how long his parents had lived here before coming to get them.

Their mother killed and dressed a chicken, fried it up. There were baked potatoes drowned in butter, fresh string beans. His mother's biscuits. Blackberry pie. Milk cold from the ice box.

Mac ate everything and too much of it too fast but couldn't stop. He threw it all up then ate the rest of the chicken.

That night, his father stood in the doorway of Mac's bedroom, his very own bedroom, while his mother came to him and sat on the bed.

In the morning, she said, we'll go into town and buy you some real nice clothes. You've grown so much. And then we'll get you signed up for school. New shoes too, two pair. Would you like that?

Mac hadn't been to school yet, as Nim had for two years in Oklahoma before the mule died, and he really wanted to go. Nim and the older boys at the orphanage always complained about their classes, how stupid the teachers were and how much they hated all of it, but their stories only made him more curious. Occasionally Nim sneaked Mac into the small library and tried to teach him to read, and Mac already knew his ABC's and could print them with a pencil.

His mother swept her hand over his forehead, kissed him on the cheek, tucked him in.

She said, Sleep tight.

His father said, Don't let the bed bugs bite.

Now he wanted to cry. But he waited until his parents left.

The bedroom was too dark and too quiet and too big.

A while later Nim crept into Mac's bed, and they sank toward each other in the middle.

Don't get comfortable, Nim said. You know we'll have to leave.

But this is our farm, Mac said, Dad said so. We have a horse.

For now. We don't belong here. You know it. It's too good.

But we're never going back there, Mac said.

A waxing moon peeked in the bedroom window.

No, Nim said, I won't let that happen.

But we can stay here.

Not for long, Nim said.

They did stay, however, for seven years, and the farm did become, for that long spread of days, Mac's home.

NCO Club

We were expecting a visitor. A Navy buddy, Lt. McDole. In Key West he and my father had led a submarine rescue team aboard the U.S.S. Penguin. It was rare, I was told, for an officer and an NCO to fraternize, frowned upon by brass, close to an infraction. But McDole and my father had become fast friends anyway, diving together on the weekends, going to Joe's, their favorite, a red-brick bar near downtown, and sometimes our two families had dinner together. They were meeting up for the first time since we'd moved back to San Jose, though my mother and Mrs. McDole wrote letters and sent Christmas cards. McDole was on a two-week training assignment at Moffett Field, where we bought our groceries every Saturday.

My father told me I had met McDole in Key West, that he had a son, also named Robert, about the same age, and that we all used to wade together in the coral shallows behind base housing, hunting for conch and longooster.

I didn't remember anything about Key West. I carried images of a stark white expanse with no trees, a few pale stucco buildings, the thin horizon of the sea, me in a crib with Sparky parked nearby. But these images were also in the photo album in the living room, all in black and white.

The day McDole was to arrive, late spring, a Saturday, my mother dressed me in my Easter suit, and I hated it, the clip-on bow tie, the shoes I was not allowed to run in. My mother was also Easter got up, in a turquoise dress and a long string of fat pearls, Grandma Cleaves's pearls, which my mother borrowed for special occasions. My father wore his new, shiny green-black suit, a red tie with golden lassos stitched in, his Navy tie clip. We were going to dinner at the NCO Club.

My father went to the porch to wait, so I waited with him. Sparky was out roaming the neighborhood. It was late afternoon, coolish.

Lt. McDole pulled up in a pale green Ford Falcon sedan, Navy initials and numbers stenciled in black on the front doors. Every Navy car was the same.

Before the car stopped, my father was moving to meet it, almost running.

McDole, you ol' sonnuva bitch!

Then McDole got out and he yelled, Mac, you Okie rascal you!

They shook hands, in the street, for a long time, each clasping the other's shoulder.

McDole seemed much younger than my father, which surprised me. He was an Officer, superior by rank to every Non-Commissioned Officer. I assumed he'd be older than my father. Lt. McDole was dressed in civvies, a tight black suit, white shirt, black tie. Crew cut. He could have been one of the NASA technicians who sat tensely in front of the switches and dials at Cape Kennedy.

Here's Robert, my father said. Sproutin' like a weed.

McDole shook my hand the way all my father's friends did, a crushing grip, meant to show, I thought, that I was a man now. But it always embarrassed me, made me feel more like a little kid.

Bobby, McDole said, my Bobby says to say hello.

Hello, I said.

C'mon, my father said, Olive's dying to see you.

My mother was on the porch, looking quite unlike my mother.

Lieutenant, she said, and curtsied half an inch.

Olive.

McDole kissed her on the cheek, and she blushed.

Bobby, McDole said, there's a bag in the front seat, would you mind.

I wanted to ask him to call me Robert, but there might have been gifts in the bag.

Yes. A box of chocolates for my mother, Cuban rum for my father, but a conch shell for me. We already had a conch shell, taken from our backyard in Key West. It sat on the mantel and lit up. My father had drilled through the back of it and inserted an orange Christmas tree bulb.

Robert, my mother said, say thank you to the Lieutenant.

Thank you, sir.

Sir? McDole said, laughing. Sir. That's rich. Not anymore, Bobby, your dad's a civilian now. About dinner.

The NCO Club, my father said, on me.

Now, Mac, McDole said, I've already made reservations at the Officer's Club. Have to pull rank, I'm afraid.

Hogwash, my father said. They've done a bang-up job on this one, and I want to show you how good us NCOs have it these days.

We took the maroon Chrysler 300, black rag top, our new car, as big a car as we'd ever owned, power windows and air conditioning. My mother sat in the back with me, the men in front talking Navy. The sky was striped pink and blue with high feathery clouds.

I could not figure out why McDole had driven the twenty miles from Moffett Field, where he was staying, only to go back to Moffett for dinner, only to come back to Flood Drive and get his car, only to drive back once more.

My mother explained that when we returned from dinner, the men would want some time alone and probably talk far past my bedtime.

We slowed at the entrance to Moffett Field, stopped at a stucco and tile guard house flanked by squat palm trees and the American and Navy flags. The guard, a Marine corporal, stepped forward, examined the decal in our front window, stepped back and executed a sentry salute, only chest-high, we were free to pass. Then the guard offered my father a full salute, slow and perfect and impassive.

In front of us, but far across the base, was the dirigible hangar, a silver-sheathed structure as long and as high and as mounded as two dirigibles, with enormous sets of doors at each end. Through one of the Chiefs he knew at Moffett, my father had sneaked me in for a tour last summer. There were no dirigibles any longer, but dozens of planes in perfect rows, F-4 fighter jets, fully armed. I did not imagine that any building could be larger than this. I shouted into the metal girders, giddy with my echo.

But today we turned before we got to the hangar and parked near a grove of skinny palms.

The NCO Club was a round white-stucco building with a red tile roof. We only ate here on the most special occasions, birthdays or Christmas or New Years, even once on Thanksgiving. We'd come only a few months before, my parents' anniversary.

The maître d', in a fancy short tuxedo, greeted us. He wasn't military, none of the restaurant workers were, but they'd been versed in rank and respect.

Chief Macoby, welcome back, sir.

Our guest tonight, my father said, Lieutenant McDole, active Navy.

For a moment I worried Lt. McDole might not be allowed in. He was an officer, after all, and we were NCOs. Sirs, the maître d' said, it will only be a moment. My father beamed.

The dining room was a scattering of white tablecloths under dim lighting. Other NCOs, some in uniform, some not, sat together in small groups, or with their families. It was a room full of Chiefs. A single glass-globed candle burned in the middle of each table.

Our waiter approached with a stack of thick black menus. Sirs, the waiter said, this way if you please.

I allowed my mother to go first, as I'd been taught, then followed her, while my father stopped every few tables to introduce the Lieutenant to his fellow Chiefs. There was a lot of standing and saluting.

Lieutenant, the waiter said when he'd seated us, would you like to start with cocktails tonight? He leaned over McDole's left shoulder, pen raised over his pad.

Yes, we would, my father said, raising a finger. Double Canadian Clubs, over, for myself and the Lieutenant. Ginger Ale for my lovely wife and a Roy Rogers for the boy.

Sir, the waiter said. He nodded then backed away.

The three of them talked over their drinks, catching up on Key West news. How was Betty? The Laughlins? And that boy of yours?

My father told McDole about GE and the nuclear reactors they were building.

Now isn't that something, McDole said. The pay good?

I watched the two men. I saw that my father was no longer in the Navy. The way he sat, leaned back in his chair, his gestures loose, a storyteller. Lt. McDole's every move and sentence were as precise as his crew cut. My father sipped his drink with his eyes closed, as if listening to a song on the jukebox. After each sip, McDole examined his glass for structural flaws.

The waiter returned.

Lieutenant, have we made our dinner selections?

My father snapped his menu shut.

He had yet to look at the menu.

Let's see, my father said, we'll have rib-eyes for the men, and he looked over at me and winked. Rare as they come, I wanna hear that cow moo. And for the lady? Olive, chicken or fish?

Chicken.

Chief, the waiter said.

Oh, and a bottle of red, my father called, your finest.

We never drank wine.

Iceberg and tomato salad in Thousand Island dressing, fat-shrouded steak, scalloped potatoes, creamed spinach, a basket of sourdough. Chianti in a wicker wrapped bottle.

My mother had half a glass of wine and giggled.

During dinner the talk turned back to the Navy, to a submarine rescue off the Bahamas that nearly killed twenty-three men. I had never heard this story. I watched the men's eyes, to find the real story, saw how pinched they became when the faulty release valve was mentioned.

Chief, McDole said, you were the only one who was right that day. You saved those men.

Thank you, sir.

A different waiter came by and scraped the breadcrumbs from our table with a tiny silver knife.

The first waiter returned and placed the lone dessert menu in front of my father.

Port for the men, Sanka for my mother, a hot fudge sundae for me.

My father and McDole talked on. My mother swiped spoonfuls from my sundae.

So, my father said, what brings you all the way to Moffett?

Mac, I wish I could tell you but I can't. Classified.

Now, hold on there, L.T., you can tell me, we've always spilled secrets. Never let the suits come between us. It's NASA, isn't it?

Mac, I just can't. You have to understand.

But it's Moffett, I know these guys.

Chief. That's quite enough.

Just a tid-bit? my father said.

Chief.

I finished my sundae as quickly as I could.

When we got back to the house, we stood in the kitchen, and my father pulled a bottle of clear alcohol from the cupboard above the stove, and two squat glasses.

Remember this beautiful moonshine, L.T.? he said, I reserve it for only the finest occasions. Sit down, take a load off. We'll have a snort. Maybe two.

Have to decline, Chief, I'm pretty bushed. What say next weekend, you and me, we'll hit the Officer's Club, just the two of us, my treat this time.

My mother left the room.

Sure, L.T., sure. That's good.

When I woke up the next morning my father was asleep in his recliner. His tie was undone but he hadn't got his jacket off. The moonshine was half empty, and the ashtray overflowed.

Strangers

Who were your friends?

The family, naturally, in San Jose, all my uncles and aunts and cousins, Grandma Cleaves too, they occupied most of our socializing, Christmas, New Years, Easter, Memorial Day, Fourth of July, Labor Day, Thanksgiving, and all the birthdays, weddings, births. Hardly a day left over.

You and Mom had friends from the Navy, men you'd served with, families from the same base housing and similar rank. But those were pen pals by the time we got to San Jose, Mom keeping current, the letter writer for you both, signing each letter in her perfect blue cursive with the word Mizpah, which she said meant strong friendship. And every December the tide of Christmas cards going out and coming in, a major family undertaking, me on stamps and flaps. My Godmother was someone named Anne Peabody, from Navy housing in Key West, though I couldn't remember her. Every year on my birthday she sent me a card with five dollars in it. You spoke of Navy buddies with respect, then told outlandish stories of the shenanigans you'd all got up to, but only once did one of them visit, Lt. McDole, an officer who'd been a friend, though when he visited that time it was awkward and you both seemed disappointed, and I was sad for you. The Christmas cards seemed enough to tie you to that past.

In San Jose, there was one family we were close to, the Phillips, Art and Zora, who you and Mom had known since the war, when you and Art were stationed in San Diego, and Mom and Zora became best friends. There were three Phillips kids, Art Jr., as old as Ricks, Susie, a few years older than me, and Mike, my age, and they all had red hair. They lived on Blossom Hill Road, which traced the top of the first ridge of the valley's western foothills. I loved seeing the valley stretched out like that, Mount Hamilton and Lick Observatory, to the east, visible and tempting from across the broad valley, and even on smoggy days, when it was hard to see the eastern slopes through the brown air, it was beautiful.

Their house was two-story, with a driveway that swooped down steeply from the street. We drove up here during Christmas to see the colored lights on the houses that had replaced the orchards. I liked Mike, but we went to different schools and were only friends because of you and Mom. Mike and I played Slinky on their stairs, rode bikes down the steep driveway. But they rarely came to our house, and I understood it was Mom's friendship with Zora that brought the two families together, Mom and Zora Navy wives at seventeen and eighteen and lonely in San Diego. Art only served one hitch in the Navy, and you two, so similar in appearance, had little in common. I thought you didn't trust him.

Yet you were always making new friends, at work, at bars, on fishing trips. You liked talking to strangers, as much to listen to their stories as to tell your own. You were always introducing me to your new friends, and you always brought their best stories home with you. Your wallet, soft and once-black, at least two inches thick, was stuffed to the gills with names and phones numbers, business cards and scrap paper and bar napkins, though I never saw you call any of those numbers.

When we were on vacation, always driving, never flying, whatever town we were in, you looked through the White Pages for any unknown Macoby. Once in Winnemucca, Nevada, you found a Macoby, called the number and spoke at length with Donald, who owned a dry cleaners on the edge of town. Donald had grown up in Oklahoma too, and his family had originally come from Alabama, where the Macobys had lived a long time ago. Surely we were related. Late that afternoon we drove to the Lucky Seven Dry Cleaners and Martinizing, where we'd meet Donald then follow him to his house for dinner, you and me and Mom.

You marched right up to the counter, put out your hand, and said, Mr. Macoby, I'm Mr. Macoby, we spoke on the phone. You both shook hands with gusto, then broke out in hearty laughter, and Mom laughed and so did I. We were probably not related. You were white, and Donald was black. At dinner at the Macobys, you and Donald talked at length about Oklahoma and sharecropping, and shared stories of Alabama that had been handed down by your grandparents, compared the very different wars you'd both served in, you a diver and Donald on KP. You told Mrs. Macoby, Carla, that her fired okra was the finest you'd had since you were a boy and which you'd dreamed of for decades. Mom and Mrs. Macoby formed their own little corner of stories. I played with the twin girls Violet and Ivy, a little older than me, and Tracy, a year younger, Mousetrap and Sorry and Operation. When we were in the car on the way back to the motel, you said, Come to think of it, I believed we are related. Mom and Mrs. Macoby traded Christmas cards forever.

But did you have a best friend?

Dale Dickeson was my best friend from kindergarten to second grade, but when he started at a new school, I met Jim Bryant who was my best friend forever after. Jim and I told each other everything, built a science lab together in his garage, and dreamed of becoming astronauts. Until I met Rich Davis, who played drums and listened to The Beatles.

Who did you talk to?

I worried that you didn't have a friend to talk to. Was the family enough? Your work and bar pals? Christmas cards from the past? Sparky? Me? Your brother Nim, my lost uncle, he didn't count, how could you talk to him if he wasn't there.

There were some new friends, in San Jose, though I was often mystified by them, not as people, but where they came from, how you met them. These were not bar friends. Or bowling friends, bowling friends were Thursday nights at Moonlite Lanes. Maybe these new friends were friends of Mom's from the County Assessor's Office, the job she took after your first heart attack. I didn't know.

Once we drove to the east side to have dinner with a couple you'd recently met, and I was given my own plate and soda and snacks and stayed in the living room by myself while the four of you had dinner and drinks and played cards. Their house was a much nicer house than ours, fancy and sleek, like in a TV show, and this confused me as well, confused me about who these people were and what you talked about. They looked like somebody else's friends, I felt like we were trespassing. But I was happy that night, alone and feeling grown up, watched Robinson Crusoe on Mars on NBC, Crusoe on the desert planet waiting for the aliens.

You went out with this couple one more time, dinner in a restaurant, Finally, a real night out, you said, and you and Mom wondered if I would be okay at home by myself, for the first time ever at night. I was nine and said, Yes, of course. But The Saturday Night at the Movies movie I watched in our family room that night was The Haunting, about a house that made terrifying noises that made the actors do awful things to themselves and one another. When you came home, every single light in the house was on, including the porch light, which is where you found me, on the porch with all the doors open at midnight.

Another time, a year or two later, we went to a luncheon in the Santa Cruz Mountains, at a house I could only think of as a mansion, white and pillared and set against a dramatic hillside, a horseshoe-shaped driveway. There were many adults at that luncheon, and everyone was dressed too fancy for the daytime. I had to wear a tie, clip-on. What was the occasion? Why were we there? There was one kid my age, ten or so, and she was deaf, and I'd never known a deaf person, and she was interesting, so we wrote notes back and forth. She was pretty, wore a black velvet smock with a white blouse underneath, a single pearl on a silver chain. I thought she and I would become friends, but we never went to another luncheon.

Then suddenly, at the end of sixth grade, we were spending time with the Brooks, whose oldest son Greg was my age, but how did you know them? They lived in a regular house, like our house, but one set down oddly in the middle of walnut orchards and which had nothing to do with the orchards. They had a built-in pool, and that summer we were always swimming, many big BBQs around that pool. I even spent summer weekdays with the Brooks, both you and mom at work, and Greg and I took guitar lessons at the community center in a nearby park, Leaving on a Jet Plane, and Greg taught me to ride his mini-bike. Greg used to come visit me that summer, and I introduced him to my school friends, but he got a crush on Cheri Miller when he met her, when I already had a crush on Cheri, but it was okay, she didn't like either of us that way. Then school started, and Greg was too far away.

The friends of yours who troubled me most were Bob and Renata. I did know how you met them, I was there, in Yosemite, in the ski lodge, and after that, we saw them all the time, at their house and ours. There were two boys, Ernst and Karl, and I played with them because I was supposed to, even if they were a little annoying because they were little kids. Renata was born in Germany and came to California after the war, then met Bob. She was tall and pretty, with short blonde hair, and reminded me of Mrs. Larkin from the end of our street. Bob was short and mean looking, and he was mean, to everyone. I saw him cuff Ernst once, hard across the back of his head, and Ernst cried and ran away. We were playing croquet.

So I knew where they came from, but not why we saw them all the time.

Bob is a mean drunk, you told me, sick with drink. You always looked like you wanted to punch Bob. Renata needs a friend, you said, so you became her friend. I didn't think Mom liked Renata very much, but Mom was always nice, wasn't she. Except around Bob. And Bob was always there. Why didn't you make him go home? I knew why you liked Renata, she was quiet and warm, but I could never figure out how that was supposed to help her, you being her friend.

She was the last new friend you made.

Basic

My brother had a broken arm, and I hadn't seen him in the nine weeks since he'd started Basic Training. That's where he got his broken arm, Basic.

We drove to San Diego for his graduation, my father and mother and I, and Rick's wife Jan, who was pregnant. They'd been high school sweethearts and were married now. She got pregnant after Ricks enlisted but before Basic started. My sister was already married and did not come with us.

It was Family Day when we arrived, the Thursday before Friday's official ceremony. The entire battalion of new Marines had gone for a three-mile beach run after breakfast that morning, a Boot Camp tradition, but now had on-base liberty to be with visiting families.

We met Ricks in an airy lounge, couches and easy chairs and tables, in one of the yellow stucco buildings that dotted the base. The base reminded me of Camden High, where my brother had graduated two years before. Ricks was showered and dressed in his fatigues, but a short-sleeved blouse, to make room for the angled cast over his right elbow. The official term, I knew, was blouse. Other recruits from his platoon had gathered here too, waiting for their families. Outside, it was overcast, and the lounge was well in shadow.

When he saw us, he snapped to attention and saluted my father with his broken arm, holding his salute until my father returned his. Then he ran to Jan and carefully held her, kissed her for a long time. I had been watching these two kiss since I was five and was used to it. He turned to my mother and kissed the top of her head. She pulled back, held his face in her hands and simply gazed.

Little brother! he called and pulled me into a light-hearted headlock. I was delirious but tried to hide it, so I examined his cast. White, no signatures, fresh. He'd only broken his arm the week before. But my relief at seeing him had little to do with his broken arm. I was overwhelmed to recognize him, the brother I had always idolized. His letters to me from Boot Camp, on thin blue APO stationery, blue ink, did not sound like my brother. He repeated, in these letters, that he had joined the Marines to Save my little brother from the Commies. He wrote that he wanted to Kill Gooks, so that I could live a life of freedom. That was not my brother, and these were things I did not want him to do on my behalf.

But there, in the shadowy lounge, was my brother. Some mistake had been made with those letters, it was clear. Here he was, restored, as I knew him.

We went outside for lunch around one of many barbecue pits, each sheltered by a wooden patio roof and open on all sides and surrounded by green picnic tables. Hamburgers and hot dogs and all the soda I could drink. Ice cream sandwiches. Ricks rounded up his buddies and introduced them to the family. He always said My little brother Robert, and he always said My beautiful wife, and The best mother ever, but when he introduced my father, he grew more formal. Chief Petty Officer Elwell Ricks Macoby, Sr., retired Navy. My father swelled with each introduction and salute.

A few of Ricks's Marine buddies had no family there, and my father made them sit with us and tell us all about their families and where they were from. Errol Spoke from Reno, Oscar Hidalgo from Santa Fe, Otis Masters from Seattle.

I got to wrestle with Ricks for a bit, out on the lawn, and we mimed a few football plays, but then it was time to leave. We would see him tomorrow.

We checked into The Dolphin, ate at a Sambo's across the street, then I swam by myself, alone, in the motel's pool, diving into the lighted turquoise water and emerging in thick blue dusk. Back in the room, we watched TV together, the four of us on two beds in the same room, reruns of The Wild Wild West and Hogan's Heroes. Jan let me touch her belly, and I felt the baby kick. She rubbed my back until I fell asleep.

When we woke up, the sky was pink, the whole world was pink.

Blood Tide, my father said. We were looking across the pool toward the harbor. An algae bloom, intense and red, the sky caught its pink from the ocean. The color of the sky and the color of the ocean were linked, my father often told me.

By the time we returned to the Marine Corps Recruit Depot, the pink had intensified. It was muggy now and close.

The four of us sat at the top of the metal grandstands that faced the enormous parade ground. To one side were the yellow stucco buildings, to the other a reviewing stand in front of a grid of pale metal Quonset huts, the recruits' barracks. Beyond the Quonset huts, orange and red PSA jets landed and took off from Lindbergh Field. Vacationers arrived in San Diego, Marines departed. And beyond the airport, the Blood Tide harbor.

On the reviewing stand a hundred Marine officers and NCOs, and one general, all in dress greens. A forest of flags withered tiredly behind them. People spoke over the loudspeakers. There was applause.

The Marine Band entered from the open end of the parade ground, all in dress blues and white hats. They were playing The Halls of Montezuma. I sang along, knew all the words. The band made a circuit of the parade ground, passed in front of the reviewing stand, then came to a halt.

The battalion of recruits entered. Every recruit wore dress blue slacks, red striped, but with short-sleeve khaki blouses, and on the sleeves, the fresh insignia of rank, a single chevron, khaki and outlined in red. PFC.

I knew the order of command by heart. A battalion, 800 men, was graduating, and these 800 entered in companies, 200 hundred to each company, with each company comprised of four platoons. At the head of each platoon, a drill sergeant and one Marine carrying the company's ensign.

The battalion entered, separate but marching with one mind, 800 Marines marching as one.

The companies passed the reviewing stand then found their spots, splitting into its platoons, sixteen perfect grids on an otherwise empty tarmac.

There was no music during the processional, only the shouts of the Drill Instructors and the synchronized steps of the battalion. One-two, one-two, hut-left!

I spotted Ricks right off, pointed him out. He was the only recruit with a cast on his arm, glaring white, like a target, or like a flag of surrender. The sharp angle of his cast mirrored the sharp angles the other Marines maintained.

He'd broken his arm during a drill session in which recruits climbed a fifty-foot knotted rope while carrying a fifty-pound pack. At the top of the rope, each recruit had to slap the cross-beam, loud enough for the Drill Instructor to hear. My brother lost his balance reaching out to slap the cross-beam, though he'd done this drill a hundred times, and fell the fifty feet, landing on his elbow. He knew immediately it was broken and went to the DI. Sir, permission to report to the infirmary, sir.

You're hurt, are you? the sergeant said. Well, let me give you something to cry about, you big baby, you fucking cockroach, you pussy, you faggot, you maggot. Dead Man's carry, one mile.

I knew exactly what words the DI had said that day because my brother told me over the phone. When my brother phoned us from Basic, he called collect, and we refused the charges, then phoned the pay phone we knew he would be standing near.

The DI then pointed to another recruit, it didn't matter which one, just a body. My brother flopped the recruit over his left shoulder, like a long sack of potatoes, and ran with him, for a mile, two laps around the training field. Then Ricks was allowed to go to the infirmary. He returned to drill sessions two days later.

The ceremony ended after more boring speeches and more military music. My brother was no longer a recruit but a Marine, PFC, Private First Class.

We met up with Ricks in the lounge again and took Instamatic snaps of us all, then he returned to barracks to change into his civvies. He had off-base liberty for 72 hours, and we were going to celebrate with a fancy steak dinner at the Imperial House, and later a separate hotel room for him and Jan.

Headed to downtown San Diego in the car, my brother gave me a present, a record still in its bag. The new Lovin' Spoonful album. Just came into the PX this week, he said, thought you'd like it. I did. I was the only one who got a present.

We drove through downtown in the lowering pink dusk, the high-rises capturing us in their canyon.

I tore the shrink-wrap off the album, studied every word and image, slid the record from its sleeve and pored over the label. As I was re-examining the cover, the wooly vests and striped shirts and rust-colored bell bottoms and long hair of the band, their new single came on the radio, Summer in the City, hot damn, summer in the city, back of my neck feelin' dirt and gritty. It was hot and humid here, and it did feel gritty, in this strange city we drove through.

I sang along. I knew all the words.

Vacation

I had a map so I could keep track of everything. The Western United States. Two horizontal creases, eight vertical, I practiced folding it until it got soft, clipped on a ball-point pen to trace the route as we motored along. The map showed the cities and towns, and the roads and railroads that connected them, showed the vast spaces of mountain and desert where no one lived. On the back were drawings and descriptions of the sites that were to be seen. The Redwoods, Crater Lake in Oregon, the Space Needle in Seattle, Yellowstone, the Great Salt Lake, Las Vegas, Four Corners, the Grand Canyon, Hollywood. We would visit some of these, my father promised. Sixteen days in the car, north to Canada then east to Montana, then south to Yuma, Arizona, on the Mexican border, then west to San Diego, north again and back home to San Jose.

On our last trip to Yuma, the summer before, when Jan was still living on base with Ricks, with their daughter Kim, the Barracuda's engine blew up the first day, just outside of Los Banos, in the valley. After a night in a din-gy motel with no pool, my parents bought the Chrysler 300 off a lot, only a year old, the newest car we'd ever owned. The biggest too, like a living room, maroon with a black rag top, chrome details off a rocket. Power windows and air conditioning, unheard of.

After dinner one night, while the three of us pored over my map, my father said, This is our big trip, and we've got the car for it.

We would leave June 3rd, the Tuesday after Memorial Day, avoiding the get-home traffic, putting us into Yuma on Flag Day for Ricks's platoon's BBQ. The night before we drove Sparky to Aunt Mimi and Uncle Don's house, where Lory and Meri would watch her, they loved her, and Sparky knew their neighborhood well. We woke up at four the next morning, packed the trunk with our suit-cases and green and silver aluminum cooler, stopped by the Winchell's on Foxworthy for donuts and milk and cof-fee, and headed for 101, easing onto the freeway. No one else in the world was awake yet, except the KLIV deejay, and it was still mostly dark.

Making good time, my father said.

He flicked his cigarette out the window, like someone in a movie. My mother looked back at me and smiled.

By the time we passed Moffett Field and the enormous dirigible hangars, the sun had crested Mount Hamilton, and the traffic began to thicken. Along the western shore of the Bay, passing Candlestick Park, where the Giants played, and then into San Francisco, cresting a hill and curve there, the city crowded and white and yellow, then over the Golden Gate Bridge, where on the bay two garbage scows chugged past Alcatraz.

With my Instamatic I took the first picture of the trip, out the back window and up at the tall towers. Then I marked our progress on the map.

101 North, through hills still a little green but mostly gold, a few towns and one city, then more hills, dense oak forests encroaching on the freeway, the freeway narrowing, and along until the oaks gave way to pines, short and scrubby but taller as we moved north, until the pines gave way to redwoods, which kept the car and the road, 101 only two lanes here, in dappling shade. The roadside stands, redwood burl and chainsaw sculptures of bears and eagles and Big Foot.

We stopped for lunch in Leggett at the Drive-Thru Tree and drove through the trunk of the Chandelier Tree, a redwood that was 2,100 years old and 315 feet high and 21 feet in circumference. The Chrysler barely fit, and we stopped for a few minutes with the bulk of the entire tree hovering above us. We ate ham and cheese sandwiches from the cooler, sodas from the gift shop. We walked a wooden path through other redwoods, but I couldn't see the tops of them. The pamphlet said, World's Tallest

Creatures! The light here was green and blue with shafts of gold and orange infiltrating.

It's so beautiful, my mother said, and she was right.

Long stretch ahead, my father said, so I lay across the back seat and listened to the radio, which scritched in and out. Only I could hear it because the Chrysler had chrome buttons on the dash that turned off the front speakers. Through the back window the green and gold flashing redwoods, and when I closed my eyes, these became orange and purple, and the image of a blonde woman rose up out of that. She was dressed in black lingerie, and I could see her perfectly, one of the women in the magazines my brother had left behind.

We came out of the redwoods, and I sat up and popped my head on the bench seat, between my mother and father. There were four lanes again, and we passed the lumber trucks that had slowed us, each truck carrying an enormous section of redwood trunk. A river flowed close, then away, an eagle coasting along its course, then a paper mill town. Then The Trees of Mystery, and the giant statues of Paul Bunyan and Babe the Blue Ox, but we didn't stop because we'd been there a few years back. Then the ocean, but far away, across the sandy sloughs outside of Eureka, until, past Arcata, the real ocean coast, rocky and right there. The sun was going down and the fog was coming in like a blue pearl, and the waves blasted the rocks.

Naked ladies! my father called out, but they were only pink flowers along the roadside. We were in Crescent City, right on the water, a tidal wave had hit it in 1964, and we stopped at my father's cousins Bascom and Effie's diner. Chicken fried steak with all the fixings, banana cream pie.

I slept on the couch in their living room, but we woke up early to head inland to Medford, where my father was going to show me the farm he'd lived on as a kid, a couple of hours of winding green roads with no redwoods.

The farm was still a farm, and it sat in a small round valley. There was all the farm stuff, barns, a few horses, a tractor, though all the buildings were washed-out gray and rickety. We walked the perimeter of the barbed-wire fence, and my father told me again about life here, Jody the horse, and Ivan the dog he'd had to shoot when he was nine and Ivan broke his leg in a gopher hole. My father had been bitten by a brown recluse once, and his arm swelled twice its size, a story I'd not heard. A cow came up to us and licked my hand. My father said, So much has changed.

On a beach on the Rogue River, we met Bascom and Effie's grandkids, all boys, seven of them, younger and older than me, we swam all day in a shaded swimming hole and ate rigorously, a pirate tribe. The grown-ups happily ignored us, drinking beer and playing cards. A huge campfire, with ghost stories. I sat between my mother and father, and we listened. Slept in a tent and sleeping bags of Bascom's, and my father and my mother and I played shadow puppets to the hissing Coleman lantern.

In the morning we ate bear sausage Bascom had shot and Effie had made, peppery and dark, along with eggs and pancakes, but left too early, no swimming, north on 5 to Olympia in Washington, the highway so new the tires zinged.

I watched the world go by and marked the map, watching the green turn greener, shades I'd not known, and the gold of California dissolved into more of that greener green. The radio was clear now, the stations were different, the songs the same, Crystal Blue Persuasion, Sugar Sugar, I Can't Get Next to You, Grazing in the Grass, Bad Moon Rising, Everyday People, Aretha's Eleanor Rigby.

We stopped at The Rock Shop for a parking lot picnic, and I bought my first souvenir of the trip, an egg-shaped geode cut in half, its interiors highly polished, its crystals pink and purple, millions of years old. It was overcast, but why would it rain in summer. The Rock Shop sat on a big flat plain surrounded by low hills covered with evergreens, and I'd never been to this place, and California and Flood Dr. were far away, there was only this new place. I couldn't even remember the names of the kids I'd gone swimming with yesterday.

We passed from Oregon into Washington over a river. My father pointed upstream and told me this was where he'd learned to build ships and where he and my mother had gotten married. Not enough time to stop, though, so my mother blushed and frowned.

By four we arrived in Olympia, the Olympic Mountains tall and spiked and that darkest green, even a few still snow-capped in June. Puget Sound lay ahead, fingers of it, the watery world, a briny scent. The sun, high in the sky, sparkled everything.

We drove past all the motels and went to the Olympia Brewery, my father's favorite beer, took a tour of the brick castle and learned how beer was made, then my father had a free tasting, even my mother had a small glass.

Checked into The Captain's Quarters, we went across the street to Sambo's for burgers and shakes and Oly. In the motel room my father looked for Macobys in the White Pages but found none, so I went swimming by myself in the pool, and it was already ten o'clock, but the sky was light still, that's how far north we were suddenly. I watched the cars go by and dissolved in the aquamarine water.

Vamoose, my father said, today's your mother's special day, get the lead out. Driving north along the Olympics, greener and greener, it started to rain, I didn't know it could rain in summer. Drove right onto the green and white ferry in Port Angeles, through big water dotted by blue islands. I stood at the rail and saw it all and it was sunny again, golden shafts breaking the clouds, and we drove off the ferry into Canada, through Victoria toward

Butchart Gardens. My mother said Booshart and I said Butt Chart.

She read to us from a pamphlet that arrived in the mail, and I was ready to be bored, but then she said Sunken Garden, and I was ready, the gardens were sunken, and we walked down into the old quarry surrounded by colors and shapes and all the green around them. My mother insisted everything was so beautiful, Grandma Cleaves would love it here. We drifted along the paths, up and down, the golden sky dripping on us. In the gift shop, my mother bought her first souvenir spoon of the trip, for her collection which hung in our kitchen.

But my father was up to no good, I could tell because he winked at me in the rearview mirror as we drove past every motel. We begged him to stop, we were starving. On the waterfront, in front of a huge building that should have been the capitol of Canada, my father unfolded one of the twenty city maps he'd brought and stared helpless, until he finally said, Oh, Ollie, I'm afraid we'll have to stay here tonight. We drove up the Empress Hotel's driveway, and my mother nearly fainted at my father's big surprise. We had never stayed in a hotel before. We were motel people.

Yes, there was a pool, but first the room, a castle room, all wood and pink and gold, two beds, no cot, a marble bathroom. In the fancy restaurant, I wore the jacket and clip-on tie my mother made me bring. Steak and lobster for everyone.

I swam in the indoor pool, like a pool from Citizen Kane, and never wanted to leave, but the next morning we drove straight to the Seattle ferry, three more hours of islands and gray skies, no rain, then houses and a city, and the Space Needle but there was no time for that this time, driving straight up the Cascades, then down onto vast plains of golden wheat, and the sun sliced down, and that was all there was for hours.

Time took forever.

Somewhere we stopped for gas, near two grain silos and railroad tracks, one take-out diner, where we stretched our legs. I wandered away from my parents, ate a lemon custard soft-serve cone, and let the sky and the wheat fields and emptiness fill me up.

Spokane on the river, already dusk, alone in the pool after dinner, until almost eleven, the sun refusing to set.

More golden fields, then arid mountains, then redder mountains, all day to Yellowstone, where we slept in tent cabins, and my father grilled burgers for us from the cooler, which we'd stocked in Bozeman and where I bought a beaded Indian belt. The spray of the Milky Way, we ooh-ed and ahh-ed.

A Yellowstone day, Old Faithful, bison, a bear, and more grilling, and the next day, an early morning trail ride, me and twenty other kids, no parents, following steep ridges down into river valleys, nose to tail, my parents off somewhere, and when they picked me up, the car was packed and we headed to Salt Lake City, the grand Tabernacle all lit up, and the next morning, we passed by the lake before heading out.

All day to Las Vegas, the hills bare now, exposed and worn here, jagged and threatening there, rock bending back on rock, where the earth had buckled while forming itself. I counted the striations, the layers of all that time.

I swam in the Atomic Motel's pool in Vegas that afternoon, the sun stretching my skin when I left the water, the only one in the pool. That night the brand-new Circus Circus Casino, the kids' mezzanine where I played carnival games and won a few tickets, but ended up watching from above while my mother watched my father play Blackjack. None of us won anything.

As we approached the Grand Canyon the next day, with a quick detour across the bald-faced Hoover Dam, we passed through a town, straight down the middle of it, with trees thick on either side of the road, and it felt like the loneliest town, and I really wanted to live there, I could feel the north rim of the Grand Canyon a few miles to the south.

Nothing prepared me for it. We checked into our Cabin in the Trees, though the cabin was among the trees, not in them, and ate another fancy dinner, at the lodge, then sat all evening on the patio, the three of us, and watched the

Grand Canyon fill with layers of color and then dusk, the stars rising up out of the canyons, and I knew, because I had read it, that we were looking back in time. Four million years.

Nine hours to Yuma through the desert, white-hot and endless. The radio and the back seat and thinking of my brother who I had almost forgotten. Ricks.

We called him from the motel, the Thunderbird, and made plans to meet him in the morning, and I swam in the pool, of course, and the cars went by on the street until my father finally called me in.

Ricks brought me a present, he always brought me a present, this time a yellow U.S.M.C. sweatshirt with red designs, official, but the long sleeves cut off, like his own, and even though it was already ninety degrees in the Denny's parking lot after breakfast, I put it on and wore it all day.

Today was the big BBQ for Ricks's platoon, some celebration for all fifty of them. We drove onto Marine Corps Air Station Yuma, the sentry waving my father in as usual, then, just past the gate, three sixteen-foot white missiles, Hawks, bunched on one trailer and aimed at the sky. This was what my brother had trained on, to use in Vietnam, but that never happened. But here they were, in person, gleaming and lethal.

We followed Ricks to a big park in the middle of the barracks and the yellow and red-tiled buildings, where the platoon was setting up the picnic. There were shaggy pepper trees around the edge of the park, and picnic benches under these. The men were loading up the grills with briquets, popping kegs of beer into metal tubs and covering them with ice, setting up black loudspeakers stenciled U.S.M.C. and connecting those to a record player. The platoon wore green fatigue pants and yellow U.S.M.C. sweatshirts with cut-off sleeves, just like mine. The satisfying tang of lighter fluid.

We were the only family there, and Ricks introduced us to everyone, including his best pal, Sgt. Brophy, who we had heard so much about. I hovered near Ricks all day, while my parents sat at a picnic table and were served beer and ice tea and burgers and potato salad and strawberry shortcake, and the men came by in small groups to talk to them, borrowing family.

The music blared all day, the music I'd been listening to in the car, and everyone sang along, but there was also new music I didn't know yet, Jimi Hendrix and Janis Joplin, Hippie music, my father called it.

We played softball, even my father for a few innings. I played first, which was my Pee-Wee League position and managed to make some outs.

The day had no time to it except the colors of the sky. When we first arrived, at noon, the sky was scoured aluminum, impossibly flat, and the world squinted white. But as the day moved on, blue crept back into the sky, with gauzy rooster-tail clouds inching into the east, and it was almost like the hottest day ever in San Jose. The afternoon brought in sudden soft oranges and yellows, painted almost, with a thin band of brown smog around the horizon, and the world took on depth again, and I found vast spaces between myself and the trees and the far-away barracks, the air around me, beyond me, sparkled with mote and dust.

The Beatles Get Back came on, and my brother moved to the loudspeakers and stood near them, and stared off somewhere far away, and everyone left him alone. When Brophy tried to talk to him, Ricks waved away his best friend.

Then football, tag football, Marines against Marines, and I thought I would play, but my mother said no, I was too small, and my father agreed. We watched from the sidelines while the men threw themselves at one another, and it wasn't tag but tackle, men bleeding when they were hit.

Something happened. Under the trees, near the BBQ grills, a cloud of Marines swarmed in a tight knot, and the dust, orange and red, rose up around them, and my brother began to shout orders and run toward them, and the football players followed him and dove into the cloud. It was furious, this cloud, and green and yellow flashing, streaks of red, a fight, a brawl, no one not fighting, fists and motion, and my brother trying to shout over all of it.

My father got up to go help, but my mother sat him down. I had no choice but to stand and watch.

The platoon stopped fighting when they got too tired.

What happened, I asked my father.

It's what Marines do, he said, what they're trained for.

That night my mother and I stayed in the motel alone, while my father and brother and Sgt. Brophy went out for a drink, and the next morning, just as the sun was coming up, they all three tumbled, still drunk, into the motel room. Ricks had a bandage on his left forearm, his first tattoo, a Marine bulldog with a drill instructor's cap and smoking a cigar. Brophy had the same one on his forearm.

My father pushed up his shirt sleeve, his right arm, the heart with a banner over it, with my mother's name, which had once been another woman's name, and to which he'd added my sister's and my brother's names. He was laughing when he told me that he'd had my name added, so I should have known, but was still disappointed when he revealed it fully, only to find he was joshing me.

He took me out by the pool and apologized over and over, he hadn't known it would hurt me. He held me until I stopped crying. He said, I'm sorry, Robert the Bum, I'm too old for that foolishness now.

My father slept all day in the motel room while my mother and I went to the Yuma Territorial Prison historical site, stark adobe buildings in the middle of nowhere, and the sky aluminum and flat again, but inside, though uncovered, the walls were so high and the shade so deep, the prison yard was almost cool, and long shafts of light smacked the ground around us. There were desperadoes here, and hangings.

The next morning, after one last dinner with Ricks, who promised he'd be up on Labor Day, we set across the same-looking desert, stopping in Calexico where I bought a black bull whip and a cowhide stool on a wooden tripod.

Made San Diego in the afternoon, and for an hour in the car, I could smell it coming, the ocean, then that blue ocean was right there, nowhere left to go in that direction.

Drove around the Navy base, where my father had learned to dive before shipping out to Espiritu Santo. My mother said, These were the happiest years of my life. The war, she meant.

The next morning up early to Mission San Diego, the last of the twenty-one missions we had yet to visit, and arrived just as they opened, and the ranger let me ring the morning bells, but we had hours to go to get home that night, all the way, a straight shot, twelve hours.

Through the smog of L.A., along the coast to Santa Barbara, then back inland to Atascadero, where my father and mother first met, where my mother grew up, I'd been there before. Just outside King City, we stopped at a roadside stand for plums and oranges and artichokes.

At the far end of the gravel lot was a mound of abalone shells as tall as me and as long as our car, nothing but shells, glistening pearl and rainbow in the lowering sun. Twenty-five cents each, so we bought five more for ashtrays, and one for my desk.

On the gravel in the warm afternoon light, I saw it, sensed it, Flood Dr., in the dark, the kitchen window lit up yellow.

We were almost home, I knew then. We had made good time.

Leaving

After seven years in Oregon, Mac began to believe the family had made a real home. The apple and corn and bean crops were successful, for the most part, and the weather was ideal, proper rain and proper sun. The chickens and their eggs were abundant, and the cows gave milk. His parents no longer fought all the time, and his father stuck around, for the most part.

There was even enough ease that now and then their father gave them a twenty-dollar bill, crisp and clean, and drove them to town to spend a dollar each of it, on whatever they chose. Their father methodically counted the change.

Nim and Mac both went to school, a one-room schoolhouse only an hour's walk from the farm, where they learned to read and do sums and make friends. The teacher, Miss Ethel, took a special shine to Mac, and he graduated seventh grade. Nim stopped going to school when he turned fourteen, to help around the farm, but also cutting out whenever possible, often gone from Saturday through Sunday morning just before church. Once Nim didn't return home until after church, and their father made him pay for that disrespect with his fists.

The best of life on the farm was the horse Jody, for which his parents had traded four fat shoats. Jody's coat had been red at some point, but she was old now, faded orange, white muzzle. The crops were plowed with a rusty tractor, so Jody's main task was to haul a wooden cart, produce and supplies. On Sundays after church, Mac was allowed to take Jody into the foothills. She was slow, a bit swaybacked, but never minded Mac on her and knew all the trails. They tromped everywhere, and in late summer foraged for blackberries, bringing home bucketsful, and everyone sat together on the porch and stained their mouths purple while churning ice cream.

Sometimes Mac and Jody went to the creek, to the deep swimming hole, Mac flying underwater through the green and yellow and black shades. Then he might do a little frog-gigging. Mac preferred to go without Nim, or anyone else, on these days. He liked being alone, liked drying off on the warm table-rock at the pool's edge.

Jody, school, the farm dog Ivan who showed up one day and never left, cousins Bascom and Effie and their brood only a few miles away, Mac's best friend Phil Chapman from the next farm over, his mother and father always at home, and Nim at home too, for the most part. Home.

Their father left for the last time early one Monday morning in November, a thick and drenching rain. He was gone before anyone else was awake, left a note on the kitchen table, Don't wait up for me. He took the car and one suitcase, left the banged-up truck.

Mac's mother pushed the boys out of the house and locked all the doors, then proceeded to break things. Mac and Nim stayed on the porch and listened to every last splinter and shard. Mac had never seen his mother in such a state. Usually when she was angry, she sat black and quiet in her rocker and filled the spittoon with her chaw.

The house was then quiet for a good while.

When their mother came out to the porch, she said, We better get some breakfast on and get to work.

Mac stopped going to school.

Their father did not return. Their mother never spoke of him and stopped any question with a vehement expectoration.

When Mac asked Nim about their father, why he'd left, why he didn't like the family anymore, Nim only said, That's just his way, the bastard.

Two months passed, rainy and muddy months, and the three of them worked the farm every day, except for Sundays when Cousin Effie picked up their mother and drove her to Medford for church. Mac and Nim had stopped going, though their mother didn't seem to mind, as if their absence at church meant that much more Jesus for her. Every night at dinner, We just want to thank you, Lord Jesus, we just love you so much, Jesus.

One morning their mother got in the truck and set off for town, Going to make a phone call.

When she returned, everything began to move faster. They sold the farm and everything on it, for cash, including Jody, loaded up what they needed in the back of the truck, wedged in anything else that fit, and by March were headed to California, to Modesto.

Saying goodbye to Jody was the most difficult moment Mac had ever lived through, far more painful than being abandoned at the orphanage.

We're going to build our own house, their mother told them.

They purchased a vacant lot in an unincorporated section of Modesto, in the heart of California's long valley, a few other houses going up around them, pale dust everywhere, the slapping of hammers. To the east, thousands of acres of farmland and orchard, the snow-capped Sierra Nevada a mirage.

First they dug a hole for the outhouse, then built the outhouse over it, from scrap wood they'd picked up outside the Modesto freight yard. They pitched a leaky tent where they'd sleep until the first room, the main room, was done. After that they'd add the other rooms.

Mac and Nim laid a rugged foundation on posts, then laid a crude floor and raised some simple beams, constructing the slat walls, inside and out, from discarded orange crates a trucking company was happy to be rid of. Late one night they spliced electricity from the street's overhead wires. A Franklin stove for heat. Their mother built a chicken coop and run, raised a fence around the backyard.

All they did was work. But by late July, the main room was finished, and the three of them celebrated with grocery store steaks. They turned on the lights. Everything worked. The radio too, their mother's great splurge. She spent the last of their money on that, which Mac thought was more than reasonable.

Lying in bed indoors that first night, Nim snoring delicately beside him, Mac tried to imagine that this, finally, was their home for good, had to be, no one left to leave them behind. He listened all night to the freight trains.

Nim, who was eighteen now, left a few weeks later. Like their father, up and out before anyone else was awake. He'd left a note for Mac on his pillow.

Little Brother, it said, there's nothing here for us, you know that. I'm off to find real work. You should too. Here's some money. Don't ask. I'm headed south, but let's meet back here in a year, in August, and we'll team up again, things will be better then. Tell Mom I love her.

When Mac showed the note to his mother, she read it, tossed it in the stove, and withdrew to her rocker and spittoon past dinner.

Nim was right, there was nothing for Mac in Modesto. Through a cousin, their mother found a job in a canning plant, and the money was good, but there was no place for Mac, too many adults out of work these days. He looked for work everywhere in Modesto, but nothing. School didn't start until September and didn't seem important any longer. He was fourteen after all.

Mac left in late August, while there were still dry months ahead. He left a note too, but hidden under his own pillow, promising to write when he found work. After dinner that night, he told his mother he was going out to see a friend. He turned in the doorway and looked back. In this one little room, in her rocker, with her spittoon, the radio on, Major Bowe's Amateur Hour.

He retrieved his bindle from under the house and began hitching up and down the valley, looking for work.

There was day labor here and there, picking and packing, burning debris, digging irrigation ditches, most of that work paid in scrip. Nothing steady. There were too many others suddenly, all looking for work, families in overloaded trucks and cars. From Oklahoma and Texas and Arkansas, crossing up and down the long valley.

Nights he slept in soft orchard dust near the side of the road, bathed in irrigation ditches before dawn. A few times he was corralled by a family who insisted he join them for dinner, around the campfire near their car, no one should eat alone, they said. He accepted these invitations with some guilt, having promised himself that he'd spend none of Nim's money yet, but with gratitude for a home-cooked meal and company. He always washed the dishes and set up the morning coffee as partial payment. Mac was at ease with these people, their voices, that twang, and he could almost return to Oklahoma. He slept in the warm circle of these families.

One night, one of the fathers, Tybo Hauck, described for Mac how their Texas farm had turned to dust and how the bank re-possessed it. Their journey since, five months on the road, half a job here, a day's work there, the children always hungry.

Mac offered his own story, it only seemed fair, though he never mentioned all the leaving.

Here's a thing, Tybo said, got a cousin near Bishop, owns a horse ranch, always got room and board for a youngster like yourself, least when he wrote last. You get to Bishop, you mention my name. He's a Hauck too, Boone.

Where's Bishop?

T'other side of the Sierras, mighty pretty.

You think honestly? Mac said.

I do.

The next morning Mac hitched a tomato truck to Modesto and hopped the first of many freights, up to Sacramento, through the Sierras, down to Bishop.

Horses.

Sparky

She was my brother's dog for four years in Bayonne, he'd picked her out of a cardboard box in front of the PX there. But when we transferred to Key West, when I was two weeks old, she abandoned him. He never forgave me for stealing her from him, that was the word he insisted on, stealing, and he never let me forget. There were photos from Key West, in the albums in the living room, of me in a playpen with Sparky parked outside, calm and vigilant, in the shade of a palm tree with white coral and dark sea in the background.

According to the story, when my mother and sister brought me to Key West, two weeks after my father and brother had already arrived and set up house, Sparky at once hunkered beneath my bassinette and allowed no one to approach. She snarled at strangers who came to see the new baby, allowing only immediate family to approach. She'd already had one litter of puppies by then and knew how to mother.

She was, my parents said, a mix of Border Collie and standard Collie, though who knows. She was the shape and size of a Border Collie, with that shorter snout, and white all over but with Collie-colored tan and brown and black splotches on her butt and the tip of her tail and face and mane and ears. Her fur was longer, like a Collie's, and in the early spring, when she shed, it came out in matted clumps like thick pieces of felt. She was as smart as a Border Collie, but with an easier temperament.

I grew up only knowing that she was my companion, always there. By the time we left Key West, when I was four, and moved back to San Jose, Sparky was, without question, my dog. My poor brother.

What Sparky did most was listen to me, the two of us often on the floor of my bedroom, where I recounted and railed and confessed and jabbered. She heard much from me about the unfairness of my parents. We frequently shook hands, her best trick. I depended on her constancy.

What I did for Sparky, I fed her cans of K-9 dog food, the can opened and turned over, making a delicious sucking sound before the food plopped into her bowl. I bathed her as often as she would allow, picked up her messes from the backyard. I took her with me whenever I left the house, walking or on my bike, Sparky trotting alongside, her dog tag jingling against the collar's buckle. We traveled the streets near Flood Drive, and through the orchards, while there were still orchards, and in the open construction sites after the orchards were razed and before the blocks of identical new houses sprouted. But if we'd gone too far and I wanted to keep going too far, or if there were bigger, more dangerous streets to cross, I'd say, Go home, girl, and point, and she'd jangle away, waiting for me when I returned.

Sometimes she met me at school when the day was done.

My father and I took her camping and fishing with us. She guarded the camp site while we went out for the day. Once at Lake Pinto in Watsonville, it rained all night, heavy and cold, and the Army surplus tent, thick green canvas, began to leak in the earliest hours of the morning, so just before dawn, my father and I conceded, stowed the gear and the tent in my brother's red Fairlane station wagon, and set out for home. Sparky, soaked skinny, reeked, my father said, To high heaven. Her rank, oily scent, just a tad sweet, filled the station wagon. I did not dislike that scent. I had breathed in Sparky my whole life, and this wet pathetic morning seemed the essence of her.

But Sparky was often on her own, the side gate always open, the front door too, she had territories to tend. Once when my father and I were walking home from Buy th' Bucket, our usual Saturday stop, Sparky met us halfway, then fell into step and accompanied us. She hadn't been looking for us, we'd simply run into her during one of her rounds. When she was in heat, she would disappear for days at a time, and at least twice came home pregnant, though I didn't remember the first time.

The second time, I was eight, and Sparky chose my bedroom closet for her nest. She gathered old towels and shirts my mother left out for her, and made a precise oval of them a week before giving birth. Then one midnight she woke me with her whimpering, and my father and mother and brother, we all watched her deliver six dark puppies, four brown and two black. Labs, my brother guessed, and that seemed right.

That night was wonderfully long, each puppy sliding blue-black and blood-covered into the nest. Sparky licked each blind pup clean. My father cleared away the after-birth, my mother laid in a new nest of old clothes, and the puppies suckled.

The puppies lived in my closet for eight weeks, and I tried to heed my father's advice, Don't get too close and don't name them, that makes it harder to say goodbye. So I helped Sparky care for them and did not name them, and one Saturday, after my father placed an ad in the Mercury, Six Puppies! Free!, six families came to our house and took the puppies away, one by one. It made me happy that Sparky did not growl or bark when we took the puppies from her. It meant I was still her boy.

In the spring of my sixth-grade year, Sparky, sixteen now, developed a tumor on her belly as big as a golf ball, and grew lethargic, wincing on her worst days. The vet removed the tumor, which I knew we could scarcely afford, and she was her old self again. I kept her thick stiches clean. But the tumor returned over a few months, and even I knew that she was in pain and dying. So we held a family pow-wow after dinner one night, and agreed, ruefully, it was time to put her to sleep.

Robert, my father said from across the dining room table, it's best for Sparky, you know that. I know, he told me, how hard it is to kill an animal you love.

I had heard the story before, that when he lived on the farm in Oregon as a boy, he'd had to put down his favorite dog, Ivan. My father was only nine at the time. Ivan had broken a leg in an animal's deep burrow, and my father's father insisted that my father take the dog behind the barn and shoot it with the family rifle. He did. Once, in the head. And then he buried Ivan all by himself. He didn't think he'd ever get over that, the image of Ivan bloodied and dead, but he knew too, even then, that it was best for Ivan, the end of his pain.

That night I listened to my father, intently, and knew there was only one choice.

But, my father said, we'll go to the vet, and he'll give her a shot, and she'll just go to sleep.

I nodded, afraid to say yes, as if my silence might stop time.

She's your dog, Robert, he said, it's up to you.

My twelfth birthday was three days away, and I thought if we could wait until the day after my birthday, then somehow time would not only stop but go backwards. So I asked.

Of course, my father said, and my mother reached out and touched my hand.

The morning before my birthday, I woke early and headed to the kitchen, but down the hall I saw Sparky's body in the middle of the living room. She had died in her sleep. I called my parents.

After we examined her and each had said goodbye, and I petted her one last time, my father brought an old blanket in from the garage. I knew I had to be farther away for this, in the hall, outside my bedroom door.

From there I watched my father roll Sparky onto the blanket and wrap her. He knelt and lifted her, cradling her as if she were a sleeping child. He kissed her once on the head.

He carried her to the car, put her in the back seat, then drove to the vet.

I stood alone in an empty house.

Abbey Road

You had no idea who I was becoming or wanted to become. But how could you?

At the beginning of seventh grade, I was who I had been for so long. I was your best buddy, of course, and still held all the dreams you had helped me cook up. I could not become an astronaut, that dream dead when I was nine, thanks to my astigmatism, though I pondered Astro-Physicist as a back-up. Or I would play in the NFL, an offensive guard like my brother. Or I would join the Marines, like my brother. Or the Navy like you. And some small notion, because of my knee-jerk hamminess, that I might become a stand-up comedian. None of those dreams survived past twelve.

The summer before seventh grade, I stopped getting the usual military-grade crew cut, though my hair was still a regulation Boy's cut when classes started, close on the sides and back. I wore straight jeans, but no Levi's,

Lee or Wrangler, and my shirts looked as if I lived year-round at summer camp.

Then: Once.

October. I was walking with Rich Davis between classes in the morning, beach fog from Santa Cruz a pan lid on the valley, overcast we called it. And I heard The Beatles' Come Together over the P.A. in the open corridor of Ida Price Junior High, my new territory.

I stopped and listened, confused.

What is that? I asked Rich.

The Beatles, dummkopf.

Oh, yeah. As if I knew.

I did know who The Beatles were, but not these Beatles. You and me, when I was six, and Mom and Ricks, we watched them those first two times on Ed Sullivan, She Loves You Yeah Yeah Yeah. Judi was married by then and living with Dave. You thought The Beatles were amateur musicians and that their hair made them look like girls. But a few months later, I didn't care about The Beatles anymore, moving on to other kid things. I missed Sgt. Pepper's completely and how much The Beatles had changed, gone were the mop tops. My favorite song the year Sgt. Pepper's came out was Bobby Goldsboro's Honey. You and I both liked its schmaltzy wallow, perfect for a barroom jukebox.

What I heard that morning in the corridor with Rich Davis, even as it was muffled by the school's tatty p.a.

and had to break through the junior high chit chat, that riff that opens Come Together then shimmers all the way through it, shoomp doomp boodle-a-bing, that sound shocked me with its alienness, and seduced me with it too. A door too long closed, I felt, had been opened and would not be shut.

And Rich Davis. He was a brand-new friend, a brand-new best friend. Thin and jointed like a doll, he had buck teeth, a really bad attitude toward adults, and long blonde hair parted in the middle. Long long hair. He wore bell bottoms and light suede cowboy boots just like Creedence Clearwater Revival wore. I adored him as much for the fun we had making fun of everyone else as for the signpost he was, directing me to where it seemed I wanted to go. And he was a drummer. Had his own kit. Pearl Ludwig with Zildjian cymbals and hi-hat.

I went to Rich's house after school that October day, crammed into the room he shared with his older brother Wayne, where he played me all of Abbey Road, Sgt. Pepper's, The White Album. What other day would shape my life so clearly? Rich played his drums for me, and that's probably when I fell in love with him.

It took a month, but I finally talked you and Mom into buying me Abbey Road. You were stubbornly against it for an unidentifiable reason. One torrentially rainy Saturday, we drove to the Gemco near our house, but they were out of stock, though the man in the record department was nice enough to call the Cupertino store. So you drove us there, despite it being all the way across the valley and in such nasty weather too. On the way home in the car, I gazed at the cover, front and back, burning it into my brain, almost hearing the songs, leery of tearing off the shrink wrap too soon.

I woke up early every morning to play Abbey Road, both sides, before I went to school. I played it very loud, on my blue and white suitcase GE record player, as loud as I'd been instructed to play it, Rich's doing. For a week or so. Until you burst in one morning while I Want You (She's So Heavy), last track, side one, rolled on maddeningly.

Turn down that funeral music! Your exact words. Was this the first time we truly yelled at each other? Not the last. I yelled back at you, something about privacy, but really pure barking, and you slammed the door.

But it wasn't only The Beatles, was it? I was twelve, after all, bound to move away from you and Mom, mostly you. I had discovered masturbation that summer, another miracle, all stoked by years of poring over Ricks's stash of Playboys on the top shelf of his closet. I began to play the fool for Cheri and Terry and Jeri. Or any girl. I'd always been a ham, but that ham became impossible to tame. That was one secret among many I kept from you.

Then the urge to grow my hair long consumed me. As long as The Beatles, as long as Rich Davis. Longer.

You and I argued about my hair a lot.

I was thorough, determined, preparing my arguments in advance, which I knew were watertight. Hair was just hair. Jesus had long hair. Everyone had long hair these days. What was important was on the inside, in your soul. We'd save money on haircuts.

But you trounced every single point. You didn't listen to me at all, didn't use any dissembling logic or reverse psychology. You squashed me flat.

No son of yours.

Angry, frustrated, I would leap to the offensive, and it was always the same weakness I poked at. Your smoking.

Your smoking will kill you, I was not afraid to shout. My hair wouldn't hurt me at all. How could you even. You weren't being reasonable.

From then on, mostly barking. Top of our lungs, twelve feet apart barking. Mom disappeared during these arguments, though she might offer a conciliatory Now, Honey before leaving. We never knew if that Now, Honey was aimed at you or me.

Once, one Saturday. You stood by the dining room table, I stood at the kitchen sink looking out to the front yard and the Liquidambar tree. Coming on a blue, warm, and cloudless dusk. Barking and barking, dogs at sunset. I finally fled, to the bathroom, got under the shower, and continued my now pathetic defense, arguing with you with you not there.

Oh, look at me, I'm going to smoke until I die, but you can't grow your hair long, Robert, because you're just a stupid little kid. Then I veered into the most common adolescent rhetoric, self-pity. Fine, then, don't worry about me, maybe I'll start smoking and then I'll die and then you won't have to worry about me anymore, I'll show you, I bet you won't even cry at my funeral.

What I didn't know was that you and Mom were on the front porch, ice tea for Mom, Oly for you, on the bench directly under the window in the shower, which window was open.

Then I heard you both laughing, clearly laughing at my performance, and I was filled with shame and rage and went to my room and slammed the door and stayed in all night, gnawing on my righteousness.

Our fights were about long hair and smoking, but also not. We were fighting because wasn't that what fathers and sons were meant to do. I'd seen plenty of it between you and Ricks, when I was younger and he still lived at home. My arguments with you were nowhere near as ferocious, though. When you and Ricks fought, it was a battle, and on more than one occasion, bloody.

But the fights didn't separate us, not for long. We were still pals, you still took me with you, to bars, yes, but also to see slices of the world I'd not yet seen. Steel mills, dive centers, valleys and hills far off the main highways, a nuclear reactor, an aircraft carrier, a destroyer, and once,

SEALAB II in dry dock at Hunter's Point. We still talked about everything else too, the war and how you'd softened to it, what a deadly fiasco it was, you were relieved Ricks was leaving the Marines. We talked about the war a lot. And everything else. Between arguments.

That February, you relented, tired of the barking, I supposed, but only a little bit, allowing me to grow out the short sides and back of my Boy's haircut. Nothing over the collar.

Still, I went on changing, every day, sometimes by the hour.

Maybe you did see me changing, maybe that's why you were so adamant about the length of my hair, maybe you didn't want me to change. I should have given you more credit. How could you not notice all the changes, you were too smart not to. Maybe you did know who I was becoming and wanted to stop it, not because you didn't like who I was becoming, not because you didn't like the me emerging from me, but simply because you didn't want me to change. And now that we were arguing so much, you were worried about what would become of us, us pals. You may have seen something darker ahead for us, a darker future I could only feebly imagine.

After all, you did buy me my first bass, from the PX, a Japanese knock-off of a Hofner violin bass, just like McCartney's, maple sugar brown and yellowing gold sunburst with white trim. You came to the seventh grade play, a campy melodrama, and told me after that I was really funny. You let me start a band with Rich Davis and our new friend Keith Epstein, who had a beautiful hollow-body Gibson, deep red-orange. You even let us practice in the living room a few times, which must have been torture for you and Mom. You let me hang out with Rich Davis, even though you didn't like or trust him. You let me go farther and wider on my bike.

All that year, I changed and changed. When Ricks came home from the Marines, I commandeered one of his fatigue shirts, cut off the sleeves, and sewed patches all over it. Peace Symbol. Ecology Symbol. Sgt. Pepper's. The Frito Bandito. Those patches were both signal and armor, This is who I am and nothing will change that.

That spring, in the dusty and minute Ida Price library, the librarian gave me a copy of The Strawberry Statement, about the Free Speech movement at Columbia in New York. I read it, was enflamed by it, but never shared it with you, even though I should have.

There was more and more music coming from my room, louder and sharper. My door stayed closed all the time. You had to knock now.

But you were changing too. Weren't you? I knew you were out of work that spring, when Mom didn't. I knew you had a new friend, Renata, the unhappy wife of a family we'd met in Yosemite the winter before, and who lived in Los Gatos. You two were good friends, you told me, she needed a friend, her husband was a monster, he hit her and their sons and drank too much. You started dressing in a new way, as if you were taking us to the Atomic Motel in Vegas for the weekend. You bought a pipe, for some reason, with a space age design to it. You chased your Oly with Schnapps.

You went new places you never told me about.

Shore Patrol

It was off-season at The Boardwalk, March, a few of the rides open, The Giant Dipper and the Wild Mouse and the Jet Star, and most of the games too, but the beach was littered with only a few families, a scattering of surfers past the breaks. There were no lifeguards on duty. It was sunny but not warm.

My father and brother and myself, a boys' day out, that simple. My brother, Ricks, was fresh from training school at Camp Pendleton, home for a 72-hour leave before transferring to Huntsville, Alabama, where he would learn to fire Hawk missiles, surface to air. I was ten and idolized him, had written pages of a story about his courageous exploits in Vietnam, where he had yet to go, but would soon, he was certain.

Ricks wore his Marine Corps dress greens, a heavy wool jacket, wool slacks, a soft green garrison cap peaked front and back. PFC stripe and the red ensign of a Sharpshooter. He had to wear the uniform, he told me, because even though on leave, he was considered active duty. Maybe, I thought, because also he wanted to piss off my father, retired career Navy, because the Navy and Marines despised each other. Why he had joined the Marines in the first place.

It was the end of the day, afternoon creeping across the beach, The Boardwalk emptying.

Ricks was the one who started it. At the Rifleman booth, live .22 ammo, paper targets with bull's-eyes. He was showing off, for me and for our father, his expertise, his competence to kill. There was one other person at the booth, clearly a hippie, bell bottoms, flowering feminine shirt, and long long hair. I liked the way the hippie dressed but sensed this was a problem. Ricks and the hippie agreed to shoot against each other.

The teen who ran the booth, one foot on the front counter, stared out at the bay, bored with being bored. When the short sharp pops evaporated, the teen gathered the targets and tallied the score. The smoke was so acrid it tingled in the back of my throat. My brother, of course, was the winner, no doubt.

Maybe, Ricks said, sighting down the barrel of the toy-like rifle as if preparing for inspection. Maybe, he said to the hippie, if you cut your fucking faggot hair, you'd hit something.

The shouting started, the distance between Ricks and the hippie closed, face to face.

My father wrapped his arm in front of me and pulled me behind him.

None of the words mattered, I thought, it was just barking, playground barking. But the fangs were bared, and the dull afternoon suddenly crackled with a charge.

The words did matter.

At least I'm not a baby killer, the hippie said, and my brother and the hippie were throwing fists, and my brother was winning, how could he not, trained to do so.

I'm going to Vietnam to kill gooks and save my little brother from Communism, Ricks had written to me from Pendleton on blue, almost transparent military stationery. I wrote back and asked him not to.

There was blood already, the hippie's nose, when my father joined in, and he and Ricks had the hippie on the ground and were beating him.

Shrill whistles sliced through the cloud of fists.

Shore Patrol, my father said calmly, and he grabbed my brother by the collar and me by the collar, and we ran.

I looked back, just like in the movies, and there were two Shore Patrol chasing us, green fatigues, black boots and armbands, white helmets, silver whistles, .45s unholstered.

We ran to the nearest exit, crossing under the Giant Dipper, then along behind the boardwalk, until we found a curved ramp that would take us into Santa Cruz and away from the Shore Patrol. My brother and father whooped, so I did too.

We drove back to San Jose then and told the story all night, to my mom, to my brother's pregnant wife Jan, to one another.

I remembered, but did not say that night, that while we were running away, all of blue-green Santa Cruz before us, the exhilaration of being on the run with my father and brother. I was running with them into a future that seemed certain, inevitable. We flew.

Rider

Although the sun had not yet risen, the Bishop Diner was crowded. Real cowboys, it seemed, men in cowboy hats and boots and thick wool jackets.

The smell of eggs and bacon and coffee.

Mac hitched himself up on the last free stool, tucked his bindle under his feet, nodded blindly to the man next to him. The counterman slid a menu across and poured a cup of coffee without saying a word. Mac felt as if everyone in the diner were watching him, some poor kid on his own, too many of those these days.

Yes, please, he said, four eggs, sunny side up, sausage and bacon, hash browns, white toast and jam, and more coffee, please. Orange juice if you have it.

Mac had saved the money Nim had given him, but this seemed a good time to spend some, the horse ranch so close and after two days on trains with nothing to eat. He peeled off a dollar bill and fished out a quarter, slapped them down as he'd seen the other men do, then asked the counterman if he knew where he might find Boone Hauck. He was a cousin of Boone's, from Texas.

Pert near there, maybe fifteen, twenty miles, I'll draw you a map.

While Mac was eating, the sun had lipped over the softer and more distant eastern mountains, and to the west, tinged the steep close slopes of the Sierra Nevada orange and salmon, the snowfields on the summits blazing. Nothing, Mac thought, could get over those mountains. Or were they cliffs?

The view stopped him in the street, and he regarded the Sierras through the veil of his own breath.

His mother must be thinking of him, wondering why he hadn't returned or even written, it had been weeks already. He thought about where Nim might be, pictured him on a beach down south, posing and smiling that smile. His father was merely gone.

Bishop was like all small towns, three blocks long and two blocks wide, a bank and a post office and a movie theater, Laurel and Hardy in Bonnie Scotland, and soon he was on Round Valley Road, headed across the scrubby plain toward the granite wall of the Sierras. It took the entire day, not a single car or truck to hitch from, but it was pleasant once the shadows lifted, and he shed his thin jacket. Here and there, the road touched a narrow winding river, but the mountains refused to get closer.

Dusk had deepened by the time he stepped onto the porch of the yellow lighted ranch house, though he could still make out the two corrals, the long stables, seven horses at rest in an open field, a mess of outbuildings, three trucks. The sweet scent of hay and manure.

Before he knocked, a fear that embarrassed him, because he had failed to consider it, swung down on him. He had not considered that Boone Hauck might send him packing. Mac could not sleep rough out here, he'd freeze.

Boone himself answered the door. He was short, pudgy, as Mac's mother would say, a tight black vest, his hair matted with sweat from a cowboy hat. Real cowboy boots, cracked and uneven.

Young man, Boone said, I trust you didn't come all this way to try and sell me something. What you got? Hoovers, Fuller brushes, encyclopedias, Bibles? We ain't buying, no matter the miracle.

Boone laughed at his own joke. Mac liked that.

Tybo told me to look you up, Mac said, and that was all it took.

Boone swept Mac into the kitchen where the crew was wolfing down dinner, chicken and dumplings, boiled greens, pan-fried potatoes. Mac was ordered to help himself to a plate, then was introduced to the seven other men, some not much older than himself, whose names he promptly forgot.

At the crew's insistence, he told his story, meeting Tybo, his history with Jody and the farm, and this time he did not leave out any of the leaving.

The oil lantern over the table chased the shadows into corners.

Men? Boone asked the table, and it was unanimous that Mac would join the crew. A jug was passed around, and Mac took a quick snort, relieved he had not coughed.

After dinner, Boone took Mac out to the porch, where they smoked, his first cigarette since leaving Modesto. Mac was astonished by the vast and bright throw of stars across the moonless sky, the mountains so black he thought they might swallow him.

Long as you understand, Boone said, I can only offer room and board, maybe a little fun, certainly endless doses of hard work. And we'll get you some warmer duds. But it's a good crew, and if you want to learn about horses, ain't no place better. Deal?

They shook on it, and Boone led Mac to the bunkhouse, where he took up the last bed, bottom, nearest the window. The crew introduced themselves again, and Mac would not forget. Charley, Barlow, Tex, Nipper, Levon, José, Ray.

Just Mac, he said.

No one had a last name.

They offered him a seat at the table where they were playing poker for matches, and smoking, and the jug kept going around, and when he was called out of his bunk at dawn, Mac ran out the door and threw up the entire night, the crew howling behind him. It was not his first drunk, but clearly his worst, and there was no mercy to be offered.

He dunked his head in a barrel of rainwater, dressed and went to breakfast, which he tried and failed to eat. The crew scattered to their tasks, and Boone led Mac to the long stables, twenty horses under one roof. The stalls were empty though, the crew warming up the horses in the attached corral.

Here's the shovel, Boone said, and there's the shit.

For the next many weeks, all Mac did was shovel shit, carry what needed to be carried, dig what needed to be dug, strung and re-strung fences, but always keeping one eye on the crew and the horses. He memorized every word and gesture.

The crew worked him hard but fairly, nights in the bunkhouse were easy, though no one went out of his way to teach Mac anything about horses. Except for José.

José was the next youngest, seventeen, as short as a jockey, but wiry, and maybe stronger and smarter than anyone on the crew. He was from Sonora, grew up on the family horse ranch, but two years before the horses had been stolen and the ranch burned to the ground. José had been in town that day, to purchase supplies, and felt lucky to be alive. He assumed his family was dead. So he kept riding.

Besides their youth, what he and Mac shared was a mutual distrust of the bullshit the other crew members frequently peddled.

José knew everything about horses and was eager to teach Mac. On slow afternoons, and on Sundays, he taught Mac how to comb and pick the horses, tie the necessary hitches, blanket and cinch a saddle, read a horse's eyes, sense when it might kick or rear, speak to it softly. He also taught Mac Spanish commands. José believed horses were more inclined to Spanish.

By October, Mac was ready to ride, and one Sunday, José took him out on the range, Mac on a Palomino mare who'd been broken that summer. José rode his own horse, a Bay named Carmen. They toured the ranch's boundaries, José showing Mac where the wild herds gathered, these the horses they would break next spring. At the western edge of the range, Mac stared up at the blue-gray face of the Sierras. It seemed as if the mountains stretched back over him.

Jody, Mac said, I'll call my horse Jody.

If you must. Don't get attached.

On Saturday nights, the crew regularly went to Bishop for drinking, for whoring, for getting off the god damn ranch. Mac never went, claiming he needed to write his mother, and José often stayed with him in the bunkhouse, where they told each other every story they'd ever heard. The truth was that while Mac enjoyed his nights alone with José, he didn't go to town because he knew what happened in town and didn't know if he knew how to do it. Even while he wanted to. José stayed to save money.

The main entertainment in the bunkhouse that fall consisted of fighting. Fights, bare knuckle and full speed, broke out out of boredom, though, rather than dispute, and could break out almost any night. These were real fights, though not intended to harm, but, it seemed to Mac, to bone up, train, stay fit. These were nothing like the boyish fights at the orphanage, or on the school yard in Medford, these were painful, and Mac learned quickly when to jab and when to duck. He earned respect for a wicked left hook. No one ever got hurt badly enough, though there was one time that Charley went too far and Mac left him bloodied on the ground, unconscious for hours.

Smoking, drinking, poker, fights. The boredom was all right by Mac, there were always horses the next morning.

One week after the first snows fell, Charley left, along with Nipper and Ray and Barlow, just Mac and Tex and Levon and José left behind, and Boone in the big house.

That was Mac's first true winter. Deep snows, freezing winds screaming down the mountains' stone faces, short days, lots of time in the bunkhouse, the crew practical-ly hibernating. They patched and repaired what needed it, fed and cared for the stabled horses. Ate and drank and smoked and played cards, wrote letters home, but the fights ceased, too cold for that. No one went into town, the town closed up for the winter.

What Mac most loved that winter was delivering hay to the wild herds. The crew stacked the truck bed high and got as close to the herds as the two-track roads permitted. The crew that followed on horseback loaded up travois with bales, Mac and Jody wading through the powdery snow, the wild horses pawing and hungry and wrapped in their own breaths.

The winter seemed endless, though Mac appreciated that. His mother did not write to him.

In the spring, when Nipper and Ray and Barlow returned, though not Charley, the ranch worked without ceasing. First the broken horses were sold and picked up, then the crew rounded up twenty from the wild herds and brought them in for breaking. Over three long days, Mac broke his first horse, a spotted Mustang, and everyone was impressed, though Mac was sore for weeks, with bruises from succeeding horses piled on. This continued into summer.

One night Boone asked Mac to stay after dinner for a drink and a smoke, a touch of business to conduct.

You're a horseman, Boone said, and a good one for your age. We all like having you here, but I'm wondering if you're getting ready to move on. You're young, a long road ahead. And there ain't no girls out here neither.

Mac was set to return to Modesto in a month, meet up with Nim, see his mother, and though he missed them both, this life, here, he'd wanted it so much and now he had it. But Nim.

I've got to get back to Modesto, Mac said, in August, see my family, I promised. That's the plan at least.

And you're going?

Yes, sir.

Well, that's good then, you should. Family and all. Here, this'll help.

Boone handed over a wad of bills.

Your pay, he said. I know I said room and board only, but you've earned it. I only say that room and board crap to scare off the ninnies anyway.

It was twice as much money as Nim had given him.

On August first, Mac said goodbye to the Palomino Jody, tried to make it brief and not to cry. Then Boone and José drove him into town and stood with him at the side of the highway. Boone shook Mac's hand and got back in the truck. José hugged him, slapped his back. Hasta luego, chico.

Mac put out his thumb and waited.

He caught a ride to Reno, then hopped trains back to Modesto, laid the money before his mother, and asked her to forgive him, but he'd written, he said, written every week.

Yes, she said, you did.

She sat in the rocker all weekend, then on Sunday afternoon fried up a chicken and began to ask Mac questions, and to listen to his answers.

Finally, she said she was proud of him. He was a man now. She said nothing about Nim and did not ask after him.

His mother had finished two new rooms in the year Mac had been gone, a bedroom for her and a kitchen. Mac went to work on a second bedroom. He tried not to think about his brother.

Nim showed up four days later, with presents for their mother, a new watch and a gold cross on a gold necklace. They had grocery store steaks that night.

For a few days, it was something like home.

But Nim had a plan.

The Army, Nim said, it's perfect for us, can really give us a leg up, there just ain't any other work, I've looked. Whaddya say?

I'd say I'm only fifteen.

But you don't look it, not at all, you're a man, and my brother, and that'll slide us right on in. They're begging for recruits.

I don't want to, Mac said.

Buddy boy, Nim said, my little brother, I've got news for you.

I'm sure you do.

At Camp Ord, where we'd get trained up, there's a cavalry regiment, the last one in the Army. I've talked to a recruiter friend, he says we're a cinch. Cavalry, Mac. Horses.

They went downtown to the recruiting office, and when they returned, just as dinner was being laid, they announced to their mother that they had enlisted. Leaving in two weeks.

Mount Umunhum

There was always the same plane in the sky, no matter the time of day or night, that plane passing over our house on its way to passing over Mount Umunhum, and from there out to and around the Pacific. It felt like the plane passed over every two minutes, but it was really once an hour. The sky always held one plane.

The P-3 Orion Turboprop was a submarine hunter, launched from nearby Moffett Field Naval Air Station, where we bought our groceries and our clothes and got our film developed and I bought my first guitar, the privileges of my father's Navy retirement. Saturday mornings at Moffett, on our way to the PX, the Post Exchange, we first drove past the hulking dirigible hangar and then the gridded fleet of P-3s that waited idling on the white tarmac.

Painted battleship gray, with black and white insignia, the P-3 ascended, strenuously, west over the broad Santa Clara Valley, where it nearly scraped the concrete cube of the Air Force weather and radar station on the summit of Mount Umunhum. From there, the P-3 would circle the Pacific, ten or more hours at a time, searching for Russian submarines armed with nuclear warheads. Soviet submarines. Communist.

Skimming the ocean from a razor-thin height of 200 feet, the crew monitored every beep and bing from under the waves, decoding red and green shapes in their blacked-out cabin and the hiss and tongue of intercepted radio. When the P-3 returned, gliding over our tidy streets, that forest of TV antennae, I knew that at least twenty-three other P-3's continued their vigilance of the Pacific. This was a war, we knew. Were told.

Our house, on Flood Drive in Cambrian Park, on the western edge of the valley, in the shadow of Mount Umunhum, was directly under the P-3's flight path, and the constant ascending and descending became a metronome to my days. More regular than the sun, more precisely incremental, the P-3 offered certain knowledge that our world was safe. But I also understood, because my teachers told me again and again, that the nuclear warheads might have already been launched and we might only have ten minutes before the big white flash.

I would look up, of course, when the P-3 passed over, at school, in our front yard, out the car window, frozen by the fat gray plane and its impossible scaling of the mountain of air. In the earliest morning, when the sky was stretched to milky blue, during the red and orange sunsets of winter and the smoggy purple sunsets of summer, at summer's white noon or winter's sharp blue noon. Even on black-gray rainy February days coming home from school, when I slanted into the storm in my yellow rain jacket and the plane almost impossible to see.

On quiet nights, when there was cloud cover to echo the noise, I heard the P-3's low engines while I lay in bed and imagined myself in uniform and on full alert. After the plane passed, I waited expectantly for the necessary ten minutes.

Movies

The film appeared one day when I was eleven, as if it had once belonged to someone else, only discovered by chance while my father was searching for an official piece of paper, a mortgage or a birth certificate. It was in the bottom back of my parents' bedroom closet, and though I often rooted there when they were out of the house, especially in the weeks leading up to Christmas, I'd never seen the film before, or even heard it mentioned.

It came in a dark green, wax-coated box held secure by canvas straps with black buckles. A paper label, peeling, said CBS: Submarine Rescue, 06/19/56, when we were still stationed in Bayonne, a year before I was born. The metal reel inside, spooled to the edges with black film, was at least four times as big as the plastic Super 8 reels that showed our family's vacations and parties.

Sixteen millimeter, my father said, shame we don't have the projector for it.

Submarine rescue? I asked. Are you in it?

Yup, he said, The Bushnell, out of Bayonne, before you were born. CBS filmed us doing a training exercise.

It was on TV? Did you watch it?

Sure, he said, and he pointed to the date on the label. Haven't seen it since, he said, stole this copy from the C.O. when we left Bayonne.

You never told me.

I forgot.

I had seen my father on film before. Our Super 8 home movies, my father clowning for the camera by the BBQ, my brother and I running football plays in the front yard, my mother shying from the camera at every turn, my sister and her husband and kids getting out of their car, me and Jim Bryant skiing in Yosemite and falling down a lot, my father dancing off the cold that day, my father smiling and drunk in the chaise longue in Aunt Mimi's backyard, Sparky trotting across the camera's field. Our camera, Bell and Howell, had to be wound with a silver crank in order to shoot.

We played these movies as soon as they were developed at the Moffett Field PX, on our own roll-up screen and an olive-green Bell and Howell projector, watching ourselves from two weeks in the past. Watching these movies, it felt as though once we viewed them those moments were truly in the past, separated from the present forever. I don't think we ever watched any home movies twice.

My father had also been in two real movies. The Navy loaned him out as a stunt diver and technical advisor. The pay was good, he said, hazard pay, and he laughed at this. These were real movies, first in theaters then on TV, which is where I saw them, usually on Saturday afternoons, in the family room with the drapes pulled tight against the sun. As a family we pored over the TV Guide every Tuesday when it arrived in the mail, and when my father found the listings for these movies, we watched them together, my father and my mother and I, Sparky too.

The first was Operation Petticoat, with Cary Grant and Tony Curtis, stars whose names and faces I recognized and knew that my parents admired. But this movie was silly, a comedy about a pink submarine, and I couldn't understand why the submarine was pink when the other ships were gray. But at one point, the captain needed a scuba diver to swim along the sub's keel, on some vague mission, and that was my father, in shorts and mask and tank, and I knew it was him because I recognized his legs and his underwater swim-kick. The movie was in Technicolor, because of the submarine. I tried to tell my friends at school about it, but they didn't care and didn't know who Cary Grant or Tony Curtis were.

The second one, the earlier one, was best, Battle of the Coral Sea, a war movie, in black and white, with battles between us and the Japs, detailed models of warships churning and firing artillery in a studio-built ocean. Stock footage from WWII naval and aircraft battles was added to make it seem more real. I knew the ships were fake, but I didn't care. There were actors too, but they didn't matter, only the ships and the battles.

My father played one of two Japanese divers assigned to attach explosives to an American sub. They'd shot his scene in the ocean, live action, though the sub was clearly not moving and near the surface. The scene was dark, muddy, the divers approaching from aft, swimming along the hull, chains of bubbles trailing. Then there was a close-up of the divers as they attached the bricks of explosives, then another long shot of them swimming away as quickly as possible. The divers wore full wetsuits and hoods, and I could not tell which was my father. I didn't care. There he was. For weeks I played that scene in my head, pretending I was him pretending to be an enemy diver. Every week I checked the TV Guide for the movie and saw it several times after.

But this new film, we had the wrong projector. I watched my father looking at the reel, saw he very much wanted to see it again, and I needed to see it too, not a home movie or a made-up movie, but a real movie about real things.

So the Monday after my father found the film, I asked my teacher Mr. Addington where the projector we used in class came from, I knew it was sixteen millimeter, and he sent me to the janitor, who was also in charge of the school's A.V., projectors and TVs and film strips and record players, moved from classroom to classroom on metal stands with rubber wheels. Mr. Amato, tall and a little spooky, was clear that I could not, under any circumstances, borrow the school's projector. But there was another way, he told me, the public library loaned out sixteen-millimeter projectors, which is what Fammatre School used when ours was in the shop.

So after school that day I rode my bike to the Cambrian branch and found that the library did loan projectors, and all you needed was a library card, but you had to go the main branch downtown and be an adult.

So my father called that night and reserved a projector, and on Saturday we picked it up from the basement of the great beige cube of the main branch. On the way home we stopped at Carlito's for tacos and coke and beer, where we sometimes went after Saturday trips to Orchard Supply Hardware.

We had decided it was a special night, so my mother made tacos, which my father and I did not protest, and when we were finished eating, I set up the white, sparkly screen in front of the fireplace. I threaded the film through the projector's sprockets and onto the wind-up reel, turned off the lights.

The film, black and white, showed a training exercise, but I knew that my father had actually saved real sailors from real disabled subs, so it was easy for me to imagine the peril.

A few miles from shore, a submarine, The Grenadier, hovered at 125 feet. The sub's crew guided the Bushnell to their location via radio, then released an emergency buoy, which the Bushnell homed in on. The crew hoisted the buoy from the sea to the ship's deck, and with a welding torch, severed the buoy's cable. This cable, its other end still connected to the sub, was now attached to the cylindrical diving bell on deck. The cable would guide the diving bell to the submarine's escape hatch.

The diving bell was lowered from the side of the Bushnell into the sea, where it bobbed in five-foot swells. Deep sea divers examined the diving bell from below, to ensure the fastened cable. Then my father and two other divers, Barbieri and Sartorette, Good men, my father said, excellent divers both, all three crossed from the ship to the diving bell with short leaps, opened the top hatch and climbed down into it. My father wore only tennis shoes and white swim trunks.

Sailors onboard the Bushnell readied and double-checked the cables that carried oxygen and communication to the diving bell. The deck swarmed with activity.

The camera man leaned over the ship's railing and caught my father and the two other divers waving up at him. My father wore his inevitable goofy grin. They drew the hatch closed and secured it from inside, while another sailor sealed the hatch from outside. That sailor banged on the bell with a wrench, three times, the diver's signal, good to go. Then the long slow descent began, my father disappearing, down through the fishes and the sharks and the open ocean, but there were no windows in the diving bell.

Most of the film was a newscaster interviewing the Bushnell's crew, mostly officers, each describing a different facet of the operation. At one point there was a close-up of my father explaining, while using his hands, how the diving bell latched onto the sub's escape hatch. Once the diving bell was attached, the water in the space between the two vessels was cleared with oxygen from the diving bell, then both hatches were opened, a clear passage into the sub. My father sounded like he did when he showed me how things worked, slow and careful, and I knew to stay focused on his hands. There was a caption in white letters, CPO E.R. Macoby, Master Diver.

Back to an officer who explained that the diving bell could only bring up three sailors at a time, that it would take all day to rescue the sub's crew, diving and surfacing and diving again. Most of that time, he said, was taken up with attaching the diving bell to the sub and then releasing that connection.

The last shots of the film were of the diving bell at the surface again, the hatch opened to reveal three submariners climbing up out of it and onto the ship. And there were my father and Barbieri and Sartorette waving up at the camera again, all smiles, my father's face and arms and chest grease-stained, him sweating all over, soaked, the strain and fatigue visible on his body, but still with that grin. Even if not on this day, on other days he had saved drowning sailors. This was what he did when he went to work. This work made him happy.

The film ended, the last inches of it clack-clacking as the wind-up reel continued to spin. The three of us stared at the white empty screen, the past having made its escape.

Transit

There were horses at Camp Ord, but none for Mac or Nimion. There was, as Nim had promised, a cavalry regiment on the base, but these were real soldiers, and Mac and Nim were given nothing but drilling and running, basic training, after all. Mac should have known better. Only a few times in his weeks there did Mac see the cavalry, in formation across the distant chaparral, charging, and now and then he'd get a tangy whiff of manure.

Arriving, heads shaved, showered and de-loused, Nim and Mac were sent to separate quarters, as at the orphanage. Mac secured a bottom bunk, knew the protection that offered, a respite from Nim too, a place to not be seen. The uniform was to his liking at first, the boots and spats and natty campaign hat, crisp and clean and his. His own rifle and bayonet and pistol. That first day, the world seemed taut and orderly.

But order gave way to habit, and for six weeks, Mac and the other recruits, not yet soldiers, ran up this hill and down that, marched and presented themselves, spent days at the firing range, where Mac found that his squirrel hunting, assumed in Medford, served him well, high marks, and when he graduated, a badge, sharpshooter.

They bayoneted canvas dummies, hurled dead grenades at wooden silhouettes of armored tanks. Drill and kill. Repetition. Numbness.

The worst of it was the daily morning run, under full pack, fifty pounds, across the highway and over the dunes, running on the gray curved beach that led to Monterey and the wharfs there, the one tall hotel, the low scattered adobes, and the forested mountain up which the rest of the quiet city spread. Santa Cruz to the north, at the other end of the moon-sliver bay, as distant as Japan. Beautiful but distant. They ran on the dry sand, not the wet-packed, and the sand was trudgerous.

All that season the skies remained overcast, stubborn high fog off the Pacific, a kettle lid on the land and the ocean, the ocean's surface wind-whipped. Unusual for fall, the drill instructor told Mac's platoon, but be grateful it's not hot.

The recruits were too tired at the end of their days to fight much, and little booze to prompt. So nights in the wooden and drafty barracks, cards, of course, and letter writing, outlandish stories of girls left behind, passed-on magazines and dime novels, newspapers, one battered radio to huddle around, and forever dreading reveille. Mac played cards and swapped stories with the other recruits, good guys for the most part, but no one, not even Mac, pretended Camp Ord was anything but transit. He would forget all their names. There were a few scuffles, though, here and there, because, Mac saw, this is what men did given half an ounce of energy and a too small square of space and time.

Never once did anyone question Mac's age. He must be a man now.

He rarely saw Nim, even at meals in the clamorous, grease-scented mess hall. He was still angry that Nim had hoodwinked him with the promise of cavalry and would not seek him out. Mac wrote to his mother every Sunday, Sunday a half day and never once a leave to Monterey, which at night he could see lit up, enticing and disturbingly near, the yellow lights of the city, as if put there only to tempt. Some nights, Mac swore he heard the music and clinking laughter.

Basic required as much exertion as the horse ranch, but nothing got done, nothing made or fostered, as with picking fruit or breaking horses. Just more exertion, day after day. There was no work here, merely routine. Nothing came of anything.

Then it was over. Mac hadn't realized how stupid and insensible he'd grown in six weeks, until on the last day, graduating to soldier, he and Nim both sporting sharpshooter badges, Mac looked up and around and found the world still waiting, followed by the sudden and tiring thought that the three-year Army hitch he'd signed onto would be exactly the same dull sheen as basic.

Their orders arrived that day, both Mac and Nim shipping out to Hawaii, the Schofield Barracks, infantrymen.

Hawaii, little brother, Nim said, ruffing his hair, you and me, believe it or not, watch out, you fine Wahine, the Macoby brothers are coming to your luau, beaches, Mac, girls, every boy's dream, paradise on a stick.

Mac thought, Leaving will be easier this time, all the goodbyes have long been said.

They rode the train to San Francisco and boarded an aging liner, the SS Arabic, which had been converted to troop transport, 750 soldiers. It was painted Navy gray now and fitted with guns.

From the dock, Mac stood under the ship's prow and gazed up into its height and heft. There had never been anything this large. When he climbed the gangplank with his pack and duffel, the world seemed to fall away, as if already at sea. Gathered on deck with the others, awaiting lifeboat instruction, he rapped the ship's thick walls with his knuckles, heard the steel echo that seemed to course through the entire ship, down through the engine rooms and up through the hull. The ship was an enormous bell.

As they set sail, Mac and Nim moved to the rail, near the bow, while the Arabic passed under the half-finished Golden Gate Bridge, the Pacific all before them, and they

smoked, and Nim talked, kept talking, about all what hell
the Macoby brothers would raise in Hawaii, God damn,
Hawaii, Mac, a fucking paradise, I told you. Mac watched
the ocean race under the ship. He'd only ever been in the
ocean, near it, wading, never on it. Beneath the blue-gray-
green surface, what lived there? Seagulls tracked the ship
for hours, until it passed the Farallon Islands and there
was nothing but ocean anymore.

At night, lying in yet another bunk, his fellow soldiers
snoring, Mac let the sea roll under him, that comforting
swell more solid for its movement than land often was.
Mac felt the depth of the ocean, the solidity and life of it,
no longer gliding along a dusty surface, but connected
down and through it.

During the dull sea days, Nim got up card games and
produced more stories, while Mac roamed about, going
wherever anyone would let him. The cargo holds, the engine rooms, round and round each deck. The big gun em-
placements, their shining cylinders, motorized turntables,
and the smaller guns, too, the machine gun nests. The
heads, the galleys, the infirmary, the brig. He touched everything, the hull's huge steel plates, studied the welds
and rivets, the incredible fact of them, how the ship
held together. The smell of diesel in the engine rooms,
the sweating engine rooms, the bludgeoning noise, the
men there who knew what to do and did it instantly and

always, real work making real change, pushing this city block across the ocean.

Eventually, inevitably, but differently too, he eased toward Nim, and they ate together and stood at the railing, only Mac listened now and spoke too, brothers again. After all, this ship and Hawaii, who knew what would come next. He forgave Nim without saying so.

The voyage took nearly three weeks, but the monotony did not dilute the excitement, the possibilities. Mac toured the ship constantly and asked questions of any sailor who would answer. Nights smoking at the rail, with or without Nim, the crack of the Zippo, a flare of orange light.

When the ship approached Oahu, Mac knew he'd arrived in a different country. The bright green and smoky blue mountains, the turquoise and white-foamed shallows, a sky he could not recognize or name. And then, as the Arabic eased into Pearl Harbor, Mac saw what he'd only heard before, all that talk in the barracks about war, another one, a bigger one, reading from the newspapers, the radio reports, scuttlebutt and hunches. Here it was.

The harbor was filled with destroyers twice as large as the Arabic, aircraft carriers that seemed islands to themselves, scores of smaller ships, and subs, and tugs, and on the docks, cranes and trucks and jeeps, and men racing about, as if war had already been declared. All that talk, all that b.s. soldier talk about war, Mac suddenly knew it was real, there it was, before him, the great industry of

Pearl, the urgency, even this late on a Sunday evening. It was all building up to an immensity that Mac knew would not be stopped, could not be, and here he was, no longer in transit but arrived.

Uniform

You must have loved the uniform, the first one and the others that followed. After those ragged years, the flour sack dresses as a child in Oklahoma, the orphanage make-dos in the year you sprouted from five to six, the hand-me-downs from your brother, patched and frayed overalls and thread-bare shirts, and later, whatever jackets and shoes you scrounged from church bins and bus station lost-and-founds as you roamed the West in search of work.

The uniform, when you wore it, surely gave a new form to your life, containing you.

First, at your brother's coaxing, was the Army at Camp Ord near Monterey, you only fifteen and pretending to be older, that uniform initially a disguise to maintain the charade, if a uniform then clearly a grown man. That uniform, perhaps, was the first set of new clothes you'd ever owned. You were inducted, shorn to skin, showered and scoured, then given a duffle with all your worldly needs. Vagabond to soldier in one afternoon. Khaki knee breeches, buttoned khaki spats, new black boots you shined and shined again, a khaki blouse, matching pack and field shovel, utility belt, and a campaign hat, brown with a wide, round brim, its dome indented four times, like Smokey the Bear's. There would have been no mirror in the barracks that first day, but you wouldn't have needed one to sense the eager precision of the uniform, an elegance alien to you.

A rifle too, brand-new and your best friend.

But infantry training at Camp Ord was nothing more than running and marching, shooting at wooden tanks and bayoneting straw men, only the back of the soldier in front of you visible, all in that summer's fog, nothing to see, and never once leaving the base for the shimmer of Monterey across the scimitar bay, a dim glow in the night fog latent with promise.

Once you boarded the ship to Hawaii, your first time on a ship, first time at sea, you had the leisure to notice the thousand other soldiers crammed on board, all in the same uniform, each of you alike, but knowing that underneath the uniform, every soldier, like yourself, was not anything at all like the others. You and your brother, for instance, smoking at the railing, looking west, happily bored, in uniform, and with the family resemblance, perfectly identical, though the two of you were different in all ways. So it was belonging, on the ship, that's what you saw, the cohesion of this many-celled organism, the Army, to which you all accrued, and which protected every individual soldier.

At Schofield Barracks, just north of Honolulu, you glimpsed a broader vista. Against the green mountains and blue skies, whose colors you had never imagined, you saw platoons marching in concert across the vast parade grounds, in step and in uniform, the beat of a thousand boots keeping your time. Then, at the end of each day, you and your platoon buddies, back in the barracks, unbuttoning, undressing, breathing loose, such ease only possible because of the uniform that had straightened you all day. And each night folding the uniform and packing it in your trunk, then polishing your boots, cleaning your rifle, brushing your campaign hat, tomorrow laid out pristine.

At Schofield you learned to read other uniforms. The number of stripes on a sleeve, from PFC to SGT Major, and the brass hardware of lieutenants and captains and majors and colonels. The different headgear and what they meant, the chest candy of campaign ribbons, the cloth badges that signaled fields of expertise, who wore suit jackets and straight slacks and dress shoes. Each of these uniforms was a clear signal, how to behave. It was a comfort to know what was expected, depending on rank, a comfort to know who to salute and how crisp a salute was required.

When you first took leave in Honolulu, after three weeks at Schofield, your brother towing you, the uniform became something else. A second one was issued, active off-duty, dress shoes and straight slacks, khaki dress blouse, khaki tie and brass tie clip, the tie tucked into your blouse, a soft garrison cap folded over your belt. Nearly civilized, you told me your brother told you that first leave. As you wound through the throngs of soldiers and sailors and civilians, you knew, even at fifteen, that you weren't unique. Nonetheless there was a status made obvious by the uniform. Everyone who saw you knew your place in this more colorful and fluid world, and for the most part, with the exception of drunken sailors, respect followed, not suspicion.

Three years in the Army at Schofield Barracks, and the uniform never varied, always the single chevron, PFC.

After, with the CCC in Yosemite, another uniform, civilian, more like a Boy Scout's but loden green, wool pants and a thick cotton shirt, a cap like a baseball cap, a set of fatigues, aptly named. You showed the others how to wear a uniform and respect it, all those out-of-work boys, ragged and formless. But when you were building the stone-by-stone guardrails on the winding mountain roads, none of you, you told me, kept your shirts on, too damn hot, wife beaters for everyone. Still the uniform prevailed, an orderliness, the back-breaking labor made easier by the uniform, all of you laboring on something larger than the next stone you lifted or poison oak you uprooted. It was an easier uniform to wear, but definite.

Then you drifted to Atascadero, met Mom, then up to the shipyard in Vancouver, Washington, then married Mom and enlisted because the war had started, and there found the uniform for your next twenty years, Navy.

At basic in San Diego, the blue-black wool bell bottoms and sailor's blouse, white spats, the white sailor's hat called a dixie cup. Another new rifle. This uniform conferred a fresh definition, a stature you were yet unfamiliar with, accomplishment, because the war was on now, and the uniform never let you forget that responsibility.

On duty in San Diego, after basic, and then on Espiritu Santo, the chambray work shirt and denim bell bottoms, always and only that, until you rose in the ranks, became Chief, then a long series of other uniforms, more insignia, more rank, a further definition, who now had to salute you, who jumped when they saw your three stripes. Later, as CPO, a white dress uniform, strictly formal, for occasions when other NCOs and officers dressed up and listened to speeches and a Navy band, the transfer of a ship's command, visiting admirals and politicians. That uniform was camouflage.

And my most favorite, which I only saw in the photo albums in the living room, the black dress uniform, more imposing than the white, and as regal as a parade marshal's, sober, with the white Chief's ensign and red-stitched Navy eagle, your campaign ribbons, Master Diver's insignia, your history clearly inscribed, more armor than uniform. Which you wore at your retirement ceremony.

All along the way, the khaki day uniform of a Chief, slacks and blouse, short- or long-sleeved, a light khaki jacket, a black-visored cap with a khaki crown. In photos from Key West, your slacks are often wrinkled, the blouse untucking at your waist, but still your uniform, the announcement of you, the experience and expedience of you. The ease with which you wore the uniform then.

Even after you retired, when you were a welder and no longer a diver or Chief, a civilian again, you wore something like a uniform. Civvies, you called it. Black Ben Davis work pants, thick enough to staunch the sparks from welding, and a pullover Ben Davis shirt, pin-striped, with a short zipper. Your lunch box, always the same, pale green by Thermos. Every day you left the house in this uniform, and like your other uniforms, it told you where to go and what was expected of you there.

Grand Ole Opry

Summer Saturdays on our front porch, we listened to The Grand Ole Opry, live from Nashville. Tex Ritter, Loretta Lynn, Tammy Wynette, Willie Nelson. This was after my sister and brother had moved away. And of course, Sparky was on the porch too, always with us.

There was a big transistor radio in the garage, on which we listened to Giants games when my father and I puttered there, but for the Grand Ole Opry, my father and I dragged his mother's old radio to the front porch and ran an extension cord into the kitchen through the window. It was an enormous cabinet radio, as old as any radio I'd ever seen. The wood was worn smooth, and on afternoons in the living room, when the sun poured in, it shone blonde in the mote-haze. The dial glowed yellow. The radio took long minutes to warm up, and we only ever listened to it on the porch, and the only signal I could ever fix was The Grand Ole Opry.

The radio, my father told me, had a richer sound, warmer, all those tubes and no transistors. It was the first major purchase they had made, his mother and brother and himself, when they moved from Oregon to Modesto after Grandpa Macoby abandoned them for the last time. Grandma Macoby, with help from her sons, built that house herself, out of orange crates scavenged from a local packing plant, then to celebrate bought the radio with the last of the money from the sale of the farm. When she died in that house, when I was six, the radio came to us. It reminded my father of Oklahoma, he told me, and reminded him too of when he was a boy on the farm in Oregon, and of course Modesto. It was hard for me to puzzle out that thinking. Was it the music or the radio, or merely his mother's presence?

Those summer Saturdays were always the same. The lawn near the street lit by sun, the porch already in shade. The sky was blue, the air hot but with a lacy breeze, and the newly mowed lawn filled the air with that particular scent. The forest of TV antennae above all the houses. Barely any traffic on our little street.

My mother and father sat together, my father's arm around her, on a short white bench he'd built and she painted. I played waiter. Ice tea for my mother, the ice clanking in her favorite purple aluminum tumbler. Oly for my father, in a frosted glass, from the pony keg in the icebox in the garage. I learned early how to ferry a perfectly tapped beer. My father smoked, tapping ashes into an abalone shell.

No one said much, we listened to the music, the afternoon's quiet called for that. Even my mother listened, who never seemed to care much for music. I wandered and bounced about the lawn but listened.

Once.

My father, during the Opry, made me a wager. I must have been talking too much that day. If I found a four-leaf clover in our lawn, he'd buy me a Slurpee.

I lay on my stomach on the lawn, the Kentucky Bluegrass sharp and tingly. The lawn also had big patches of crabgrass, islands inhabited by the spherical burrs that caught on my socks and pants. And little trails of volunteer clover running through. Pill bugs, ladybugs, ants, furry brown spiders, beetles, an occasional grasshopper. Birds alighting nearby.

Sparky lay next to me, paws crossed and calm, staring off into the world, always alert to it, what sound or scent or flicker, because that was her job.

I tried to trick my father and presented a three-leaf clover I'd made into a four-leaf by pinning a spare leaf with my thumb. Ya bum, he said, get back out there.

Then I found one, a true four-leaf clover. I turned to the porch, about to shout out, but stopped. My father was far away, his gaze lifted but seeing nothing in this yard or across the street or above the trees. Something like a smile. The radio had taken him away, to some other home it reminded him of, but was it Texas, where he was born, or Oklahoma, or the Orphanage, or Oregon, or Modesto, or the Army base in Hawaii, or Atascadero before the war, or San Diego or Espiritu Santo, or Harlem or Norfolk or Bayonne or Key West, or maybe even this house here, our house on Flood Dr. in San Jose. I watched him for a while, and he never saw me watching him.

Look, I called finally, I found one.

I grabbed his wallet from their bedroom but stopped in my room and left the clover on my desk. I was going to frame it.

From his fat fist of a black wallet, stuffed with notes and phone numbers, he gave me a dollar and told me to keep the change.

I refilled my mother's ice tea, pulled a fresh beer for my father. Lit a Parliament for him, just to feel the heft and gravity of the Zippo, to breathe in the tang of lighter fluid. I waited for the Opry to be over. It felt wrong to leave early.

We moved the radio back to the living room, then Sparky and I headed out for the 7-11.

Be back soon, my mother called from the kitchen window.

The sky was layering pink and orange and purple, and down Leigh Ave., far away, the North Star made itself visible.

Buzbee

Sparky waited outside while I stepped into the cool blue air of the 7-11 and ordered my large Cola and Cherry swirl. Then back out into the warmer evening, my shirt sticking to my skin.

We walked back home, not any traffic on Leigh, the only sound Sparky's dog tag clinking against her collar's buckle. Above, a Navy sub chaser struggled into the sky toward Mount Umunhum. Turned down Flood and were home.

But I stopped, out on the sidewalk, and just looked at our house. It had always been painted turquoise, my mother's insistence, a bright shade of motel swimming pool, and in the sunset's lights, it seemed to glow, emanating something I felt but could not name. The kitchen window was warm and yellow.

On which porch where, I wondered, and listening to what music when, might I one day sit and try to reclaim this home here.

Tattoo

If life in the Army were to be as monotonous as at Camp Ord, the Schofield Barracks at least offered Mac more space than he'd ever known, and pleasure too, in a way. In the long barracks rooms, there were only single beds, no bunks, and that column of air, all the way to the ceiling, felt like his alone, and then around each bed, space, not private, but not crushed up against other bunks. There was a uniform trunk at the foot of each bed, and a bedside table, too, with a reading lamp, and room for a photograph of his mother, a drawer to keep private things.

Outside the barracks rooms, on the upper floors, Mac was on the third, broad open-air corridors, where he could smoke and watch the blue-green mountains just to the west, the lightning and the black-black clouds, and on easy days, the rainiest days, the world nothing but wet, chairs were dragged out and poker games got up. Mac liked to sit here alone, too, cracking open the Zippo and smoking and staring.

The Schofield Barracks surrounded a grassy quadrangle, where soldiers drilled in formation, set up and tore down pup tents, cleaned and re-assembled their rifles.

Each morning, another run, full pack, up the mountain trail, into the black-green and lime-green jungle, almost to the volcanic summit.

Endless hours at the shooting range.

So the Army monotony continued, amplified by guard duties at various checkpoints, and KP once a week, with never any explicit sense of what all these soldiers were doing here, getting ready for, but nonetheless, the war, its coming, always present, the vast amount of soldiers, the squadrons of planes constantly buzzing over.

When Mac did go on leave, headed into Honolulu, the base bus skirted Pearl and the ships and industry there. Beneath everything, the war, coming. At first, that alone was enough to ease the ponderous paddlewheel of the days.

And the ocean, as if he'd never left the ship, the island a ship, the island air always watery, lush and voluptuous, enveloping, that humidity, the insects, and the often fearsome rains. The island was in and of the ocean, and this also softened the monotonous clicking of days.

The first leave, two weeks after arriving, a 24-hour pass, Nim had one too, a Saturday night, they took the bus into Honolulu, skirting Pearl's great machinery, and landed at Smith's Union Bar, which everyone said was the bar everyone went to first though never the last. Mac's uniform was his i.d., no question about his age.

A shot and a beer with Nim, toasting their great adventure, toasting all the adventures to come. The neon bar was cramped with soldiers and sailors, and young women, civilian women, in long flowing dresses and flowers in their hair, dancing with and moving around and up to the soldiers and sailors, the three-piece band loud and tinny.

Was this freedom, Mac wondered? Security and freedom? To move through this space, this sound, these hours, unfettered, money in his pockets, knowing he had a home for the next three years, and something of a future too, the war, at least, pulling him forward.

After Smith's Union, out on the streets of downtown, the streets a river of uniforms, the neon calling, there was The Swing Club, then Dink's, Max's, and Ho's, all through the evening and into the night, Mac and Nim grabbing hot dogs from a cart, then continuing, and it did feel like freedom to Mac, until he woke up on Waikiki Beach, the sun sharp and unrelenting, Mac not remembering anything of that beach in the night nor how they got there. At least Nim was still with him. They managed to find the bus and get back to base with enough time for Mac to sleep a few hours before Sunday night guard duty, western gate.

After that, leave was all. Mac maintained his best soldier posture so that he would never miss a leave, and once every two to three Fridays or Saturdays, he'd be in Honolulu, with or without Nim, alone, or with others from the barracks, drinking, often fighting, those fights almost always soldiers versus sailors. Sometimes a bold stare from across a crowded street was enough to ignite a brawl, the MPs or Shore Patrol breaking it up eventually but not too early, letting these men and boys work it out.

One night, drunk again but on his own, Mac stood before Dr. Black's Tattoo Emporium, and felt that only this would settle him, make him man enough to forget the boy he was trying to shake, the boy who sometimes missed his mother and wanted to cry, but a tattoo also to say, yes, god damn it, I was here, here, here's proof. He pointed to the design on the wall, sat in the chair, and drunk enough to not feel anything but desire, watched as the hula girl in her grass skirt and coconut bra stitched into his skin. There, the artist said, she's a beaut, if you flex your bicep, she'll dance for you. And she did. Mac spent weeks, when no one was looking, looking at her in the mirror and making her dance.

Leave and duties, and scattered hours with Nim, and while Mac drank and talked baseball with the other soldiers, knew their names and stories and fought sailors with them, it was only leave and duty and waiting for the future, there were no real friends. Except his one friend, Ronald, who was not allowed to be his friend, the two could never go drinking together. Ronald was a negro, that's why, but he and Mac became friends anyway, over okra.

See, Ronald worked in the kitchens, cooking his only and sole duty, while the other negro soldiers had their only and sole duties, cooking of course, building roads and servicing jeeps, cleaning the heads and whatever else needed cleaning, transporting and stacking ammunition. But Ronald knew okra, and one night, Mac's KP duty finished, Mac found Ronald at the stoves alone, frying up what looked like but shouldn't be fresh okra, not here in Hawaii. Mac had missed okra since the family left Oklahoma. That couldn't be okra, Mac said, and Ronald nodded, and held one out to Mac, and Oklahoma opened up in him.

Mum's the word, Ronald said, but I've got a friend at Pearl who sneaks these to me, straight from the ship, take a seat. Every night that Mac had KP, and some nights when he didn't, Ronald fried up okra for the two of them, a bottle of his homemade hot sauce, sometimes fish or eggs to go with it, sometimes just a plate of okra, and sitting there alone in the kitchen, the two traded stories, Mac of Oklahoma, Ronald of Louisiana. They each missed their places. Ronald taught Mac how to perfectly bread and fry the okra, and Mac loved cooking for his friend. Besides the okra, what pulled Mac to Ronald, was his quiet, Ronald never once slapped him on the back or yelled in his ear or challenged him to some ridiculous and dangerous stunt, like the other soldiers. After their late-night meals, Mac and Ronald stood outside the back door of the mess hall and smoked and told more stories. Mac brought along beer or bourbon.

Then Rosie.

After almost a year, Rosie, there at Dink's, which had become Mac's favorite, Rosie sitting alone at the end of the bar, in a red and white sarong, her hair not done up but pretty nonetheless, and waving off the soldiers and sailors who approached her. But she kept looking at Mac and smiling occasionally with her red lipstick mouth. No one had ever looked at him before. So he had no choice but to rise and go to her and say hello, which was all he could say. Rosie said, Hello, soldier, how old are you? Nineteen, ma'am. Wonderful, she said, I'm twenty-three, Rosie, by the way, I think we'll get on fine, now let's get out of here.

Mac knew the deal, he wasn't that naïve, he had listened in the barracks, on the horse ranch in Bishop, to the fruit pickers, to his profane father and brother, he'd listened all his life.

Rosie lived in a room above Dink's, up the back stairs, a pink and green room, a bed and a vanity, a long mirror and piles of clothes and magazines, a bottle of bourbon and two glasses, the one light bulb shaded with a pink and green silk scarf. The music from Dink's coming up through the floor. Instead of Waikiki Beach, he woke in Rosie's bed, and even though he knew the deal and handed her the money, he still fell in love, which he knew he shouldn't do but did.

Rosie was from Idaho, where her family ran a grocers, but left when she was seventeen, the store already failing with the rest of the country, and Idaho Falls no place for a future to begin with, and moved herself to Seattle, where she worked for a while in a department store, but that was failing too, so she made her way, By hook and by crook, she said, on her own, to Honolulu, Don't ask, she said.

Mac told her every single thing that had happened to him, including all the leaving, including that he was only sixteen. Rosie didn't seem to care.

On the bus back to base that day, Mac knew he had to take up boxing.

Soldiers who signed up for a bout automatically got 24-hour passes, those who won 72-hour passes. Mac won his first bout, KO, won every other bout, all KO, the bouts held in the cacophonous base gym. He was allowed one match a month, on top of his regular leaves. It was easy to beat these kids, who'd clearly never been in fights before, never worked fields or with horses, not strong enough, softies with swagger, some of them college boys. Mac found he had a wicked left jab no one could see coming.

He saw Rosie at every possible turn, sometimes all weekend, three entire days, two restless nights. He knew, of course, what Rosie did the other nights.

Days they swam and picnicked on the beaches, not Waikiki, but beaches Rosie knew, secluded, and nights in Rosie's room, and boxing in between for another 72-hour pass, keeping his nose clean otherwise because he dared not miss a single hour with her. She dressed him, taught him how to dress, civvies, not uniform.

They pretended to talk about the future, though Mac was certain, yet hopeful not, that they were just pretending. They would go to Modesto, they'd open a bar in Honolulu, they might set out farther west, Singapore, Hong Kong, get out of this madness. They talked about the war, they both knew it was coming, and how they might get free of it.

Rosie was the only thing.

Then a year later, Rosie was gone. Mac wasn't surprised, though he was broken. One Friday, he took the bus to Dink's, and she was not there, went upstairs to her room but the room was empty, even the scarf over the lightbulb was gone. There was no note. He asked around and asked, but no one knew anything, no one had heard a damn thing, and Mac realized from how everyone spoke of Rosie's disappearance that they really did not know anything, she had simply up and left. He stayed in her room that night on the broken bed and drank until he could pretend to forgot.

The next day he returned to Dr. Black's Tattoo Emporium, and sober, in the muted sunshine, Mac asked for a heart with a banner, in reds and blues, and on the banner Rosie in black script, his right arm. It would do no good, he knew, but it seemed necessary, a memory, no mere souvenir, a scar to be fondled, a flag of some occupation, and in his weakest moments, a beacon, come back.

But she never. Nothing.

So the war continued to ramp up that last year, and Mac did his duties, and started to think out what came next for him, how and where to be in the war, whatever future that might be. Nim tried to convince him to re-up, Hey, little brother, life can't get no better than this, this is paradise we're living in. Mac knew it wasn't paradise.

Mac said goodbye to Ronald, then he and Nim went to Pearl and boarded for San Francisco, where they'd be discharged.

On ship, among the thousand ships at Pearl, the war was even more present, and Mac thought about his rifle, which he'd cleaned and presented for three years, and fired countless times. He did not know where he would go once he was discharged, to his mother in Modesto most likely. But that wasn't the question, really, the question was, how to be in this war, this war that was certainly coming, and he knew that his rifle, which he'd returned to the Army, was not the answer. He looked out over the bay of ships, the hustling crews, the flags and big guns. He knew he would be of the war, and maybe it was a ship that would take him there.

He cracked his Zippo at the rail and smoked, headed east to California. It was a good enough plan for now, and for the moment, he would simply step into the future again. The future was all he'd ever had anyway.

Hooky

I was in fifth grade the first time, and my father was out of work for the first time. It must have been that.

That morning he packed his lunchbox and pretended to leave for work, but before he did, my mother getting dressed to leave for work herself, he tucked a note in my shirt pocket, It's an excuse, he said, meet me at the side gate at eleven, we'll have ourselves a little adventure. He touched a finger to his nose.

I waited until I was almost to school before I read the note, as if my mother might be tailing me. My father's blocky printing, Dear Mr. Addington, please excuse Robert today. Apparently I had a dentist appointment at noon and wouldn't be back to school until tomorrow morning.

A secret. I was a spy on a mission.

My father's Barracuda was parked just past the side gate at one end of the playing fields, and I slid in.

Do I really have a dentist appointment?

Lord no, he said, much more fun than that.

Where are we going?

It's a secret.

We drove through the weirdly quiet streets of San Jose, everyone at work or at school or inside watching TV, no kids, few cars, a couple of dogs. Up to Blossom Hill Road and into the Santa Cruz Mountains, twisting roads under canopies of gnarled oak, pines and redwoods appearing as we climbed, arched patches of bluest sky flickering.

We were looking for a lake a buddy of my father's had told him about, a lake with no name or sign, but worth it, my father assured me.

How will we know? I asked.

My father tapped his temple with his finger. Everything we needed was right up there.

We listened to Country Western on the radio, which scritched in and out of range at certain corners and dips. We talked. He asked questions. I asked questions. What did we talk about? My brother, the Giants, Man o'War jellyfish, Vietnam. Everything we needed to talk about.

More and more the sun flashed down on us.

The car slowed quickly, stopped, then backed up a hundred feet, until we were looking down a bramble-bordered two-track.

My father looked at me, shrugged.

Whatta ya think? he said.

Why not?

Just a ways down that rutted road, after a sharp left, there was the lake, its blue surface flashing gold under a mountain breeze, only as big as a really big pond, but clearly a lake, and deep by the looks of it, fresh-fed, with no rafts of reeds or algae blooms. Clean blue lake.

We parked on a matted patch of grass, and I had to leap out and run down to the shore. Then just stood there looking.

My father opened the Barracuda's hatch and was unloading the fishing poles and tackle box, so I ran back up, grabbed my lunch from the front seat, my Gomer Pyle U.S.M.C. lunchbox, bologna and onion sandwich in waxed paper, an apple, three chocolate chip cookies, a thermos of milk.

We can share my lunch, I said.

Got better than that, he said.

He opened a brown paper bag and held up a sandwich wrapped in white butcher paper. I knew it immediately.

My father said, Got th' Bucket to open up early.

Crab?

Two crab salad sandwiches, a big bag of BBQ Lay's, two cans of Shasta Cola, a forty-ounce bottle of Oly.

But we'll get hungrier, he said, so bring that too, fishing starves me.

We made our way along the narrow lip of the shore, packed earth and stones, until we were opposite the car, where we found a dirt beach just big enough.

We ate everything and fished for hours and caught nothing, slid salmon roe onto hooks that came up empty. That didn't matter, only the lake mattered. Once an eagle shot over the lake and rose to the tip of a Ponderosa pine, where it sat for a while while we watched, until it broke and dove and glided over the chopped surface, then climbed noiselessly out of the lake's forest bowl and away.

Sometimes we talked, sometimes we didn't.

My father got me back to school twenty minutes before the last bell. He would see me at home, at dinner, when he was off work.

Don't tell your mom, ya bum.

For a moment I thought I'd wait for school to let out, wait for Vicky Olah, who I always walked home with that spring, but I didn't. I went in the side gate, crossed the vast grass fields and exited through the back gate. I wanted to walk through the still quiet streets alone, knowing that I was the only kid in San Jose holding on to the day that had just passed.

After that, depending on where my father was working, or wasn't, every few weeks he would take me out of school. Better than books, he said. I hooked out for the entire day now, my father picking me up at the back gate before I went in, the both of us still acting the charade that we were fooling my mother, though I doubted that. Excuses were delivered the following day.

To Livermore, where GE had built a small nuclear reactor, a test reactor my father had helped build, and where the small cooling reservoir was stocked with fish, mostly crappie, stocked by GE for the enjoyment of its workers and their families. My father must have been working at GE again, because he showed a badge at the gate and the guard waved us through. There were days when we both played hooky.

The reactor, a squat white silo with a white dome top, drew all the landscape to it, upon its hill, but we sat on the near shore with our backs turned away and looked across at the other lime green hills.

Is it safe? I asked. This was in sixth grade, and I had moved up to Boy Scouts and had earned my first merit badge, Nuclear Science.

As houses, my father said.

We caught fifty crappie that day, tiny and bony fish, nearly inedible, and filled the ice chest with them, then remembered we were playing hooky, so we dumped them back in the lake. Not all of them survived. I also caught a big turtle, twenty pounds at least, hooked its shell just inside the neck and reeled it in, believing it the biggest fish anyone had ever caught, until we saw the placid, disgruntled face rise up out of the water. We let the turtle go, of course, and it swam off as if nothing had happened.

Lots of fishing in lots of lakes, Pinto Lake, Lake Berryessa, Anderson Reservoir, Lexington Reservoir, Loch Lomond. Caught lots of fish, which we released, and caught absolutely no fish on other days. Any lake we could get back from by the last bell.

Days at foundries and welding shops, where my father knew a guy, he always knew a guy, who would show us around the enormous pieces of steel, some beams fifty feet long. The erupting cones of welding sparks that flashed in the long, tall, dark sheds, the dusty light from high windows. Every one of these shops was like all the others, the high windows and dusty light, and the smell of grease and metal and acetylene, but I never failed to be fascinated.

Then, I could hardly believe it, Sealab. Sealab II, to be precise, and I was very precise about Sealab. It had been on the ocean floor off La Jolla, down south, for two months and was now in dry dock at Hunter's Point, on the bay's shore near Candlestick Park near San Francisco. A diver my father had trained in Key West was Dive Master for Sealab, both I and II, and he'd called my father and asked if I would like a tour, and oh, yes, would I like to meet Scott Carpenter the astronaut? Second American in orbit in Mercury's Aurora 7, and now with Sealab. Yes, please, please, yes.

The vessel was enormous in its dry dock, two stories high, five cars long, as wide as our house. We entered through a large hatch at one end, climbing sea-stairs, open-grille steel stairs, steep and clangy. I had been on many ships and always loved these sea-stairs but rising up into this ship was beyond anything.

This was the diver's hatch, where, when Sealab II was submerged, divers entered and exited, and which was always open when under the sea. I knew the physics of this. The air pressure in Sealab II kept the water out, same thing with an empty cup turned over and lowered into a full dishpan. I had to imagine myself there, in scuba gear, stepping out onto the bottom of the sea.

Burnsie, the Dive Master, gave us a tour, up and down and around, the bunks, the lab stations, the engines, the mess and the heads, even up into the ballast racks. Narrow aisles, canyons of equipment and buttons and dials and wires.

After the tour, Burnsie got on the horn and asked Carpenter to come to the dive room. And I met an astronaut, and he looked like one, looked exactly like every picture I'd ever seen of him, looked like every astronaut ever. He shook my hand, answered my questions, about Sealab II and the ocean pressures, and what it was like to orbit the earth at 17,000 miles per hour, and which he preferred, sea or space. My father asked just as many questions. The biggest difference between the sea and space? More leg room, better fish.

Carpenter asked my father about his diving career, and I stood there and listened with the gravest attention. The talk turned to Helium-Oxygen, the 80/20 blend used for prolonged or deeper dives. I knew that Helium changed your voice.

Without my knowing, it was decided I should try Helium-Oxygen. Burnsie pulled a triangular Jack Browne mask from its rack, opened up a compressor, and held the mask to my face. He took it away after a few shallow breaths and told me to say the word Tequila.

My voice was a mouse's voice, and I couldn't stop laughing at the sound of my own voice.

Tequila was a song on the radio, nonsensical, instrumental until a break, then Tequila! an olé shout. We passed the mask around one time, and the four of us sang Tequila! But the helium wore off quickly. It was a Sealab tradition, the astronaut told me, all day long, Tequila!

Scott Carpenter gave me an autographed picture and an official Sealab II patch.

Descending the sea-stairs through the diver's hatch, I paused, not knowing if I were descending into the ocean in my wet suit and tanks, or floating out into space in my EVA suit. Either way, vast worlds awaited. Sealab II was, I figured, what spaceships might look like one day.

I knocked three times on the Sealab hull as we left, the diver's all-clear.

There was still plenty of time to get back home.

On the drive down Bayshore toward San Jose, I asked my father if he wished he were still a diver, still active, and if he was, would he join Sealab II and spend months at a time on the sea floor breathing Helium-Oxygen.

Yes, he said, I would, quicker than you can say Jack Robinson.

The traffic swarmed around us, relentless, all those commuters racing home.

Patio

My father had been planning the patio all spring. Sketches, in pencil, on the backs of envelopes and on lunch bags, revised and tossed then retrieved from the garbage can in the kitchen and started over. Lists of supplies and costs figured. Which new BBQ grill would be best and we could afford. Now and then he went into the backyard and stood where the BBQ would stand, just to the left of the family room's sliding glass door, as if summoning the final vision and volition necessary for this job.

The whole time we'd lived on Flood Dr. the backyard was nothing more than lawn, except for a bouquet of banana trees in one corner, but no bananas, and a forked birch in the other. Room for me and Sparky to play, room for Sparky's business, room to play catch with my father or my brother, but rarely used by the family, that's what the front yard was for, the porch and the view, waving hello to the neighbors, the slow traffic of the quiet street.

When my father spoke of the patio, there was a tone in his voice I rarely heard, some giddy hope, almost a child's, almost the voice in my own head in the weeks before Christmas when I imagined how extravagant my presents would be.

The BBQ will go right here, he said, next to the door, make it easier to pass food in and out of the house.

Even if it rains, we can still use it, and the rain will sound great on the roof, you've never heard the sound of rain on a sheet metal roof.

And the backyard, we'll put in some flowers, maybe roses, your mom likes roses, really use this space.

Maybe get some outdoor lights.

What was that tone? The belief, it seemed to me, that by building this patio my father might climb some precipice, on the other side of which the world would be, not perfect, no, rather, more whole. A reward, perhaps, for his having worked so hard for so many years. Or the feeling that, after five years of living in this house, we had finally arrived home.

It would take three weekends. I would be his helper, but he was determined to build this alone, a task only he could complete.

The first weekend, we went to Orchard Supply Hardware and loaded the supplies into a truck one of my father's buddies had loaned him. Five straight two by fours, cut to length, for the base and interior sections of the forms. Five tall four by fours for the posts that would support the patio's roof. Four lengths of curved two by fours for the perimeter of the half-moon patio. Pre-cut sheets of aluminum, for the roof, with scalloped bands of it for the trim. Steel connector brackets, nails, cement trowels and placers for smoothing the cement, earth tampers. We stacked everything in the backyard in an orderly fashion and covered it all with our Army surplus canvas tent, though it was summer and rain was no threat. Staging, my father called this. He had built bridges, ships, floating dry docks, nuclear reactors. Staging was key.

That Sunday we measured and marked off the footprint of the patio with blue string wound around simple pegs. Then we dug up the grass with shovels, about four inches deep, to form the footprint, and carted the sod to the far side yard. We tamped the exposed earth with long-handled tampers, square fifteen-pound weights. Wearing gloves, we lifted the tamper and let it fall, over and over in the same place, before moving on to a new square of earth, until, hours later, the earth was smooth and uniform and firmly packed. This, my father told me, would prevent the cement from sinking.

My father did most of the work, naturally, tamping three or four times the area I did. He worked tirelessly, and this was San Jose in July, hot and dry and white-skied through the afternoon, so he worked with his shirt off. He was tanned all over, a particular reddish hue I only ever saw on him, and which he claimed he and his brother, my long-lost Uncle Nim, had gotten during their Army hitch in Hawaii. I only saw my father with his shirt off when we went swimming, from the beach at Santa Cruz, at Almaden Pool, in motel pools, and his tan remained constant. Maybe it was Hawaii where he got it, or all those years on and near the water, Espiritu Santo, Greece, Key West, aboard ships in several seas, maybe those suns had stained him.

Occasionally I was called on to fetch a fresh-tapped Oly from the pony keg in the ice box in the garage, a two-gulp beer. Just renting it, my father liked to say.

When we were done, we dragged out two webbed beach chairs and sat in them on the tamped earth, drank Oly and Dr. Pepper, and my father smoked. We reviewed every aspect of the patio construction so far and reviewed what would come next. Sparky eyed us skeptically from under the birch. The sun began to drop at last and my mother called us in for dinner.

The following Friday evening, I helped my father more precisely indicate the shape of the patio, each of its divisions, with more peg-bound lengths of blue string, a pale ghost of the patio.

We woke up early Saturday to set the forms. The cement mixer would arrive at two, and we needed to be ready. We set the outer perimeter of the patio with the bent-wood two by fours, holding them in place with wooden shims, then connecting one to the other with steel brackets and nails. Then we set the straight two by fours, two against the cement step, three radiating from it, creating half a pizza with four slices. These smaller sections of cement were less likely to crack or buckle, my father told me. It was a lovely plan, thorough.

The cement mixer arrived a little after two, a rotating barrel on wheels towed by a pick-up truck. My father heaved wheelbarrow after wheelbarrow of cement through the main side yard, dumped them into the forms equally. My job was to distribute the cement in the forms as evenly as possible, using our own garden rake, the one with the single row of huge metal teeth. When the rake clogged with wet cement, I washed it off with the hose, mucky fun.

After the cement was unloaded, my father and I raked it some more, grossly. He used a bubble-level to check the forms, make sure they hadn't shifted, and now we were ready to level and smooth with a finer touch. We used cement placers, like mops, like a janitor's mop on a long handle, except the wide brush head was a flat aluminum blade. After, we would smooth the smaller imperfections with trowels.

We had only just started when Ynez from next door came crying into the backyard.

Mac, Mac, she cried, almost wailing, it's Ernesto, his heart, please, come quick.

My father tore away, but yelled behind him, Keep at it, Robert.

I did the best I could, but I didn't know what I was doing, and didn't have the strength to do it. I kept forgetting to rinse the blade of the cement placer with the hose, and chunks and streaks began to appear, and no matter what I did, nothing seemed level at all, I didn't know any more what level was. I got tired, the cement was thickening. I was not afraid my father would get mad at me, but I still felt foolish. A kid.

At one point, Sparky came over, sniffed the cement, and delicately pressed one paw into it. I did not smooth over that print.

My father was gone for three hours. The cement had set before he returned. I just stood there. I'd forgotten to put my name in the cement.

Our neighbor Ernesto had indeed had a heart attack, right there on his living room couch, drinking a beer and watching the Giants game. My father performed artificial respiration and chest compressions, basic to a diver's training, until the ambulance arrived, but he went to the ER at Good Sam with Ynez so she wouldn't be alone. My mother picked my father up from the hospital when it was clear that Ernesto would survive, but only after Ernesto's son and daughter-in-law showed up.

It was dusk when my mother and father returned, pink and blue and beautiful because of the smog. We turned on the single-bulb backyard light. The patio was bubbled, cracked in places, and it all titlted badly to one side. The winter rains would gather there.

My mother put her hand on my father's arm, Oh, honey, she sighed.

I knew that to fix the patio, we would have to rip it out and start all over, and I didn't think that was possible.

My father assured me I'd done the best I could, and I believed him because he was able to make light of the disaster.

At least, he said, we got a good story out of it.

The following week we sank the four-by-four supports for the roof, and my father used rivets to connect the aluminum sheeting and trim. The roof, at least, was sturdy.

Sears delivered the BBQ that Sunday, so my father cooked up steaks and shrimp for the three of us, and grilled corn and artichokes. But we ate in the dining room, not on the patio, though we kept the drapes open so we could see the patio and sigh.

While he was grilling, my father set down a lit Parliament on the edge of the BBQ, it rolled off and landed on the patio. I went into the garage and fetched one of the abalone shell ashtrays to try and stop that from happening again.

Atascadero

M ac had thought, assumed, that he and Nim would be discharged directly from the troop ship, and that he might spend a few days, or forever, looking for Rosie in San Francisco, a good enough bet. But the Army, in its infinite wisdom, directed them to a waiting train, back to Camp Ord, for the official matters. They were given severance pay and offered a bus ride to Salinas, where they could take another train to wherever these footloose soldiers might be headed. Mac and Nim decided to spend a few days in Monterey, however, before heading to Modesto and their mother. They'd always wanted to see Monterey. Why not live a little, Mackie boy, Nim said.

Just outside the discharge center, three young men in forest green uniforms, loosely worn, kerchiefs instead of ties, called to the departing soldiers. Work, they were saying, who needs work, sign up here. They were from the CCC, Mac had heard about them, the Civilian Conservation Corps, a Roosevelt deal. Mac and Nim had talked for weeks about the what next, but could only decide on Modesto, to see their mother, and from there, who knew. Mac stopped to talk to the men, listened to their spiel. From now until the beginning of the rainy season, five, six months, he could work in Yosemite, building roads and trails, room and board plus a salary to send home. No, not the military, more like grown-up Scouts. Real work, Mac knew, and time too to wait for what next, time to wait for the war to unveil itself.

Nim passed, laughing, but Mac signed the papers, agreeing to present himself in Yosemite in one week. So the two brothers hitched along the tall dunes and gray curved bay, caught a ride into Monterey, and spent two days drinking, and two nights at Flora's being entertained by those fine young women. Though Mac still thought of Rosie. He wondered if he'd always think of her.

After a few days at his mother's, where Mac gave her all of his money, what little was left after Rosie, and eating her fine fine food again, real chicken, though the okra, he had to admit, was not as good as Ronald's, Mac left one more time. He assumed he'd be back here at some point. Nim and his mother waved him off the porch as he headed out with his fatigue-green duffel.

They were right, it was more like Scouts than the military, the CCC, though Mac had never been a Scout, and he was more like a troop leader than a Scout, having worked alongside others, having done such various tasks, and he taught the younger men, though they were hardly that much younger than his nineteen, how to work and how to be. Ask Mac, he often heard. And the work was good, digging and digging and piling and piling, sunup to sunset, sweating in the knife-edge Sierra heat, the dry intensity of it, the world crackling underfoot, the trees seeming ready to explode, but the work was never monotonous because of the pale granite and deep green mountains. After a while, while he still thought about Rosie, his thoughts of her became like a last dime in his pocket, right there, he could touch it, and always remember it, but it didn't weigh him down, barely registered some days.

In October there were early rains, mild but greening the hillsides and meadows, dry lightning, and the CCC camp began to unwind, the tent-cabins dis-assembled, the men, boys really, beginning to leave. Mac was asked to stay on to the end, happily, because he hadn't yet found the what next. His supervisor, Tom, older but not that much, twenty-four maybe, asked him to step out for a smoke and a swig one night after dinner, he had a question. Mac had no idea where he was going, he told Tom. Well, Tom said, I've got a voucher here, for a CCC welding school down by Atascadero, it's the last slot. I think it might be right for you, whaddya say? You know, Tom went on, welding, as in ships, as in all the ships being built. Mac figured he'd found the what next, maybe how to be in the war.

There were twelve of them in the welding school, but no bunkhouse, only an old barn, where each of them slept in an old stall on a rickety cot. They welded all day, after morning lessons in technique and theory, and Mac proved a natural, he loved the welding, the joining, permanently, of what must be joined, how ships were made. The instructors, two older men clearly happy to have some work, any work, if not real work, also told the twelve welders how and where they would be employed when they finished, the shipyards in Vancouver, Washington, it's all been arranged. It would take nearly a year to learn the craft. Real money, it seemed, real work too.

Every day they joined pieces of metal, the sun of the torch brighter than the real sun, the heat insufferable but cleansing in an odd way. Every day after class, down to the creek and the swimming hole there, then dinner. But then. Free to go where they might, this was not the Army. Though the welders rarely went into town, to either of the two restaurants, or the one movie theater, no money for any of that. There was a bar, and sometimes, yes, there was money for that.

By asking around at the bar, The Raven, Mac picked up a part-time job driving one of the town's garbage trucks early every morning. So he rose at four, walked two miles to the dump, and rode through the quiet morning hours of the quiet morning town, bungalows with steep-eaved porches to stave off the heat, through the oak-studded hills, stopping at house after house, shouldering the dented cans into the truck. The little houses, he loved to drive past them and ponder their porches.

Then a second part-time job, weekends, rising at the same time, walking the same distance, and feeding the white turkeys at Hansen's turkey farm. These are the stupidest god damn animals in creation, Mr. Hansen told Mac, when it's raining, they look up into the sky until they drown, which Mac thought was fanciful but turned out to be true.

Indian Summer gave way to the rainy months, and all around the hills sprang to green grass, the gold of summer obliterated, and in February, the fruit trees, the plums first, later apples and cherries, began to blossom and soothe the landscape. The war had finally showed itself, though not here yet, and Mac was happy to labor, to study, to know the what next, and hoping the war, the war coming here, would wait until he could get to the shipyards. Rosie's thin dime had almost worn through.

The wheel continued to turn, and it was summer again, and there was a dance at the local grange hall, a full bluegrass cacophony, and the welders had been invited, through Mr. Hansen, and that's where Mac met Olive.

She wasn't dancing when he first saw her but standing near the punch table with her sisters Mimi and Carol. She was tiny and precise, pale skin and deep black hair, a tiny red rosebud mouth that laughed but stayed closed. So he went straight to her and asked her to dance, and she said yes, and they danced quite poorly together, but couldn't stop looking at each other. He met Olive's sisters, they drank red punch together, and Mac told them all about Hawaii, and at the end of the night, Mac asked if he could call on Olive.

She did not think so, Mac was twenty, she was only sixteen, going into her senior year of high school. Her parents surely would not approve. Ask them anyway, he said, I would be happy to offer myself for inspection, I'm good at that. He watched Olive and her sisters drive away, standing there under a gauzy full moon on this dusty and warm night, clouds of gnats swarming the one lamp outside the Grange Hall.

Olive was at the next Grange Hall dance, two weeks later, and after dancing, she invited him to dinner with her parents, who were eager to meet him, could he come tomorrow night, Sunday supper.

Her parents, Edith and Eugene, she was a nurse and he a railroad conductor, welcomed him warmly, and he was surprised by that, expected something like fear from them instead. The supper was delicious, cold roast and salads, but nervous, but Olive's family were kind enough to ask all the questions, which he answered, mostly with truth. After supper, on the porch, the long shadows crawling over the tidy bungalow, they sat quietly, the six of them, and watched the day's smaller wheel turn, and mumbled between themselves, the radio humming quietly from the living room, and finally, Eugene, shock of white hair and bemused smile, said, We do not object to your seeing Olive, that has always been her decision anyway. Mimi, the oldest, drove Olive and Mac back to the welding barn, where she waited in the car, smoking, while Olive walked Mac across the yard. They kissed there.

Every morning after that, when Mac drove by the house on Santa Ynez, though it wasn't on his route, he honked the garbage truck's horn, and Olive was always standing there waving.

This was not Rosie, they would have to be married first, which was fine with Mac, for it felt as though that waiting would bring him closer to a porch like the one where he sat every Sunday now with Olive and her parents and her sisters. Some days, short days of welding, he would walk into town and pick her up from school and they would go to the diner or just sit in the park, and on weekends there were movies and more dances, and always Sunday supper. In all the what next, this next had not occurred to Mac.

Then, in early November, welding school completed, Mac boarded the train to Vancouver, instantly at work building the big ships the war required, would require, already did in most places. He lived with the other welders in a fleabag downtown, and called Olive once a week, collect, and wrote her every day, and on his first drunken weekend there, found a tattoo parlor in Portland, and had

Rosie's name smothered under a banner of blue ink with Olive's name in bright red over it.

He and Olive were waiting until she graduated the following May, then they would figure it out, but Mac knew they would be, should be, hoped they would be, married.

The war, in December, finally arrived here, Mac had been waiting five years for it to arrive here. They advanced their plans and became secretly engaged, and in January, Olive took the train to Vancouver, Washington, and married Mac on a Friday afternoon at city hall, and they honeymooned in a nice hotel downtown, The Columbia, and on Monday she returned to Atascadero, Mrs. Elwell Macoby, and the first thing her mother said when she met her at the station, was, Show me your hand, and there it was, the slim gold band, her mother had known all along.

Two weeks later, Mac enlisted, the Navy this time, and of the proper age. The Navy because of that damn rifle he'd had to carry for three years and not wanting to carry that rifle into wherever such a rifle would lead him. All those ships, that industry, being of, would be of, the war, and he wanted to be of it, in it, but not holding that rifle. And the gleam in the recruiter's eye when Mac told him about his welding training and somewhat brief experience. There was a place for him in the Navy, the recruiter told him, they needed men like him, so once again he signed up, left out any mention of the Army and being fifteen at one time.

After a ten day visit in Atascadero with his new wife and in-laws, his last visit with Olive until she graduated from high school, he took a bus to San Diego, where he was shaved and showered, de-loused, and given a sailor's uniform.

Mom

I knew that you loved Mom, I just didn't know how or how it had come about. It might not have been my place to know. When it was you and me together, it was just that, basic, the two of us, best pals. When it was the three of us, it was our little family, both Ricks and Judi out of the house by the time I was nine, and you and me and Mom, we all enjoyed that little family, barely rancorous, the three of us on vacation, out shopping, around the dinner table, in front of the TV, on the front porch. And Sparky of course.

You called Mom Ollie, for Olive, but also after Oliver Hardy, and you played Stan Laurel, Hello, Ollie, you'd say, quizzing the top of your head with splayed fingers. She liked that you called her Ollie, it was easy to see, proud of it. The two of you often joked together, sharing private jokes just out of my hearing, you loved to tease each other into laughter. You kissed her on the top of her head, she reached up to kiss you on the cheek. Sometimes you called yourselves Mutt and Jeff.

I don't know if you two fought, real arguments with shouting and tears. You kept it well away from me if you did. Though there were silences, heavy silences, accusatory, and maybe that was a form of argument, or prelude to it.

Mostly the silences came from Mom, aimed at you, a black stare, sucked-in cheeks, the sensation that all noise was being pushed down and out of the room, the dining room, the living room, at a party, in the car, Christmas Day. These moments were easy to decode. You would have had too much to drink, and, loquacious with alcohol, grown too loud and too bawdy and too much of a sailor, her silences meant to balance out that too much of you.

You embarrassed her. Especially when you became sappy drunk and talked to her through Sparky, on the couch with Sparky next to you, You love Ollie, don't you, girl, isn't Ollie beautiful, Mac loves Ollie so much but Ollie's mad at Mac tonight. Mom would try to smile, but the silences escaped her mouth anyway.

You taking me to a bar on a Saturday afternoon, with no notice and no goodbye, that might have been the silence you countered with. Sometimes at least.

While I accepted and obeyed it, I was puzzled by your frequent instruction, Don't tell your Mom, when you and I went to a bar or you took me out of school or when we did anything approaching dangerous, diving or welding or shooting a friend's .22. Or that time you let a Corpsman at Moffett Field stitch up my dangling pinky toe, which I'd nearly severed driving your friend's son's mini bike. It was Sunday and the doctor on duty had left early to play golf, but the Corpsman had been practicing, for Nam, he told you, he was shipping out in two weeks and was pretty sure he would do a good job. You both laughed at this predicament, That's the Navy for you. Don't tell your mom.

I always wanted to tell her, though, because everything you and I did was so much fun, and interesting, especially the more dangerous excursions. But I never did tell her, even when she asked me outright. I never did tell her, even though I felt bad she was excluded from so much.

I never heard you raise your voice toward her, nor saw you raise a hand. You spoke of her to me with great affection and never once allowed me to disrespect her. You never spoke ill of her in front of your friends, even your bar friends, even when they all spoke horridly of their own wives.

There were moments when you and Mom got downright mushy. You and Mom took a surprise hunting trip to Wyoming, a second honeymoon of sorts, but a first really. You bought matching sheepskin jackets for the trip, so it had to be a big deal. I stayed with Aunt Mimi and Uncle Don and baby Cara, and spent the entire weekend on their guestroom bed teaching myself Something by the

Beatles on my new bass, though only picking out the vocal melody from sheet music, no clue at all yet what a bass was supposed to do.

You shot an elk that weekend, the first time you'd gone hunting in years, and brought back elk steaks in a Styrofoam cooler, they were spicy, a little tough, and eating them felt exotic, adventurous, I loved it. You and Mom had had a grand time. Mom blushed a lot when you told me and Mimi and Don about the weekend, the fancy hotel and dinners, time alone, a real honeymoon. I suspected why you were both so pleased, so loose, and while I knew it was none of my business, I was pleased too.

Maybe my question, then, wasn't how you loved her, because I did know that, paid attention all the time. Maybe I wanted to know why you fell in love with her, what made that happen. This question occupied me.

See, you two were so different. Your life had been so much in the world, Mom's so quiet, stable, static. It was hard for me to put you two together.

I listened to your stories about her, tried to listen into them, around them, past them.

When you met her, in Atascadero, down by San Luis Obispo, in 1941, you had already been in the Army for three years, in Hawaii, having lied about your age to enlist, and directly after that, you went to Yosemite, joined the CCC and built roads there. You got wind of a government program in Atascadero where you could study welding, hoping one day to get a job in a shipyard, there were a lot of ships being built then, the war rising up around everyone. You met Mom at a Grange Hall dance, and you danced with her, but she rebuffed you at the end of the night, she was only sixteen after all, had her eye on going to Cal to study astronomy.

But, you often told me, she was too cute and too smart, and it was love at first sight, you said, so every morning you drove the town garbage truck, one of your part-time jobs, past her house, honking once, until one morning she was on the porch waiting and invited you to dinner that night. Her parents, a nurse and a railroad conductor, wanted to meet you first.

It might have been there, at her parents' bungalow, with its white picket fence, in that small and oak-shaded California railroad town, that you attached yourself to her. The allure, impossible to ignore given your scattershot past, of that tidy home. Her parents invited you in, asked questions about you in a friendly manner, and you must have felt at home, or glimpsed some possibility of home. Her parents approved.

You married her less than a year later, Jan 2, 1942, the day before she turned seventeen, while she was still a senior in high school. You were working in the shipyards in Vancouver, Washington by then, and she took the train from Atascadero for just that weekend, then returned home. Two weeks later you enlisted in the Navy, the war at full flood, and took her along that path for twenty years, though she never really joined you in the world, stayed instead in base housing, raising Ricks and Judi alone while you were at sea or under it. Navy housing in San Diego, Harlem, Norfolk, Bayonne, Key West.

You were always in the world, she always at home, but you kept coming back until, finally, that journey ended, all of us in tow, in San Jose, on Flood Drive, in a modest house that we actually owned. You thought you would never own a home. Was Flood Drive the house, the home, you'd always sought?

I knew that there had been at least one other woman you loved, or thought you did, in Hawaii, loved enough to get her name tattooed on a banner in a heart on your right arm. Rosie, though that name you covered up, before you married, with Ollie, surprising Mom with it after a drunken overnight bus trip down to Oxnard. You told me you would never throw rocks at children in Hawaii because you couldn't be sure. But that was all.

Then Renata. We met them in Yosemite, Bob and Renata, from San Jose too. Bob was a mean drunk who beat Renata and his kids, and she needed a friend, you saw, and you became her friend, and I was old enough to know that friend could be a slippery word.

I never told Mom about Renata, how she was always nearby now, the secretive phone calls made in bars, the made-up errands, the peppermint Schnapps. You asked me not to, and I could see that it would only hurt Mom if I did say anything. I suspected what larger harm would fall on our family.

Never told Mom, even about that night at Grandma Cleaves's in Los Gatos, Mom and Grandma visiting in Atascadero, you doing some repairs on Grandma's house, and I came back from a Scout trip and up the front walk, and found you and Renata framed in the front hall and kissing. The world was dusky blue and the hallway golden.

I knew it would be dangerous, for all of us, if I told Mom, so I decided I did not want to tell her. I couldn't say anything, could I.

Or maybe I didn't say anything because I knew that however you loved Mom you still loved Mom. That had not changed.

Espiritu Santo

Basic training again, so easier the second time, and Navy too, so easier than the Army's, most said, and easier this second time because it wasn't simply to be endured but a next step, necessary, moving closer to the war. And the war, here in San Diego, on the broad blue bay, was everywhere, more and more ships, thousands, and sailors training, and down the road, Marines training, the trucks and jeeps and cranes, more of each each day, and the fighters and bombers overhead, the big liners, troops transports leaving one after the other. The wounded and recovering stretchered down the liners' gangplanks when the transports returned. Imminence.

It was easier to be away from Olive, easier than being away from her in Vancouver, because of the imminence, and so Mac threw himself hard into basic, to make it even easier, making the time pass quickly through the exhaustion of it, making the letters he wrote to Olive each night feel like tonight's might be the last letter before he saw her again.

The big difference in this basic, was all the swimming tests, floating and breathing and distance, in pools and off the piers, with re-breathers, with naked lungs, with and without masks and flippers, they were to be sailors after all. Don't buy that crap, Chief said, about sailors shouldn't know how to swim, what the hell you gonna do when your ship gets blown out from under you, swim that's what, or at least god damn float.

After the most rigorous of the tests, a long swim punctuated with sharp dives to touch the bottom of the deep pool, an Ensign, no older than Mac, pulled him aside. You like to swim, he asked, and you weld, too, it's in your file. Sir. You ever dive professionally? Sir, no, sir. Welcome to the Navy, sailor.

Excited in his letters to Olive, dive school, here in San Diego, then Seabee training in Hueneme, then, well, there was the war. Mac saw not only the war ahead, but this, this diving and welding, became something he suspected of what he might do after the war, if he survived, of course, and he would, he swore to Olive.

The first rebreather dive. Suspended, endless, in sixteen-feet of turquoise pool, untethered, isolate, the world above incapable of finding him here, with only the sound of his own breath filling his ears, an entirely unsuspected freedom. Even the first dives in the murk of San Diego harbor, visibility twelve feet on a good day, columns of warmth and chill, mote-clouds golden and silver, muck, even that offered freedom. But he'd have to write Olive tonight that he'd lost his wedding ring in the silt. There were schools of orange Garibaldi that sparkled through the murk, dolphin, harbor seal, small sharks. Not freedom from the surface world, but another world entirely. It was the opposite of Oklahoma, Mac knew that.

But the training was endless, it felt like, and Mac was aching to get to that war, if only because it had been so long he was moving toward it, should already be there, but told, with certainty, by another Chief, April next year, my best guess, that's when you'll ship out, and that's when Mac knew the war would be longer than anyone would want. He trained then with patience and urgency.

Then Olive graduated high school and that June moved into base housing with Mac, in San Diego, Mac living in no barracks and no bunk since he'd first gone to the horse ranch in Bishop, how many years ago was that. He and Olive shared a bare apartment in a yellow stucco building with other married couples, and the days became almost regular, almost ordinary, Mac leaving for dive school in the morning, coming home to a dinner Olive made for him, lunches in lunchboxes, weekends togeth-er, a not quite second honeymoon but somehow better. And friends, Art and Zora, Zora Olive's best friend, how she spent her lonely days, and on weekends, barbecues in the courtyard, with Art and Zora, and other married sailors and their wives. Knowing the war was still there, the planes always overhead, the ships calling to one another in the harbor, the respite was fine, luxurious.

After dive school, Seabee training, in Port Hueneme, four hours north, where Mac learned to weld underwater, to repair ships underwater, to maintain ships underwater, repair or replace propellers underwater, the welding torches submerged suns. Back and forth to Hueneme, but life regular, ordinary, still waiting. Until all the schools were completed, and the orders came through, Espiritu Santo, deep in the southern Pacific. Santo, the next Chief said, is where we make the war possible.

Olive was tearful of course, when Mac boarded another converted ocean liner, the SS Matsonia, and Mac cried too, but the tears were of relief in part, because the war was actually here.

Halfway around the world, days and nights, a passage more littered with storm than Mac's first two, to Hawaii and back, with sailors and soldiers sick all night and day, except Mac and a few others because, Mac assumed, he'd been in the ocean, under it, of it, and carried its rhythms, its extreme rhythms, in his body now. His ocean citizenship was made official on April 16th, 1943, when the Matsonia crossed the equator, halfway down the world, at longitude 168 degrees, 00 minutes, and Mac became a Shellback, fully initiated into The Solemn Mysteries of the Deep, so the certificate said, through hazings and silly songs and men dressed as women and babies, general tomfoolery, but solemn too, at least for Mac. Presented with the ornate certificate, calligraphed and illuminated with sea creatures, Mac read the fine writing, South on a mission of war, and mailed the certificate to Olive from the ship, it would return to her via that same ship. He did not want this lost.

Finally.

If San Diego was a city besieged by the war, infiltrated by it, conquered by it, then Espiritu Santo was a city that war had made of its own. Four hundred thousand men, they said, here on this jungle island, ships again, hundreds in the bays, and the fighters and bombers flying in and flying out, roads and hospitals, three hospitals, rows and rows of Quonset huts set among the coconut palm plantations late of the French, the orderly impossible rows of palms. Training camps for the soldiers and their damn rifles, the next step before landing on some anonymous sandy beach. Four landing strips, acres of aircraft, ammunition dumps, cemeteries. Materiel. Movie theaters and bars, post offices, and an entire island in one channel, Aore Island, with swimming pools and eight baseball diamonds. Santo was a machine.

This was it. The war.

Mac's part was to keep the Navy moving. First they built the floating dry docks, using Jack Browne masks for time and depth, the dry docks longer than the longest city blocks, Mac welding above and underwater, to hold the shell-battered ships, then under the water, Mac diving, to repair those ships. There was no training, there was no respite, only work. The ships left from here, north up the islands, toward Tokyo, battling at sea, crushing the islands with shell power, depositing soldiers unwittingly on those fortified beaches, then returning, the broken ships and the broken men. Relentless.

There were days, of course, Mac had to himself, playing baseball, going to movies, finding ways to get drunk. Swimming in Turtle Bay, the corals and shells, and purple and green and gold fishes of the reefs, the world blue and green and warm. Swimming with his fellow divers in The Blue Hole near the Fighter #1 air strip, the pristine, airless, lifeless cenote whose cerulean depth they could not reckon, freshwater. Descending to thirty feet, no more, suspended there, Mac found the place he always wanted to be now, surrounded by blue water, isolate and aware of the world at the same time, then struggling back to the surface.

He wrote Olive every night, she wrote him every day, her letters arriving halfway around the world, that miracle, in clumps of three or four or seven. Everyone was well, Olive wrote, Nim, she wrote, had been heard from, in the Army now, a paratrooper, headed to Europe soon. Every letter Mac wrote to Olive was exactly the same, which seemed the point to him, assurance, but hers carried other news, the first letter he received at Santo, she was pregnant, due in November, when was he coming home.

The closest he came to the real shooting, was on guard duty at the Fighter #1 air strip, when every Friday afternoon, this one Charlie, some poor misguided and clearly solitary Charlie, in a banged-up Zero, strafed the air strip, one single pass, the bullets pocking the tarmac. Mac and company answered with a machine gun in a sandbag nest hidden among the palms, never hitting him until the last time, when Charlie finally did find a target, Bossy the cow, a family's cow wandered onto the airstrip and ripped apart by shells and left to suffer. But Charlie got hit too and flew off to the east, over the ocean, spiraled into it and died there.

Mac put the cow out of its misery with his pistol, then started to bury the shredded carcass, but the other sailors, relieved by the night shift, laughed away and left him there. Only one other sailor stopped to help, racing from a second machine gun nest, a diver Mac recognized from a small squad of negro divers at the dry docks, though they had never spoken because that was not allowed. The two of them buried Bossy, because it felt right, and because the cow's family was looking on in pain from behind the palms.

After Mac dug up a quart he'd cached, the two men smoked and drank and told their stories, William was from Chicago, which Mac did not know at all. Drunker, Mac asked, Do you like diving as much as I do? It sure beats stacking ammo and burying the dead, William said.

The letters continued to arrive, the ships continued to need repair, the dead were buried, the wounded shipped home, and the war moved closer and closer to Tokyo, until May, two years after Mac's arrival, that other war, halfway round the world, ended, that fucker finally dead, and it was clear that this war, Mac's, would also end soon. They had done something.

In that relief, new orders arrived, Mac was headed stateside, to San Diego first, but then, almost immediately, to New York City for Deep Sea school, the brass Mark V helmets, the darker depths, the longer dives. Life after the war.

In San Diego, he met Olive again, it felt like meeting her for the first time again, and his daughter, his daughter Judi, who was nineteen months old, walking and talking, and who did not know who he was.

Payday

Payday was a celebration for my father, not simply a reward for the work he'd done for someone else, but a badge too, his pride in his work, his doggedness over the years, his ability to provide. The more exhausted he was at the end of a work week, the more his pride showed.

When he retired from the Navy, and we moved from Key West back to San Jose, my father left again, a six-month job diving oil rigs off Saudi Arabia, the pay far beyond anything he'd earned in the Navy. When he returned, he brought a duffel bag filled with presents, something for everyone in the family, my mother and brother and sister, and my cousins and uncles and aunts too. Silk scarves and tasseled fezzes and brass platters and jangly trinkets. For me, a small leather camel, finely stitched and dressed with a saddle rug and saddle of red velvet with golden embroidery and tiny mirrors, carved wooden stirrups. I had never held an object so regal. There was just the one big payday that year, but the camel was enough to make up for my father's long absence.

My mother threw a huge family breakfast to welcome him home. The toaster exploded that morning and showered the kitchen with lightning-blue sparks. He was done diving, he told us that morning. In Arabia he'd gotten two cases of the bends, twenty-four hours in the decompression chamber each time, his veins and muscles and bones twisted by pain, and he blamed the oil company that hired him for asking more of their divers than was safe. His body was no longer capable of handling the extreme pressures.

So he went to work as a welder for FMC in San Jose, home every night, no more postings. FMC, the Food Machinery Corporation, used to make tractors and combines, but when the war began, my father's war, they switched from tractors to tanks, and that's what he was building there.

The first payday at FMC, my mother and I picked him up after his shift, he wanted to show us around. From high windows in the ship-sized building, windows as high as a church's steeple, pale green light softened the half-built tanks. The welding sparked in loud vivid showers, and the other men called out to my father, Mac! Chief! Hasta luego!

On the way out, we stopped at a vending machine, brushed green metal and chrome, and he told me to pick whatever I wanted. I pointed to a package of Chuckles. I'd never had them, but they were colorful, five rectangular jellies sprinkled with sugar, five different colors, red and orange and green and yellow and black, all on a cardboard sleeve and wrapped in cellophane.

I dropped the dime in the slot, heard it tumble, then land on the other coins piled there. I drew the handle back, just like on a cigarette machine, and the Chuckles dropped into the tray. I ate them in the car on the drive home, and every payday after that he brought me Chuckles in his aluminum barn-shaped lunchbox. The thick metal snaps, the sound when they clunked open.

I never knew what happened at FMC, but a year later he was let go, or left, and for several months my father worked at the Accent factory across from Oak Hill Cemetery, near the King's Highway. Minor maintenance and repair, a handyman. Accent made a food seasoning from compounds so noxious that when my father returned from work each day, he parked in the garage, stripped down to his skivvies, dumped his clothes into the washing machine and started it, then headed straight to the shower, where he scrubbed himself raw with Lava soap. For that short time, the payday gifts stopped. Everything he touched before showering was saturated with those fumes.

Shortly after, he moved to GE, a real job again, welding parts for nuclear reactors being installed around the world. He still brought me Chuckles now and then, but GE had better vending machines, Big Cherry, Junior Mints, Bit-O-Honey, Razzles, Dots. I knew when he was almost home because Sparky always heard him from blocks away and went to the kitchen door to wait. On most days, but especially on paydays, I waited with her. Two minutes later, he'd pull into the garage.

It must have been after his first heart attack, fully recovered and full-time again at GE, that our payday ritual returned, but without candy. Now every Friday, he picked me up at the house and we drove to Hacienda Gardens, parking in front of Vann's Crafts and Hobbies, where I was allowed to choose one Matchbox car. The miniature cars were displayed in a white plastic case next to the cash register. There was a code beneath each car, like on a jukebox, E-4 or C-3. When I finally made my choice, I found the corresponding drawer in the base of the display and slid out a yellow cardboard box. Inside, a brand-new car, gleaming.

A glittery-gold Mercury with doors that opened. A black Lincoln Continental. A forest green MG. A Singer Sewing repair van. An emergency-red Sno-Cat with tinted green windows and working rubber treads.

Vann's was always empty on these visits, just the two of us and the one clerk. Model kits and glues and paints, train cars and tracks and tiny people and trees and buildings, woodburning kits, soldering irons, balsa wood and exacto knives, clay and pottery wheels. The fluorescent lights of the crammed, shoebox-shaped store always made me think it was dark outside, rainy, even when it wasn't.

Then we'd drive back to the house, pick up my mother and go to dinner at Burger Pit, where we'd stand in line to order then find a table and wait for our meals. My father always had a steak, with a couple of beers, a reward for himself.

Every Friday for three or four years.

Until he left GE. He had been asked to transfer to either North Carolina or Belgium, to work on the reactors there, but he refused to relocate and was let go. Fired. He was tired of being transferred, of constantly moving the family. He was home now.

I didn't miss the Matchbox cars all that much, I was getting a little old for them anyway. And money was tighter now, I knew without being told.

A few months later, he took a job with Mac Tools. He hated that he shared his name with the company, his customers never let him forget it, Mac MacTools they called him. He drove a yellow and white Mac Tools truck, a step van filled with wrenches and hammers and pipe-cutters and grinders and saws. Occasionally one of the small factories or workshops on his route would phone the house with a purchase order to be filled, but more often my father was expected to make cold calls. He once spent two hours with a shop foreman explaining the advantages of every piece of Mac Tool inventory, only to have the foreman purchase a single two-dollar-fifty crescent wrench, a twenty-five-cent commission. Many days when I came home from school at three, the Mac Tools truck was already parked in front of the house. That job did not last long.

Then there were no paydays at all. My father told my mother he'd found work at a welding yard on the East Side, and that GE would soon be hiring again, though neither was true. I knew the truth, he confided in me that he was not working and swore me to silence. Except for those days when he pulled me out of school to play hooky, I didn't know how or where he spent his time. But he was never home before five-thirty, quitting time, so my mother believed him.

He started to bring me presents again, every Friday, packages of Beer Nuts, we both loved them, and it was almost a return to our payday celebration, except the Beer Nuts did not come from a vending machine in a cavernous building where men shaped and joined and separated enormous chunks of metal. No, the Beer Nuts were from the liquor store a few blocks from our house.

Yosemite

We took two cars that weekend because we were all going, except my sister Judi, long married and with her own family. My brother and Jan drove up in his red VW Bug, and my father drove my mother and myself and my best friend Jim Bryant in the Chrysler 300, a rickety rented ski rack bungeed on top.

We were staying at The Valley View Inn on 120, just this side of the western entrance to Yosemite. The Valley View was a series of long two-story buildings around a restaurant and an indoor pool, all surrounded by steep mountains and enormous tall trees. It was late February, and the Sierras were dressed in snow, a gray-black pan lid of clouds over everything. Intermittent flurries.

My mother and father stayed in one room, all by themselves. I'd been allowed to bring Jim Bryant, from down the street, my best friend since second grade, the smartest guy I knew. Jim and I, this was a big surprise for me, had our very own room too, though right next to my parents. Jim and I were going to try skiing.

In a third room my brother Ricks, one month out of the Marines, and his ex-wife Jan, their daughter Kim, only three, staying with Jan's parents back in San Jose. It was, everyone said, a second honeymoon for them.

But I was confused by this. They'd gotten divorced only a year ago, and while no one had ever told me the story of what happened between the two of them, I was a good snoop and listened around corners, and sometimes went invisible so no one actually remembered I was still in the room. Ricks was my brother and I idolized him and craved every shred of gossip.

After his Hawk missile training in Huntsville in Alabama, Ricks and Jan and baby Kim transferred to Yuma in Arizona, his permanent posting. Then Jan had an affair with Ricks's best buddy, Sgt. Brophy. I knew what an affair was, no need to decode that. One day my brother came home early and found them together, and he beat Brophy so badly he wound up in the base hospital for a week. Bones were broken. Jan moved back to San Jose with Kim. Divorce.

But everyone thought it was a good idea, this second honeymoon, so what was I supposed to say. Anyway, the plan for the weekend was for me and Jim and my parents to do things together. Give Ricks and Jan a little alone time, was how my mother put it.

We got to the Valley View around five, and after dinner, my parents let me and Jim go to the indoor pool by ourselves, the only ones there. It was dark already and it had started to snow, but the falling snow was caught by the parking lot lights, and it was crazy, Jim and I thought, beautiful, the lighted aquamarine pool and the steam that rose from it, the black Sierra Nevada night, the glowing tumble of the snowflakes. And through the snow, skiers were returning to the Valley View after hours on the slopes, in their skis and boots and hats and tags, and they looked tired and hungry, their cheeks red and raw.

One of the reasons Jim was my best friend was because he would stop and look at things like this with me. Just look. Other boys, at school and in our Scout troop, would keep on splashing and jumping and yelling, miss the wonderful lighted snow. Once Jim and I spent three days in my bedroom pretending we were on a space mission, complete with science experiments and a ship's log. There was a towel tunnel from my bedroom to the bathroom, and my parents delivered food outside the door, Tang and Pop Tarts and McDonald's, but Jim and I stayed in our capsule all three days, mission accomplished.

And tomorrow, we were going skiing for the first time. Jim and I had been practicing in my living room, on a pair of wooden cross-country skis we bought for a dollar at a garage sale. We borrowed a book from the library and practiced all the moves, especially the Snowplow, and that night we practiced with our rented skis in the hotel room after our swim, practiced really hard.

Too early the next morning we goaded my parents awake, raced through breakfast at the restaurant, brought out the skis and boots we'd rented at Mel Cotton's, re-attached them to the roof rack and set out to find a hill. It had been decided by my parents that Jim and I should start on a roadside hill to see how the skiing progressed, before we shelled out money for lift tickets at Badger Pass. Jim and I thought this reasonable, and kind of exciting, trespass skiing.

We drove into Yosemite Valley, paid our day-fare, then turned south before Curry Village. It was too cloudy to see Half-Dome or El Capitan. We drove uphill toward Badger Pass, uphill all the way and twisting, the road bordered by a stone guard rail. At the first cut-out, my father pulled over. He went to the wall and touched it solemnly.

I built this wall, he said, with the CCC, back in '39, right before I met your mother. Me and a thousand other men, boys really. He had told me this story many times. They wore green uniforms and slept in tent barracks and piled stone upon stone.

Jim and I approached the wall and investigated the stones, the lichen and fungi growing on and between them, calculated how many men and how many stones and how many days to build this one stone wall from the valley floor to seven thousand feet. When I turned around,

I found my father and mother kissing. We got back in the car.

Only a few turns later, on a flatter stretch of road, we found an open and shallow hill, and stopped there, buckled on our boots, trudged to the top, flushed and sweating, and threw ourselves, just me and Jim, down the hill. I always fell back on my butt, Jim always leaned forward and landed on his face. Once Jim ran over a bush as big as him, but when I tried to hit the same bush, I missed.

My father took Super 8 movies of everything.

For a couple of hours, trudge and fall. Then me and Jim decided to give up. Skiing wasn't for us. But we still had a great time. Jim and I always managed to have a good time, no matter what. Best friends.

We drove to Badger Pass Ski Lodge, where we rented dented metal saucers to ride down Toboggan Hill. We ate lunch at the lodge and left my parents there while we trudged up Toboggan Hill and flung ourselves down it seated on our saucers on our butts. This, Jim and I agreed, was real fun. Gravity was our friend here, and we slid and dumped over and trudged all afternoon, spent so much time on our butts.

We tried to make a word like astronaut but using the word butt, buttronauts, no, astrobutts. Finally, Asstronauts, which we found excruciatingly hilarious, was fun to say, and our secret too. The grown-ups would never hear it when we said it in front of them, We're pretending to be Asstronauts.

We eventually conceded to our fatigue and joined my parents in the lounge, in front of the great stone fireplace and six-foot fire. They were talking with a couple of strangers, though this wasn't unusual. My father always made new friends, wherever we went. This was Bob and Renata, also from San Jose, they were staying in Curry Village but would join us for dinner that night. Good people, my father said, which is what he always said of strangers. Jim and I went in search of hot chocolate and pretzels.

Jan and Ricks joined us for dinner at the Valley View Lodge restaurant, which wanted to be fancy but wasn't. They were quiet, but happy, I thought, almost shy, and they went back to their room before dessert, Plum tuckered out, my brother said. Jim and I left after dessert. The grown-ups were drinking port wine, except for my mother, and they were boring, and Bob was drunk, annoyingly drunk, Hey, Bobby, Hey, Jimbo. Jim and I went to the pool and played Aquanauts.

Then the next day, instead of touring Yosemite Valley, as had been the plan, Jim and I begged my parents to take us back to Badger Pass and Toboggan Hill, We're asstronauts, we told them. My father volunteered to take us so that my mother and Ricks and Jan could tour Yosemite and its wonders, see what there was to be seen, the weather was good today. My father had seen it all before.

Are you sure? my mother asked him.

Bet your sweet bippie, he said, just want to phone Renata and see if she's okay first, Bob was a little soused last night.

Ricks and Jan and my mother left, and it was a long time before my father came back from his call.

Let's get moving, he said.

A full day of fun and gravity.

At one point that afternoon, I went to the lodge to use the bathroom, and passing through the lounge, I saw my father sitting with Renata, no Bob. She was pretty, with short blonde hair, younger than my father, I thought, but she sat with her face in her hands, and she might have been crying. My father, on the edge of his chair, seemed to be whispering to her. They had carved out a little space.

I went to them, sat on the arm of my father's chair.

Where's Bob? I said.

Tad under the weather, he said.

Is Renata all right? I tried to whisper that.

Tough day, he said, she could use a friend.

When I came out of the bathroom, I crossed the far side of the lounge. My father was closer to Renata, and he had his hand on her back now, a maroon ski sweater with white snowflakes. She was looking up at my father, a few tears.

Jim and I wore out the rest of the day, which was sunny and almost warm. By the time we'd returned the saucers and found my father in the lounge, Renata had already left.

We drove from Badger Pass straight to Yosemite Falls and met up with my mother and Ricks and Jan as dusk was closing in. Bob and Renata were there too, and a whole big crowd. We were waiting for The Fire Log.

Park rangers soaked thirty-foot tree trunks in kerosene, and every Saturday night, they lit the log, pushed it into the fast-moving river, and the log plummeted down the falls, an orange comet trailing tendrils of sparks. Or an Apollo capsule burning up on re-entry.

The log fell and flamed, and everyone ooohed.

Jim and I said nothing for a long moment, then turned to each other and laughed. So beautiful, so amazing, and over in a heartbeat. Did you see?

Ricks and Jan stood together, his arm around her, then they turned and kissed fiercely. I did not understand this very much.

My father and mother stood close too, his arm around her, though he kept looking over at Bob and Renata, who did not stand close together. Bob tried to move in and put his arm around Renata, but she pushed him away with the palm of her hand.

We ate together again that night, all eight of us, in Curry Village this time, burgers and steaks. Jim and I had two burgers a piece and split three desserts. Bob was so drunk he fell over on his way to the bathroom and swatted at my father when he tried to help him to his feet. Everyone decided to turn in early.

The next morning it was time to head back, so we woke at six and cleared out our rooms not long after, Breakfast on the road, my father said, making good time.

In the parking lot of the building next to ours, a small crowd had gathered, chattering like birds, and then I saw it. A Giant Sequoia had fallen and neatly bisected this building, three hundred feet of tree crashed down.

The people in the rooms that had been destroyed, we were told by the crowd, had left early to go cross-country skiing, and the tree had missed them by only a few minutes.

No one had seen the tree fall, or heard it, we had all slept through it. But the tree fell anyway, Jim said.

The snow and the soft branches and the soaked earth, Jim and I guessed, had muffled the crash.

Jim and I ran to the tree to investigate, pulled off bricks of the shaggy bark and examined the pale fleshy wood beneath. We tried to measure its circumference, but the tree was far too big. Jim took Polaroids, which we would annotate on the drive home.

We made our way to the thickest end of the tree, where we saw its root structure intact but popped out of the ground. We figured it out. The roots were too shallow, the ground not solid enough, then everything gave way.

Jukebox

I didn't know what excuse my father offered my mother that Saturday. Probably that he was taking me to a work site, or that he was helping a friend with a weekend project, something concrete or wrought iron. On occasion we did go to one of my father's work sites, welding shops or diving schools, and sometimes he did help out a friend. But mostly not. I never knew what the excuse was until the ride home, when he asked me to corroborate the story. And I always did.

That afternoon we ended up in a bar in Almaden, a few miles from the old cinnabar mines, where the flat valley rose up into the Santa Cruz mountains, the oak forest closing tightly over narrower and narrower roads.

It wasn't unusual for the two of us to end up in a bar, but this bar was different. Light streamed in from all sides. Wide plate glass windows. It wasn't a bar I recognized.

Most of the bars my father took me to were dark, day and night, sometimes portholes in the swinging doors, but windows were a rarity or tinted. These bars were both dark and bright inside, the neon flashing, red jukebox and blue beer signs and green pinball machines, the air and the walls and the floor more purple than black. Otto's, Buy th' Bucket, The Captain's Quarters, The Rusty Hook.

Mac! the barkeep or another customer would shout when we walked in, How are ya, y'old rascal, you sunnuvabitch, you. He only took me to bars during the day, when no one would object to a twelve-year-old, and no one did. It always felt, in these bars, that everyone was racing into the night. I loved that feeling.

But this bar, Stegner's, was as bright as a mountaintop cabin. Perched alone on a narrow triangle of land between two merging roads, it occupied the entire lot and sunshine streamed in recklessly. The light was pale yellow and warm when we entered. Sunshine glanced off the chrome bumpers of the three cars in the gravel parking lot and pinged around the room.

It must have been my father's first time in this bar too because the bartender did not call out his name or set him up with the usual. He merely nodded.

There were two other people there, sitting alone at the far end, the short end of the L, a man and a woman, who made a fort of their intimacy and never looked up. No one sat at the two or three small tables. We went to the bar for the usual introduction. The bartender reminded me of my father. I was his son, he told the bartender, No problem, the bartender said.

I climbed up on a stool, ordered a Roy Rogers with two cherries and an olive, and a bag of Beer Nuts.

My father ordered peppermint schnapps chased by Oly.

Peppermint what?

My father told me he'd just discovered schnapps, through a new friend, and found he liked it. Nice and sweet.

Peppermint?

He let me smell it. Candied gasoline.

There was a jukebox, of course. My father fisted some change from the front pocket of his khakis, and we stood over the jukebox while he plunked in four quarters. After a short scan, he punched A-15. Then he punched A-15 seven more times. He forgot to ask me what I wanted to hear. The 45 dropped on the turntable and spun. Crackled.

We sat at the bar and watched the light shift from yellow to yellower, almost buttery. It was late spring.

The song was Tammy Wynette's Stand by Your Man. I knew it, had heard it in the car, sang along. The song played eight straight times that afternoon.

We didn't talk much. I watched the Giants on TV. My father poured his beer into a frosted highball glass, took a deep first swig, then refilled it. He held up the schnapps before each sip and peered one-eyed through the shot glass, as if it were a telescope that might bring the world into focus.

He smoked, of course, Parliaments, cherry to cherry, the blue smoke twining with the yellow light, a color I knew but could not name. The crack of the Zippo.

When A-15 was finally done playing, my father gave me two quarters and socked me in the shoulder, told me to play a few of my own, he'd be back in two shakes of a lamb's tail, had to hit the head, oh, then he remembered he had to call a friend too, a promise he'd made.

I played only Beatles. Get Back, Hey Jude, Penny Lane, Nowhere Man.

The pay phone was in the short hallway that led to the bathrooms, and I could see my father there, but his back was turned. He hunched over the phone, as if whispering, and he talked until my songs finished.

When he came back, he downed the last of his beer and the last half sip of schnapps. He said we'd better get moving. It was time to go home.

After the War

Olive and Judi lived in Harlem, in a Navy requisitioned building with other deep sea divers' wives. Every day Mac took the subway to school, at the bottom of the island, and the world he'd thought was diving opened up to whole other worlds, tethered now, yes, by air and comm hoses to the ship above, but worth that tethering for the bigger freedom, dives that went on for hours, and deeper, much deeper, one hundred feet and more, with entirely new blends of air to breathe. What he loved most was the decompression, rising from the ocean floor, stopping every thirty-two feet to save himself from the bends, hovering mid-ocean, all alone, surrounded by only ocean, the surface a mirrored mirage.

But when Deep Sea school was done, after that last half of the war, Mac's war halfway round the world, Santo, had come to its inevitable end, when both wars were finished, Mac's hitch was up, and the Navy wanted to keep him now that they'd trained him again, and Mac did want to stay, explore that sphere of ocean he'd just discovered, but he and Olive decided instead to settle down, was how they put it, move back to California. Her parents were living in San Jose now, his father-in-law Eugene retired from the railroad, and Olive's sisters, Mimi, divorcing her war husband Carroll Crow, and Carol, newly wed to Frank Perry, two ships blown out from under him during his war, they also lived there, with their children, Mimi's Chuck and Carol pregnant with Joanna, and Olive thought it would be nice to have the cousins grow up together. She was pregnant again, with Ricks. Hadn't they had enough of the Navy?

So Mac opted out and they moved to San Jose, stayed with Olive's parents while he and Olive built the kit house from Sears, on the east side up against the foothills, and were just about finished with it, when Nimion, recovered, though never fully, from his wounds, gut shot parachuting into Germany, turned up. He was going to help them finish the house, until he lit out one morning with Mac's new truck and anything not nailed down.

There was welding work in San Jose, but it paled next to diving, had lost the urgency that war had once given it. So a few months after Nim hightailed it, Mac re-upped, was reinstated with all privileges, and Olive and Judi and baby Ricks were transferred to base housing in Norfolk in Virginia. Almost immediately Mac shipped out, to the Mediterranean, cleaning up the leftovers from that other war, mines and scuttled craft, the skeletons of dead sailors and soldiers, and sometimes just people.

He did one six-month tour, then another six-month tour six months later, and this went on for a long time, home then away, home then away. The Greek soldiers that chased him in Athens, the Portuguese Man o' War that scarred him off Sicily, the Navy life, orderly but also drunken and rowdy, though mostly the diving, the ocean never once ending, always opening.

Crossing the Atlantic time after time, one storm so treacherous, fifty-foot waves, that the boat stood up on its stern.

Then at home, with Ricks and Judi, and trying to enjoy that homeyness, be part of that life in that cramped Navy housing, but always wondering what part of the ocean world he'd see next.

He began to train other divers, was promoted to Chief Petty Officer, then made Dive Master, that pinnacle, which happened in Bayonne, New Jersey, where they'd been posted after Norfolk, and for all those years after the war, it was diving that occupied Mac. When he dived he forgot about the world, when he was at home, on dry land, he craved the ocean.

Then, another transfer, to Key West, Florida, Olive surprisingly pregnant again, with Robert, twelve years after Ricks. A plum spot for a diver, Key West, scuba research and warm waters, and training, submarine rescue training, and no more war to be cleaned up, only the occasional corpse to be reclaimed, and when they arrived in Key West, in the cramped base housing there, yet another too small apartment, there was the lovely backyard, which was the ocean, the crushed coral beach, longoosters and conch fished out for dinner. There was a bar in Key West he loved, a Navy bar, all red brick and faded photographs. Judi in high school, Ricks playing baseball, Robert learning to walk and talk. Yes, a plum spot, well deserved, Mac thought, after all he'd done.

But on the day the transfer to Key West first came through, Mac also knew this would be the last posting, the last insufferable base housing, the last move. He told Olive so, and she cried. So they would go to Key West, the children would grow, Olive would hang on despite her fatigue, and Mac would dive, then he would stop. The pressures were getting to him. He was tired, his arms and legs heavy. When this hitch was up, they would leave Key West, Mac would move them back to San Jose, that family there, and after all this time, all this time of service, of diving, he would haul himself back on land, for good, and stay there.

But for now, for four more years, he would lower himself into the ocean again and again, diving.

Premonition

Did you know that you would die this Monday? Was there some shudder in you, or a weightiness perhaps, did your body let you know that it was done? Or had a shadow followed you, as if some huge black bird traced you from above, the world below gray-tinted? Was there something someone said, me perhaps, when I went off with the Scouts Friday afternoon, did I ignore your farewell or hold you too closely, or you saw some cracked glint in my eye? Something Mom said on her way out of town with Grandma? Or being alone in our house, was that it, you there, alone, for the first time in no one knows how long, all the blue shadows in that house foretelling?

Or did you just know?

Did you give in?

Was it the fatigue of your life, all that roaming, constantly, that ever roaming and uncertain youth of yours, followed then by the discipline and uniform boundaries of the Navy, the brass of that diving helmet, the pressures of the deep you swam through, the constant labor of welding and re-welding? Was it simply too much work for one life? Tote that barge and lift that bale, you often sang. Had the world needed too much of you in order to keep it spinning?

Was it the frustration? The disappointment? That after all that work, raising yourself up from the harsh Oklahoma-nothing of a life where you'd started, then up and up, through the Army, then Navy, obedient, always obedient, focused, willing to risk yourself, your body, in that service to your family and the moving up, until finally, a house, a house you owned, in a beautiful and prosperous valley, your children better off than you could ever have imagined, and everything settled, it seemed, until the last few years when you found the struggle was not over, that you were out of work, and unwanted too, and so still had to struggle?

Or maybe. Maybe it was that once the struggle did seem over, accomplished, the house on Flood Dr., Ricks and Judy both launched in the world, and me showing signs I might too, that you were disappointed to find there was no more struggle? No more adventure, retired and tired, no more next to come? Just here, on Flood Dr., with the red and orange summer sunsets and the green lawn and ease, and the ease might have crushed you in some way?

I had seen it in you for some time, felt it, a gnawing, as if I were privy to the premonition, not you. I saw it on occasion in how you held yourself, how you sometimes walked, shoulders stooping, the last few years, something was changing, especially when you were in and out of work. But only glimpsed here and there, you walking back to the car when I spied you in the rearview mirror, mouth open and slack, or at a family get together, me spotting you across the room when you weren't looking and something dying in your eyes, or in a bar, looking up to find you not watching the game, not looking at me or the others, but at that faraway place where maybe you saw something no one else could see. Were you looking, at these moments, into the past or into the future?

You never let on. Even when, especially when, you were out of work, first and then again, and again, never ever letting Mom in on our secret, never once, and you sticking to the stories you told her when you would say to me, The shop's a little slow these days, I could use some R and R, let's play hooky, I've got a line on a real solid thing, any day now. You needed me, your best pal, so at least someone knew, someone you could talk to even if in talking to me you never really said what you might have said. You confided in me but you didn't want to disappoint me.

How long had you carried that weight? How long had the black bird traced you?

Two days ago, Sunday, when I got back from Kirby Cove and camping with the Scouts, Mom and Grandma

still in Atascadero, the day was tumbling to evening, but
already there because the overcast from Santa Cruz made
the world blue and electric, each little hidden bit of color
wildly insistent, Grandma Cleaves's irises, yellow and purple, and the little red flag on her mailbox. It was beautiful.

You and Renata stood in the hallway of Grandma's
house, close together, the front door wide open, the kitch-
en you'd freshly painted behind you, yellow and glowing.
Perfectly framed.

I saw you draw her to you, hold her, then I watched the
two of you kiss, a long kiss. But you did not see me.

I wondered if you thought this kiss would save you
from your premonition, that all weekend you had hoped
she would come visit you, and she did, and the weight, the
shadow, the shudder, whatever it was, might stop. Was
this another last chance?

I walked away before you saw me, not because I was
angry or embarrassed, but because, because of the beauty
of the evening and its clarity, I thought that yellow light
in that blue evening and Renata's kiss would save you. I
thought she might save you.

She did not.

That was Sunday. You died last night, Monday becoming Tuesday.

This morning I sit in Aunt Mimi's blue kitchen and eat
bite after bite, slice after slice.

Sunday, May 3, 1970

M y father picked me and Jim Bryant up after school on Friday and drove us to the parking lot of the Cambrian Community Center, where our weekly Boy Scout meetings were held in that dark and old basement. Jim and I had packed our packs and sleeping bags the night before then put them in the Chrysler's trunk. There were five fathers taking us to Kirby Cove, just over the Golden Gate, camping and hiking. Jim and I would ride in Kit Viale's father's car, along with Len Miyahara. Jim and I were still Tenderfoots, but Kit and Len, a year older, were already First Class. All that week Jim and I had said to each other, It's going to be far out, wicked. We'd bought new cowboy hats for the trip, white for Jim and black for me.

My father was not coming. My mother and Grandma Cleaves were in Atascadero for my mother's twenty-eighth high school reunion and to visit old friends from when they lived there, so my father decided to stay home and do some painting and plumbing at my grandmother's house in Los Gatos, getting it ready to sell so she could move into the little cottage behind Aunt Mimi and Uncle Don's house. I didn't mind my father not coming.

My other and newer best friend, Rich Davis, thought Scouts were stupid, naturally, and couldn't believe I was still doing it. He made fun of me for this, and I almost believed him. But Jim was going, and I'd known Jim forever, we had done Cub Scouts together, and this last year Boy Scouts, and last summer he and I had danced in my garage and kissed for practice because we'd heard that seventh grade was different. Rich said he and Keith would have to practice without me that weekend and that that sucked because I obviously didn't care about the band. I did care about the band, of course, but liked Scouts too, had already earned my Nuclear Science and Astronomy merit badges. I was caught in the middle but went anyway.

My father talked with Mr. Viale and the other dads while we loaded up the cars with packs and tents and stoves, then he came over and gave me a swift hug, which I really did want, then walked back to the Chrysler. I waved after him. Troop 318 piled into the cars and headed north on 101. School was nearly over for the year, I'd be going into eighth grade, and without my father along, and with my mother so far away, something stirred the air in me and made the world feel bigger.

At Kirby Cove we settled into a campground just above the beach. The sun was still up, but the campground sat in a shallow bowl of high pines and was deep blue and gray. By the time we set up the tents and made dinner on Coleman stoves and lit the big campfire, it was evening, so we all walked down to the little curved beach and watched the Golden Gate Bridge light itself up, and the city across the bay also lighting itself up, warm yellow against now blue buildings. The sunset behind us was clear and almost white.

That night was all campfire and hot chocolate and ghost stories, as usual, which ended when Kit Viale, telling a story about a man with a hook for a hand, stood up at the exciting part and threw a tin can's worth of gasoline onto the fire, a loud whoosh and two-story flare that sent us flying backwards off our logs. The fathers said it was probably best if we all went to bed now, lights out, tomorrow, after all, was a big day. On Boy Scout trips, tomorrow was always a big day.

We spent the morning hiking through the concrete artillery bunkers on the west side of the headlands, looking out over the Pacific. The bunkers had been built at the start of the war, to defend the bay from Japanese invasion, but had never fired a shot. Though the big guns were no longer in place, we could walk through the bunkers and imagine ourselves as soldiers during the war, play Army. The walls of the bunkers, inside and out, were covered with spray-paint graffiti, done by people like us, so and so had been here.

After lunch we drove part way up Mount Tamalpais and hiked a good two hours uphill, through scrub brush and manzanita, all the way to the summit, where we stood in the shadows of the Air Force radar station and took in all of the bay, from Richmond down to San Jose, and I thought I could almost see Moffett Field from there there was so much space around us.

After dinner, the fathers retired to their big tent, and the scouts broke into smaller groups and squeezed into tents to play poker, Boy Scout Poker, deuces wild. For pennies. No campfire tonight. In our tent, Kit and Len and me and Jim and Randy, Kit's other best friend. I looked over at Jim, and we smiled, and I knew he also felt more grown up around these older kids.

We played poker and they talked about girls, which they always did these days, and a lot of their talk had to do with boobs and how they all three had touched some. Jim and I smiled and nodded. Suddenly Randy turned on us, So what's with the dorky hats, boys? We grimly smiled and kept our hats on but our heads down.

To make up for Randy, it seemed, Kit decided to show us something new. This here, he said, is a new merit badge we all need to earn, Joint Rolling. We knew about joints, me and Jim, and pretended to know more. Far out, man. Kit pulled out a packet of rolling papers, slid out one Bible-thin sheet, and held it between his fingers so it formed a little trough. Learned this from my brother, he said, Kit's brother Allen already a senior in high school. Kit pulled a handful of shredded grass, ordinary hillside grass, from his other pocket and filled the trough with it, rolled it into an even tube, licked the gummy edge and finished it, twisting each end. So we all tried rolling one, and did pretty good, though mine looked like a humpback whale. Jim's was a perfect column.

If this was real grass, Kit said, we'd be flying high by now. Together we sat back and pretended to smoke our joints, and I felt like Huckleberry Finn.

When we left the next day after lunch, all the fathers and cars stopped at the north end of the Golden Gate Bridge to walk across it. Halfway across, Jim and I were leaning over the railing, watching an enormous gray Navy destroyer headed under us and out to sea. The wind swelled then, and Jim's brand-new hat, the white one, flew off his head and spiraled down and down to the bay waters, we watched it all the way. All we had left was my black hat.

Mr. Viale dropped me and my pack at my father's car, a few doors down from my grandmother's house in Los Gatos. I dumped my pack in the back seat of the Chrysler, then went to the little gate that opened into Grandma's yard, but before I could step through, I saw my father and Renata, it could only be Renata, standing in the front hall, the front door wide open, and behind them the kitchen lit up all yellow and shining. I stopped because some hush told me to stop. My father and Renata were facing each other, and he pulled her close to him, into him, and they kissed a long time, and they did not know I was there. I watched them for a moment, then went back to the car, where I pulled out an old Marine fatigue shirt of my brother's I'd cut the sleeves off of and sewed patches on, Sgt Pepper's, the green ecology flag, the stars and stripes peace sign. It was chilly for May.

I waited a few minutes, then strolled back to Grandma's, calling out to my father, loudly, and when I got to the gate again, he and Renata were waiting for me on the porch. I stepped through the gate, into the darker shade of the big oak, and moved toward them.

Robert, you bum, welcome home, how was camping, look who's here, Renata, she came over to help out. My father squeezed my shoulder, and Renata gave me a half hug. Ready to go, my father asked, Renata was just leaving, and since your mom won't be home until tomorrow, I say you and me head to Buy th' Bucket, whaddya say.

At th' Bucket, we had a pepperoni pizza and a pint of Crab Louie, then another pint of Crab Louie. Cokes and beer. I told my father all about the bunkers and the gasoline and Jim's hat. He told me how much work he'd done, then he said, Boy, am I crapped out, let's go home.

Sparky was waiting for us outside. The house was dark and cold, and felt huge to me. Then Ricks showed up, he and Jan had had another fight, could he stay for a few days. Of course, we were used to it, it had been happening a lot lately.

Ricks went straight to bed, probably drunk, but my father and I stayed up to watch the news, check the Giants' score, as we always did. My father drank Oly and smoked Parliaments.

Though it was Sunday, there was some real news. Students at Kent State in Ohio had been protesting what the newscaster called The Cambodian Incursion. We were invading another country, it seemed. The protests began Friday, and on Saturday the Governor called in the National Guard. A group of protestors had started a fire at the ROTC building on campus, there was tear gas on campus and downtown, the bars were shut early, and a few students had been injured by National Guard bayonets. Martial law had been declared in Kent, but a protest for Monday was scheduled to go on. Would the students brave the National Guard, would martial law be enforced, the newscaster wondered. One thing was clear, he said, America was a nation in turmoil, and there seemed no end in sight. Stay tuned.

Idiots, my father said.

I looked at him with a question.

Not the students, no, the other ones, the old men, they don't know what they're doing.

We talked about martial law for a while.

The Giants beat the Dodgers, swept the series at home.

Suddenly we were talking about the blue-green Mediterranean, my father's time there, diving after the war. He told me about a moray eel he'd surprised while removing war debris from the ocean floor. Stupidly, was the word he used, he reached through the window of a sunken destroyer escort, and the eel bit him, this yellow-green eel, took a chunk out of his bicep. I'd not heard this story, so he showed me the scar to prove it. I'd never noticed this one, a u-shaped set of needle teeth. I touched it. It felt like a fresh scar.

My father opened another beer, lit another cigarette. It was getting late, and I had school in the morning, but I wanted to keep him talking forever, to tell me story after story.

Acknowledgements

My deepest thanks to
the Indefatigable Allison Remcheck
the Invaluable Katie M. Flynn
the Inimitable Isabel Breskin

About the Author

Lewis Buzbee is the author of *The Yellow-Lighted Bookshop*, *Blackboard*, *After the Gold Rush*, *Fliegelman's Desire*, and *First to Leave Before the Sun* (with Dave Tilton), as well as three award-winning books for younger readers, *Steinbeck's Ghost*, *The Haunting of Charles Dickens*, and *Bridge of Time*. His essays, poems, stories, and interviews have appeared in *Lit Hub*, *GQ*, *The New York Times Book Review*, *Paris Review*, *ZYZZYVA*, *Black Warrior Review*, *Best American Poetry*, and elsewhere.

A long-time bookseller and publisher, he lives in San Francisco with his wife, the poet Julie Bruck, and not far from their adult child Maddy.

lewisbuzbee.com
@buzbeebooks

www.ingramcontent.com/pod-product-compliance
Ingram Content Group UK Ltd.
Pitfield, Milton Keynes, MK11 3LW, UK
UKHW020345180225
4635UKWH00001B/41

9 798822 946842